Hot Arabian Nights

*Be seduced and swept away
by these desert princes!*

You won't want to miss this new,
thrillingly exotic quartet
from Marguerite Kaye!

First, exiled Prince Azhar must decide whether to
claim his kingdom *and* beautiful unconventional
widow Julia Trevelyan!

Read
The Widow and the Sheikh
Available now!

When Sheikh Kadar rescues shipwrecked mail-
order bride Constance Montgomery, can a
convenient marriage help him maintain peace in
his kingdom?

Find out in
Sheikh's Mail-Order Bride
Available soon!

And watch out for two more tantalising novels,
coming soon...

To secure his kingdom's safety, Sheikh Rafiq must
win Arabia's most dangerous horse race.
His secret weapon is an English horse-whisperer...
whom he does *not* expect to be an irresistibly
attractive woman!

Daredevil Christopher Fordyce has always craved
adventure. When his travels lead him to the
kingdom of Nessarah he makes his most exciting
discovery yet—a desert princess!

There could be absolutely no mistaking the desire in his eyes now. For some extraordinary reason this prince—this man—was attracted to her. *Her!*

She reached up her hand and touched his cheek, just as he had touched hers. His skin was rougher than she had expected, warmer. She ran her fingers through the short, soft silk of his hair.

'Tell me what you are thinking, Julia.'

His voice had a ragged edge to it. He really did want her. She'd walked away from the chance to kiss him once—she wasn't likely to get another. 'I'm thinking that I'd very much like you to kiss me,' she said.

He was surprised into a low rumble of laughter. 'I believe they call that serendipity,' he said, 'because that is exactly what I propose to do.'

THE WIDOW
AND THE SHEIKH

Marguerite Kaye

First published in Great Britain 2016
By Mills & Boon, an imprint of HarperCollins*Publishers*
1 London Bridge Street, London, SE1 9GF

Large Print edition 2016

© 2016 Marguerite Kaye

ISBN: 978-0-263-26307-7

Marguerite Kaye writes hot historical romances from her home in cold and usually rainy Scotland, featuring Regency rakes, Highlanders and sheikhs. She has published almost thirty books and novellas. When she's not writing she enjoys walking, cycling (but only on the level), gardening (but only what she can eat) and cooking. She also likes to knit and occasionally drink martinis (though not at the same time). Find out more on her website: margueritekaye.com.

Books by Marguerite Kaye

Mills & Boon Historical Romance and Mills & Boon Historical *Undone!* eBook

Hot Arabian Nights

The Widow and the Sheikh

Comrades in Arms

The Soldier's Dark Secret
The Soldier's Rebel Lover

The Armstrong Sisters

Innocent in the Sheikh's Harem
The Governess and the Sheikh
The Sheikh's Impetuous Love-Slave (Undone!)
The Beauty Within
Rumours that Ruined a Lady
Unwed and Unrepentant

Stand-Alone Novels

Never Forget Me
Strangers at the Altar

Visit the Author Profile page
at millsandboon.co.uk for more titles.

Chapter One

Kingdom of Qaryma, Arabia—spring, 1815

It was late afternoon. He had travelled all day through the unrelenting heat of the blazing desert sun, barely stopping to rest, driven on by the knowledge that his destination was within touching distance, anxious to complete both the journey and the unwished-for task which awaited him. A difficult, potentially painful task but one which would provide its own reward. Ten years ago he had left and vowed never to return. This time when he departed, it truly would be for ever.

Azhar brought his camel to a halt and shaded his eyes. The view of the desert was never static. The rippling sands shifted continually, as if the landscape itself were alive like some vast writhing serpent, as the bone-dry winds constantly reshaped and remoulded the dunes. Today, the colours varied from gold, to burnt orange, to a deep chocolate-brown where the sun cast shadows in the valleys between the vertiginous cliffs of sand. The sheer vastness of the landscape, the vibrant celestial blue of the sky, and the searing, white-gold heat of the sun, filled him with awe and a painful nostalgic ache. His trading missions had carried him across many a desert landscape throughout Arabia, but there was none that tugged on his heartstrings as much as this one.

Had once tugged on his heartstrings. Ten long years ago, he had exorcised this place and its people from his heart. In the intervening period, he had refused to allow himself to think of it, to remember it, to allow it to impinge on the new life he had carved for himself, the life that now defined him. His business gave him independence. He was beholden to no man. He was accountable for no one and to no one. Concluding matters here in Qaryma would finally make him free.

Far below, nestled in the valley, lay the Zazim Oasis, the contours of the lagoon delineated by the belt of lush vegetation which surrounded it. The perfectly still pool was silvery-green, reflecting the ridges of the highest dunes with the clarity of a painting. Though it was a forlorn hope, for the oasis was a well-known respite for weary travellers, Azhar had wished for one last night of solitude before discharging the obligation which had led him here. Consequently, as he descended into the valley, the unmistakable evidence that he would not have the oasis to himself irked him profoundly.

The sole tent was pitched at the far end of the lagoon, in the shade provided by a grove of palm trees. It was constructed in a similar manner to the one his own mules carried, a mix of heavy wool blankets and animal skins stretched over a simple wooden frame, but this tent was larger, more akin to the type used by Bedouins, not a man travelling alone. It was then that he noticed the absence of any signs of life. No one would abandon such a precious possession willingly. The thick quality of the silence left him in no doubt that there was neither man nor beast here, but if experience had taught him one thing, it was always to be prepared, to expect the unexpected. As his camel, the string of mules in train behind it, began the slow descent, Azhar's hand went instinctively to the hilt of his scimitar.

* * *

Julia Trevelyan awoke with a start, sitting straight up on her bedroll. Her heart was beating so rapidly it felt as if it were in her throat. Her linen shift clung to her skin, damp with sweat and gritty with sand. It was stiflingly hot. The air was so dry it hurt to breathe. The bright glare of the desert sun glinting through the seams and gaps of the musty tent told her it must be well into the afternoon, but that was quite impossible.

Her head was pounding. The inside of her mouth felt as if it had been coated in camel hair. Reaching for the goatskin flask of water she kept by her bedclothes, she struggled to undo the cap, her fingers were shaking so much. She drank greedily, so desperate to slake her thirst that the precious water trickled down her chin on to her chest. The ache in her head flared into a searing stab of pain. Her brain felt like it was on fire. She tipped the remaining contents of her flask over her head in an effort to cool herself. Hanif, her dragoman guide, would be horrified at such flagrant waste of a precious resource, but Julia was beyond caring, and besides, the oasis where they were camped had a plentiful supply.

Where was Hanif? Why had he not woken her?

What time *was* it? Julia fumbled for Daniel's pocket watch, which she kept by her bedroll, but it was not there. She must have set it down somewhere else. It was not like her to misplace such a precious object. She frowned, causing the band of pain around her head to tighten. She couldn't even remember going to bed.

The silence struck her then. She listened intently. Nothing. Not a rustle. Not a voice. Neither the shrill bray of a mule nor the plaintive bleat of a camel. Despite the stifling heat, she shivered. She was being foolish. Hanif and his men were being very well paid for their assistance. They would not have abandoned her here.

Alone.

In the middle of a desert.

A wave of panic sent her heart pumping wildly. She was being ridiculous. Julia pushed back the blanket and got to her feet. Too quickly. The tent swam. She staggered. Shooting stars of light sparked before her eyes. Was she ill? Too much sun, perhaps? Not enough water?

She lurched to the front of the tent, sticking her head through the gap between the goatskin flaps. The sun cast a blinding white glare over everything. The day was well advanced. In utter disbelief, she gazed at the space where the encampment had been. There was nothing left, save the cold embers of last night's cooking fire. All of the camels were gone. All of the pack mules were gone. The water of the oasis lay completely still. Not a frond on the shady palm trees stirred. She was alone, quite alone.

Anger and confusion dissipated the worst of her fear. Why had she not woken sooner? Hanif and his men could not have packed up the entire camp in silence, and she was a notoriously light sleeper. Why hadn't she heard anything? Only now, turning back into the tent, did she notice that her clothes were strewn all over the floor. The large leather-bound trunk in which she kept them lay open, empty. Julia's stomach lurched. Where was the other trunk? The trunk that constituted the sole reason she was here, so far from home, so far from England. She almost couldn't bear to look. 'Please, please, please,' she whispered, as she made her way to the rear of the tent.

It wasn't there. But it must be. It must be somewhere. Her knees shaking, she stumbled into the darker corners, but there was no sign of it. Frantically now, she began to search, pulling up her bedroll, shaking out her pillow, casting petticoats and skirts into the air in a fruitless attempt to find the small trunk and its precious contents. But it was gone, and with it the drawings of desert flowers she had so meticulously made, the plant specimens she had so painstakingly collected, labelled and neatly stored. She had almost completed her quest. Her notebooks were alive with colour, the tiny drawers of the trunk almost full. The pledge she had made was so near to fulfilment, her freedom finally within reach. Now, all was lost.

She couldn't believe it. This simply couldn't be happening. Please let it be some awful nightmare from which she would awake. Sinking down on to the sand, Julia struggled to hold back the tears. She never cried. She could cope, she told herself firmly. Hadn't she been coping exceptionally well all these past months on her own? She had been in worse situations before. Once, the barge she and Daniel had been travelling on had sunk in the middle of a fast-running muddy river in the depths of a jungle. They had floated, the two of them, clinging to the wreckage as it tumbled downstream, she remembered, until the waters had become shallow enough for them to wade ashore. They'd lost everything then. No, not quite everything. Daniel's watch and his purse had been secured to his person. Practical as always.

Her purse! Julia retrieved her pillow from the corner into which she had tossed it in the frenzy of her search, but no amount of probing and pummelling produced the leather pouch filled with gold coins. They must have taken Daniel's watch too. A tear sprung to her eye. They had been right here, standing over her sleeping body, wreaking carnage in her tent, and she had not awoken.

Dear God, what else had she slept through? Somewhat belatedly, Julia checked her body for any signs of molestation. The relief when she found none was palpable. She began to tremble, thinking of what she had been spared. They could easily have slit her throat.

Stop!

That way lay despair, and she had no time to despair. 'No point in imagining the worst,' she told herself firmly. 'Time to take stock, not give way to a fit of the vapours.' She was unharmed. Her gold was gone, her only cherished memento of Daniel—his watch—was also gone, but hopefully her secret stash of bank notes was safe.

A soft thud of hooves on the sand outside the tent prevented her from checking. They had come back, realising the error of their ways! Relief flooded her, quickly followed by fury. She had been far too complacent, far too accommodating. It was time she made it clear who was in charge here, reminded them whose money was funding this expedition.

But Hanif already had her purse and everything else of value. He had no reason to return. In fact, he had every reason to flee. Catching herself in the nick of time from storming out of the tent, Julia instead eased open the flap a mere inch and peered cautiously out.

The lone figure sitting on the high boxed seat of a camel trailing three pack mules was just a few yards away, and a complete stranger to her. His head and most of his face was covered by a white *keffiyeh* held in place by a braid of dark-red scarves, leaving only his eyes, a pair of high cheekbones and the bridge of his nose exposed. She could only guess at his age. Not old. Five-and-thirty, perhaps less. He wore a long, loose tunic in the same dark red as the *agal* which held his headdress in place, a cloak she knew was called an *abba*, made of unbleached cotton or muslin. His long brown riding boots turned up at the toes. The simple attire, which was slightly dishevelled and covered in a fine coating of dust, suggested he had travelled far. Despite her apprehension, there was something about the man that held her attention. Was it his easy command of that highly strung beast that gave him such a forbidding presence? The hooded hawk which perched beside him on the saddle? Or the way he sat, shoulders ramrod straight, surveying the desert as if he and only he had a right to be here?

He clicked his tongue and the camel dropped obediently to its knees allowing him to dismount fluidly, his billowing robes hinting at an athletic body beneath. His hand was on the hilt of the lethal-looking scimitar which hung from a loose belt on his hips. Now, Julia thought, while he was occupied with hitching the three mules, now would be the time to run for cover in the shrubs surrounding the lagoon, or even into the lagoon itself.

She was about to melt back into the protective gloom of the tent, planning to crawl out from under the rear of it, when she saw the rangy silver-grey Saluki hound. Unfortunately the dog spotted her at the exact same moment. The animal's ears pricked, its sleek body quivered as it turned towards her. Julia retreated hastily, but even as she tried to create an opening at the base of the tent, the front flap was thrown open and first the hound, and then its owner entered.

Grabbing the first weapon that came to hand, she turned to confront the intruders. The dog was close enough for her to feel its breath on her bare feet, its hackles raised, teeth bared. 'Stay where you are,' Julia ordered, waving her weapon at its master. 'If you value your life, you will not take a step further.' She spoke in Italian, the language she had used to communicate with Hanif, for her Turkish and her Arabic were rudimentary at best. Certainly not up to the dire situation she currently found herself in.

The nomad ignored her and stepped further inside. He had not drawn his sword, but wielded a wicked-looking dagger. Julia's blood ran cold. He was at least a head taller than her, and at five foot six in her stocking soles, she had been the same height as Daniel. 'I mean it,' she said, brandishing her weapon and, in her terror, lapsing into English. 'If you take one step further, I will...'

He didn't take one step, he took several, and all of them so quickly that she had no time to move before he closed the gap between them. A firm hand covered her mouth, preventing her from screaming. A powerful arm clamped around her waist, binding her tight against a hard and unforgiving body. The dagger on the end of that arm looked sharp enough to scythe through metal, to say nothing of clothing or delicate flesh. The hairbrush she had been rather preposterously wielding dropped to the sand as Julia struggled frantically, wriggling and kicking with all her might. The dog barked, but made no attempt to savage her.

Seemingly utterly indifferent to her efforts to free herself, the man lifted her effortlessly off her feet and held her against his side while he made a quick tour of the tent. Only when he had assured himself that it was empty did he release her, pulling the *keffiyeh* away from his face and clicking his fingers to send his hound obediently back to guard the doorway of the tent.

Night-black hair, cut very short, showed his stark bone structure to advantage. A wide brow, high cheekbones, a surprisingly clean-shaven chin with a small cleft in the middle, drawing attention to the perfect symmetry of his face. His thickly lashed eyes were golden-brown in colour, rather like a setting sun. His nose was strong, but the austerity of his countenance was offset by the sensuality of his mouth, which on a less masculine face would have looked too feminine. All of this the artistic part of Julia's brain absorbed in seconds. He was one of the most striking men she had ever seen. Under different circumstances—very different circumstances— her fingers would have itched to draw him, to capture his potent and haughty demeanour, his languid physical grace.

He picked up the hairbrush and handed it to her. 'What were you planning to do with that, comb me to death?' he demanded with a curt laugh, although his eyes betrayed no sign of amusement. 'What are you doing here? Why are you alone in the desert?'

He spoke in perfect English with a soft accent, unmistakably Arabic but equally unmistakably cultured. This man was most definitely not the poor nomad she had taken him to be. Julia took a step back, eyeing the open doorway of the tent.

'I do not recommend it,' he said. 'I can easily outrun you. And even if I couldn't Uday here of a certainty could.' The hound's ears pricked up at the mention of his name. 'Uday means fleet-footed, and he is. Very.'

The dog bared its teeth, almost as if it were

smiling contemptuously at her. He and his master were well matched. Julia moved, not because she doubted that the animal would live up to its name, but because she could think of no other viable course of action.

Two steps only, she had taken, before he caught her again and set her down well inside the tent. 'Madam, you will come to a great deal more harm running in the heat of the sun without a hat or shoes or water, than you will endure at my hands.'

He was right. She hated that he was right. She was not armed, while he was armed to teeth. She couldn't outrun him, she couldn't overpower him. She had no option but to somehow brazen it out. What she must not do was show her fear. Clasping her shaking hands tightly together, Julia glared at the man. 'I have no intentions of running away. *I* am not the trespasser. This is my tent, my property. You have no right to be here. I demand that you leave. Immediately.'

He stared at her in astonishment.

'I asked you to leave,' Julia repeated, this time in Italian.

Still, he made no move. 'I heard you,' he replied in the same language, before reverting to English. 'This tent may be yours but this kingdom is not. You do not belong here. I repeat: what are you doing here?'

Julia bristled. 'That, with respect, is none of your business.'

A flash of anger illuminated his countenance. 'Do you have official papers? Who gave you permission to travel here?'

Though he spoke curtly, he had tucked his dagger back into his belt. Julia's fear began to recede, allowing indignation to take hold. The arrogance of him! She crossed her arms. 'Naturally I have papers, and they are in perfect order.'

'Show them to me.'

He held out a peremptory hand. She was on the brink of informing him that he had no right at all to make such demands when it occurred to her that he could well be some sort of official, and it would not be prudent to antagonise him any further, especially if she wished to ask for his help. 'If you will give me a moment, I'll look for them.'

Thanking the stars that she had had the foresight not to keep her papers with the rest of her valuables in her dressing case, which had of course also been taken, Julia slid her fingers anxiously into the tiny slit cut into the lining of her clothes trunk. To her immense relief, the very slim packet of papers were still there, along with the equally slim stash of bank notes, which she decided to leave in the hiding place for the moment. Smoothing out the creases of her papers, she handed them over. 'All present and correct and, as I think you'll agree, in perfect order.'

The man frowned. 'These relate to the kingdom of Petrisa.'

'Exactly. Signed by the appropriate authorities,' Julia agreed, 'including the British Consul in Damascus.' Who had recounted, as had Colonel Missett, the Consul-General in Cairo, several hair-raising incidents of robbery and murder designed to deter her from undertaking this journey. As it turned out, their dire warnings had proven to be all too accurate, but they had failed to dissuade her because they had underestimated her overwhelming motivation for accepting the risks—principally because she had chosen not to apprise either of the august gentlemen of the precise nature of her quest. It was her business, not theirs. Her life, not theirs. 'Well?' Julia demanded. 'Satisfied?'

But the stranger was still frowning. 'As you said, your papers are in perfect order. There is only one problem, and I'm afraid it's rather significant. This is not Petrisa. This is the Zazim Oasis, in the kingdom of Qaryma.'

Julia's jaw dropped. He was mistaken. Or he was lying, for some reason. Punishing her for being rude, perhaps. 'Nonsense,' she said stoutly, 'I've never heard of Ka—Kareem…'

'Qaryma.'

If he was right, then she was in deep water. She had no valid papers for this place, no permissions, which made her the trespasser, not him. She must not panic. Trespass was only a crime if it was committed deliberately, wasn't it? Julia cleared her throat. 'They told me—my dragoman said—are you certain this is not Petrisa?'

'I could not be more certain.'

His tone was implacable. He was just a touch intimidating, but her instincts told her he was telling the truth. She had no choice but to believe him. She was quite alone, and, through no fault of her own, quite in the wrong. 'It seems,' Julia said carefully, 'that I owe you an apology. I appear to have strayed over the border quite unintentionally.'

'You must have had a guide, a translator, men to pitch your camp. Where are they?'

His tone riled her. Julia wrapped her arms tightly around herself. 'I have travelled halfway across the world relying on my own initiative. I am not some helpless and witless female.' Though she was, for the moment, almost completely without resources. 'I have no idea where my guide and his men are,' she admitted reluctantly. 'They left abruptly in the night.'

'And your camels, your mules?'

'They took everything.' Saying it aloud made her feel like an absolute fool. Mortified, she glowered defiantly at the intruder. 'There was nothing I could do to stop them, I think they put some potion in my tea last night.'

His hand, Julia noticed, went to the hilt of his sword, and he said something vicious under his breath in what she assumed was Arabic. 'Did they harm you in any way?'

Her cheeks flamed. 'No. I—no, they did not. Not in any way, if I understand your question correctly.'

'For that, I give thanks. I am deeply sorry, madam, that you have had to endure such barbaric treatment. I assure you no citizen of Qaryma would behave so abominably towards a foreigner. Those scoundrels may not have violated you, but they have violated the sovereign borders of Qaryma with impunity.'

He looked both furious and puzzled by this fact. As he consulted her papers again his frown deepened further. 'You really are travelling alone, without any companion?'

'All the way from England,' Julia said, with a small smile.

The man did not seem to share her pride in her achievement, but rather looked aghast. 'You are married,' he said, pointing at her wedding band. 'Your husband, where is he? Surely not even an Englishman would expose a woman to the dangers of travelling without protection? If I were married, which I am not, I would most certainly not be so cavalier with my wife's safety. It is a matter of honour, to say nothing of...'

'...the fact that we are the weaker sex?' Julia finished for him. 'Fortunately, my husband did not share your views.' Which wasn't strictly true. Daniel's quiet assumption that he was in every regard her superior had been one of the things about him which had irritated her. Though when it suited his purposes, which invariably meant something which would be beneficial to his research, he was amenable to acknowledging talents and abilities he had hitherto denied her possessing.

'Actually, I was about to say that it was a matter of upholding the promise your husband made on his wedding day, to protect you.'

'I am more than capable of protecting myself,' Julia declared. A raised eyebrow, a sceptical look around the ransacked tent, made her flush.

'You said your husband did not share my view.'

'What of it?'

'You spoke of him in the past tense.'

'That is because I am a widow,' Julia replied. 'Daniel died of a fever contracted in South America over a year ago.'

'My sincere condolences.'

'Thank you.' Back in Cornwall, she had grieved for the loss of the man she had known all her life, as a friend, a botanist colleague of her father, and for the last seven years, as her husband. She still missed the friend, the botanist, the companion, but the husband? Distance and time, six months of solo travel, had given her a very different perspective of her marriage.

However, the fact that Daniel had been, just as this man suggested, cavalier with her safety, was none of his business, just as the surprising fact that such a striking man was unencumbered was none of hers. What she needed from him was his help, not his history. In fact, she couldn't believe she had wasted so much precious time before seeking it.

Julia smiled in what she hoped was a conciliatory manner. 'Now that you are apprised of my situation, you will understand why I must crave your assistance in pursuing the men who betrayed my trust. They cannot have travelled too far, and—and you see, they have something of mine that I must—I simply must retrieve.'

But he was already shaking his head. 'Oh, please,' Julia interrupted when he made to speak, the anguish she felt evident in her voice. 'I beg of you. I don't care about the mules or the camels. I don't even care about the money or jewellery they stole, other than Daniel's fob watch, which is of enormous sentimental value to me. But there is one other precious item that matters more than all my other possessions put together. They took my gold, but I still have access to other funds. I can reward you amply, if you will only…'

'I am not a dragoman, madam, and I most certainly neither want nor need your money.'

The look he gave her made her flinch. 'I beg

your pardon, it was not my intention to insult you, only I am desperate. I cannot tell you how— how vital it is that I...'

'No.' He unpicked her fingers from his sleeve. 'It would be a fool's errand, mark my words. Whatever they have taken will already have been sold off in a market somewhere. Stolen goods are always moved on quickly, and there is always an unscrupulous buyer willing to ask no questions in return for a bargain.'

'But...'

'I myself am a trader—a reputable one I might add, but I know how these vagabonds operate. I am sorry. I wish it were otherwise, especially in relation to the watch, but I'm afraid you must give your possessions up for lost.'

His tone was firm and quite unequivocal. Forced to accept the truth of what he said, Julia felt sick with disappointment. She pictured Daniel's trunk being haggled over in a souk. The specimens, so valuable to her, would most likely have been deemed worthless by the thieves, cast out of the drawers to wither in the heat of the desert sun. Her paints, her little trowel would be sold, but her notebooks, her drawings—no, they would mean nothing to those men. They would have no idea of their enormous significance.

Anger made her absolutely determined not to be defeated. If she could not recover her precious work, she would simply have to find a way of starting again. There was no way on earth she was returning to Cornwall without having completed her task. She had come so far, had triumphed over so many hurdles on the way, she would not—she absolutely would not!—allow a treacherous band of Bedouins to best her.

'Very well,' Julia said briskly, 'if you will not assist me in pursuing these thieves, perhaps you will help me to employ a more reliable dragoman? All I ask is that you escort me back over the border to Petrisa, assist me in exchanging some bank notes for local coin, and then I can purchase new camels, mules...'

She trailed to a halt, for he was once again shaking his head firmly. 'I am afraid there is no prospect of my doing any such thing. There is no question of my going back. I have critically important business of my own to attend to here in the capital city, Al-Qaryma.'

Julia stared at him in dismay. 'You mean you will leave me stranded here, without valid papers, without the means to make my way back to Petrisa? What on earth am I expected to do?'

It was an excellent and very pertinent question Azhar thought, eyeing the Englishwoman with a mixture of irritation and curiosity. She was older than he had thought at first, perhaps twenty-six or seven. Not in the first bloom of youth, but too young to be widowed, and certainly far too young to be wandering about alone in a foreign country, no matter how competent she thought herself.

Though he had to concede that she must be more intrepid than confident, if her claim to have travelled all the way from England alone was to be believed, and he had no reason to doubt her—there was honesty as well as intelligence in those wide-set eyes the colour of palm fronds. She might lack judgement, but she had courage, and she had resilience. In spite of his annoyance at this most unwanted distraction, Azhar couldn't help but find her—in her own unique way—appealing.

She was not beautiful exactly, her face was too long for that, her brow too high, but she was memorable, with that thick mass of dark-red hair and those big green eyes. Her body, under the hideous nightgown she wore, would be deemed too thin and too tall here in the East, but Azhar found her lean suppleness alluring. The colour of her hair spoke of a fiery temper, a tempestuous nature. And that mouth, when it was not set in a firm line, had a hint of sensuality about it.

Appalled at the carnal direction his thoughts had taken, he dragged his eyes away. As if he did not have enough to concern himself with, now he must take responsibility for a complete stranger. For he had no option but to do so. He most certainly could not abandon her to her fate. His anger flared again at the thought of the miscreants who had robbed and abandoned her. That the reprobates she had employed had had the temerity to breach Qaryma's borders with impunity astounded and infuriated him. The situation must have changed radically since he was last here. Ten years ago, no one would have dared treat the kingdom with such disrespect.

Azhar sighed heavily. One problem at a time. He turned his attention back to his most pressing dilemma. 'I cannot in all conscience abandon you here, but neither can I escort you back across the border. I therefore have no option but to take you with me to Al-Qaryma.'

She looked dismayed rather than delighted. 'But I don't have the correct papers. I'll be thrown into gaol.'

A fact Azhar himself had pointed out. He should have held his tongue. 'Fear not, I will have your papers validated when we reach the city.'

'How can you promise such a thing? I thought you said you were a trader?'

Why couldn't she simply say thank you! 'I am, and a successful one. As such I have many high-ranking contacts. Do not fear, I am not without influence, Madam…?'

'Trevelyan.'

'Trevelyan,' Azhar repeated slowly. 'It does not sound typically English.'

'That is because it's not English, it's Cornish. Both my husband and I are natives of Corn-wall, which is quite the most beautiful county in England, Mister—Sayed…?'

Sayed, the common formal form of address to which he had answered for many years. It was how he had defined himself, a nameless and root-less sir. 'You may call me Azhar.'

'Azhar,' she repeated carefully.

'It means shining, or bright.'

'My name is Julia. I'm afraid it doesn't mean

anything in particular, though I expect you think I should be called Burden or Encumbrance.'

She crossed her arms, inadvertently lifting her breasts higher under her cotton shift. To his annoyance, Azhar felt his blood stirring. Desire, which had departed entirely with the arrival of that fateful summons which had brought him here, returned now at this most inopportune time. He could not afford to be distracted. He most certainly had no time to be intrigued, far less beguiled by this English widow, especially since she was actually the complete antithesis of everything those words implied.

'What you are, Madam Julia Trevelyan, is an enormous inconvenience,' Azhar said. 'The day marches on. I am going to hunt for some food and then prepare a meal. You are welcome to join me. I will not drug you, though I may inadvertently poison you, since my culinary skills are somewhat rudimentary. I shall, however, endeavour not to. A dead English woman is the last thing I wish to have on my hands.'

'Cornish,' Julia threw at him as he left the tent, but Azhar chose not to hear her. 'So I'm an enormous inconvenience, am I?' she muttered. 'How inconvenient do you think it was for me, Mr You-Can-Call-Me-Azhar, to be robbed blind and left for dead?'

Receiving no answer from the tent flap, Julia sighed. She was being most ungrateful. At least he was not abandoning her. She considered spurning his invitation to share his food, but then her stomach reminded her that she had not eaten since yesterday. She could sit here, sweltering and ravenous, with only her pride to keep her company, or she could get dressed, grovel, and get some badly needed sustenance.

Deciding to eschew martyrdom, Julia began to pick up the clothes she had been wearing the day before from the heap they formed on the sand floor beside her bedroll.

With no shocked and disapproving husband to witness her uncorseted body, after the first few days of travel in the desert she had abandoned the daily contortions required to lace herself into her stays. There was nothing in the world, she had discovered, as uncomfortable as sand trapped against delicate skin by stiff whalebone. The heat which the combination of corsets and desert sun produced transformed discomfort into torture.

In fact, her entire wardrobe was quite unsuited

to the climate. As she pulled on a rough woollen skirt and cambric blouse over her nightgown
before adding a jacket, perspiration blossomed
all over her back. Not for the first time, Julia
wished she had had the courage and sense to
outfit herself with some of the loose tunics and
cloaks more appropriate for the conditions. She
had been on the brink of purchasing some in a
souk in Damascus, but imagining Daniel's disapproving face looking over her shoulder, she had
changed her mind. She deeply regretted that now,
as much irked by her instinctive loyalty to her
dead husband's opinions as she was by her very
British wardrobe. He himself had never been less
than impeccably turned out, whether in a man-
grove swamp or halfway up an Alpine mountain.
While Julia considered herself Cornish before all
else, Daniel had been the living embodiment of
the quintessential Englishman abroad.

No, that was not true. Above all else, Daniel
was a man of science. He'd called her his woman
of science. Back in the early days, she'd been
inordinately proud of that. Now—oh, now was
not a time for looking back. Now, it was time to
turn her mind to making good on her vow. She
had been so close, after all this time able to see

the light of true freedom at the end of the tunnel. Her duty to the past discharged, she might finally look forward to a future of her own making. For an instant, dejection threatened to overpower her, but very quickly she rallied. In this city to which she was now destined to travel, she would hire a new and reliable guide. In this strange kingdom, she might find undiscovered and rare plant specimens. Even this dark cloud might have a silver lining.

She pulled on her stockings and laced up her boots. Daniel had always derided the notion of fate, but Julia was no longer obliged to agree with Daniel's opinions. She had opinions of her own now. Fate had set her path on a collision course with this mysterious man of the desert. It was up to her to make sure she made the best of the situation.

Chapter Two

The spectacular beauty of the desert sunset never failed to take her breath away. Julia watched, fascinated, as the vivid orange and gold-streaked sky gave way to a pale, soft night-blue, as if the sun, on its rapid descent to the horizon, dragged a stage backdrop behind it. The sparse puffy clouds segued from dark grey to pewter then white as the sky darkened to indigo and the stars made their appearance, a blanket of silvery jewels hung so low in the sky that she felt she could almost touch them. The moon was butter-yellow. The desert landscape was dark and moody, the dunes clearly outlined, softly rolling, sharply falling. The air changed, from dry and dusty to soft and salty. She breathed it in, lifting her face to the sky where the biggest stars were now surrounded by pinpoints of light, relishing the soft breeze which made the palm trees around the oasis quiver.

She saw the hawk first, the bird of prey she had learnt from Hanif to be an essential companion for any desert traveller. It dropped out of the sky, seemingly from nowhere, to perch on the wooden camel saddle. A moment later, Azhar emerged from the gathering gloom, his sleek Saluki hound prancing at his heels. She was struck anew by the air of authority that she'd noted when she'd first spotted him on the camel. It was more than simply being perfectly at ease in his surroundings, but it was not quite arrogance. She could quite easily find him intimidating. She could also, all too easily, find him rather devastatingly attractive.

Devastating? Was that the right word? She wasn't sure there was a word for it, that ability of his to be both captivating and challenging at the same time. No, not challenging, perhaps imperious was a more appropriate description. Someone capable of being irresistible but not susceptible in return. Inviolate? But now she was being fanciful in the extreme. Though Azhar really did have a face that would stop any woman in her tracks. Julia longed to draw those sharp planes, the sensual curve of his mouth. Yes, it was the mouth, even more than the hard, graceful body, that made one think of searing kisses. Or it would, if one had any idea what searing kisses were. She had no doubt that Azhar knew. Odd, that she could be so certain the experience would be exquisitely pleasurable, when exquisite pleasure was as unfamiliar a concept to her as searing kisses. Indeed, she herself was getting rather hot under the collar, looking at him and thinking such unaccustomed thoughts.

It must be the desert, the sweltering heat and the savage beauty of it wielding its exotic magic. Watching Azhar as he collected various items from the mule packs, Julia felt they could be the only people here on earth under this vast canopy of stars, so far away from Cornwall, so different from the life she had known in every possible way. She could be anyone or no one. She could think wild, strange thoughts, she could even choose to act on them, and no one would ever know.

Not that she would dare. She'd felt this way once before, she remembered, in South America. Daniel had been shocked to the core when she'd kissed him passionately, had been appalled at the idea of making love under the stars, even though they were married and quite alone. As Azhar approached, the memory made her blush with mortification, eradicating any traces of her other, fanciful thoughts.

'So you have decided to join me after all,' he said.

Julia forced a bright smile. 'If there is enough food to share, then yes please.'

'Can you light a fire? The food I have foraged won't cook itself.'

Her smile slipped. It was true, she should have been tending to practical matters instead of day-dreaming, but she would rather not have that fact pointed out. 'I can light a fire,' Julia said tightly. 'I can skin that rabbit you have there, and I can even cook it. Give me it.'

The request unintentionally sounded more like a demand. Azhar's expression became haughty. How did he do that? A raising of the brows. A flinty glint in his eyes. The way his mouth set. 'It is not a rabbit, it's a hare.'

And, yes, once more he was correct. 'If it is, it's a very small hare,' Julia declared. 'In England they are twice that size.'

He took a dagger from his belt and set about

expertly skinning their dinner. 'We are in Arabia, not England. This hare is a product of its harsh desert environment.'

His hawk, perched motionless on the camel seat, watched with what Julia was convinced was a hopeful look in its beady eyes. 'You know, I am not one of those arrogant people who travel the world in an effort to prove that England is a superior nation to all others, if that is what you are thinking.'

Azhar smiled faintly—very faintly—but it was a smile none the less. Julia considered that progress. 'I have never been to England,' he said, 'which I understand is green and verdant, so I am willing to believe that the hares are bigger than they are here in the desert. Now, will you light the fire, if you please? I would prefer to eat some time before dawn.'

She set the fire quickly, coaxing it to life with what she hoped was a satisfying display of expertise, conscious all the time of Azhar's eyes on her. It was most unsettling. 'There, you see I am quite capable.'

'Indeed.' The hare lay neatly jointed in the cooking pot. The hawk and the hound were picking delicately through their share of the trimmings. From the folds of his tunic, he produced a handful of fragrant wild herbs. Pouring water over the hare to make a simple stew, he set the pot on the fire.

'You know, it is not my fault that the men I hired proved to be scoundrels,' Julia said, for his 'indeed' had rankled. Was it her fault? she wondered. Would Daniel have chosen better, more reliable guides? Certainly, if he was here he would not hesitate to make such a claim. No, what Daniel would do, was find a way to make it her fault. She recalled now, that he had blamed her for the loss of their barge. She had distracted him at a vital moment, he had said as they lay sodden, shivering, on the muddy bank of the river. Simply relieved to be alive, Julia hadn't argued with him at the time, and later—oh, later, she had done as she always did, and tried to banish the memory. She'd thought she had succeeded, too. Odd, how so many of these incidents had popped into her head lately. Which reminded her of something else.

'Azhar, may I ask you a question which has been baffling me? Why do you think Hanif waited so long to rob me?'

What do you mean?'

'I've been travelling in the desert for over a month. Why wait until now, when they could just as easily have drugged me on the first night, or within the first week.'

'A month!' Azhar's eyes flashed fury. 'That suggests that they deliberately waited until you had crossed over the border from Petrisa.'

'Why would they do that?'

His mouth thinned. 'The only reason I can think of is that they considered it safer to act here. Which would imply that the enforcement of law and order is much more lax in Qaryma,' he said grimly. 'If that is true, then things have changed radically.'

'Changed? It has been some time since you have been here, then?'

'Ten years,' Azhar said. 'I have not been home for ten years.'

'Home? Qaryma is your home?'

Julia Trevelyan was looking at him inquisitively. Azhar cursed inwardly. He had no idea how the word had slipped out. He had houses, but he had no home. 'Was, not is,' he said. 'Explain to me if you will, what is it that has occupied you for so many weeks here in the desert?'

The words sounded more like a command than a request, but they had the required effect. Though she hesitated for a moment, Julia accepted the deliberate change of subject. 'Specimens,' she said. 'I've been collecting plant specimens. I'm a botanist.'

He was surprised into a snort of laughter. 'Plants! You are here to collect plants?'

'Not so much plants as roots and seeds,' Julia Trevelyan replied haughtily. 'And what I mostly collect are drawings and notes, of the plants themselves, their habitat, companion plants, that sort of thing.'

'You are an artist, Madam Trevelyan?'

'Julia. If you are Azhar, then I ought to be Julia. I have some draughtsmanship skills.'

'And your drawings, where are they?' he asked, though he had guessed the answer.

'Gone,' she confirmed. 'Along with my paints and my notebooks and all my specimens. They were in a special trunk. It had lots of little drawers, and—and trays and—and the like.'

She was frowning heavily, clutching her fingers tightly together. Her determination not to cry was much more affecting than the sight of tears. 'It is this trunk you wished so desperately to recover, even more than your husband's watch?' Azhar asked, recalling with regret the harsh dose of reality he had administered earlier.

Julia nodded and forced a shaky smile. 'As you so emphatically pointed out, they will be long gone. I am hoping—that is I would very much appreciate if, when we arrive in Al-Qaryma, you might help me procure another guide.' Another smile. 'With your assistance, I'm sure I'll find someone more trustworthy than Hanif.'

Now she truly had astonished him. Another woman—even another man—would have been too affected by their recent experience to wish to do anything other than to count their blessings and return to the safety of their home. 'You cannot wish to remain in the desert after what has happened?'

'It is my only wish. I have to start again. Please, Azhar,' she said, gazing at him across the fire, her big green eyes wide, her expression earnest, 'please say you'll help me.'

'What did you intend to do with the specimens you collected? Sell them? As an international trader, I am aware there is a lucrative market for exotic plants, especially in light of the recent fashion for establishing botanical gardens.'

'Yes, yes, my husband and I have supplied plants to several such gardens with specimens garnered on our trips to South America, though Daniel, ever the purist, refused to sully his scientific research with commercial gain and so would not accept payment for them. I personally would have been more than happy, given our straitened circumstances—but that is beside the point.'

A husband who chose to subject his wife to poverty, whatever his scientific principles seemed a most relevant point to Azhar, but he refrained from saying so. 'What, then, is the point?' he asked.

'A book. My husband's book. His *magnum opus*. His life's work.' Julia gazed down at her lap, deep in thought for several minutes, before giving her head a little shake, as if to clear it. 'It is a treatise. A comprehensive illustrated guide to rare and exotic species of the plant kingdom. But it is not yet complete, and it was his dearest wish—his dying wish—his only wish—that I complete it for him.'

Her tone confused him. Brittle. Perhaps she was simply trying not to become upset. 'A compliment indeed,' Azhar said, 'to entrust the completion to you.'

Julia shrugged. 'My father is a renowned naturalist, a specialist in the flora and fauna of Cornwall. The illustrations for his book on the subject were mine. I first met Daniel when Papa took him on as an assistant. Even before we were betrothed, I worked on specimen drawings for him, and for almost all of the seven years of our married life I have travelled with him, taking notes, drawing and painting. So you see, Daniel did not mean it as a compliment. There is no one more suited.'

Her explanation, the toneless voice in which she spoke, confused him even further. Emotionless, or too filled with emotion? Azhar had no idea. 'This trip you have made, halfway across the world and all alone, it is then a pilgrimage of sorts?'

'It is, in the sense that it is a journey I must complete. But only so that I may then start my own journey, free from encumbrance. My husband's life's work has perforce been my life's work, and always will be until I complete this one final marital duty. But I grow weary of doing my duty. There, I have said it now. Finally, I have said it.'

She glared at him, daring him to speak, but

Azhar was so taken aback at the change in her, he said nothing.

Julia appeared to take his silence for condemnation. 'You think I'm callous, don't you?' she demanded. 'You most likely think I'm selfish and unfeeling, but you don't know the facts.'

She obviously wanted to tell him, however, and Azhar's curiosity was now well and truly piqued. 'What is it I don't know?'

She hesitated only fractionally. He could see the point where she cast caution to the winds, and wondered if she was aware of how her face mirrored her emotions in a most transparent fashion. He suspected not.

'Daniel made me promise him on his deathbed that I'd complete his masterpiece,' Julia said. 'On his deathbed, that was all he could think about—his book. So of course I promised, because how could I refuse a dying man's last wish?'

What could he reply to such a question? The parallels with his own situation struck Azhar with some force. Was the universe playing a trick on him?

Fortunately, Julia did not seem to expect him to speak. 'But that still wasn't enough for Daniel,' she continued. 'I had to promise that I'd keep it a secret, even from my father, that he had not completed the treatise himself. I had to promise that I'd come here to Arabia alone to complete the missing chapters. I had to promise that I'd finish all the colour plates, make a fair copy of everything, and have it bound into two editions, folio and quarto. Daniel was most specific about the binding for each. And the named recipients. I had to promise that I'd obtain permission from Mr Joseph Banks, the president of the Royal Society, for a dedication, and I had to promise that I'd petition Mr Banks on Daniel's behalf to sponsor him for posthumous fellowship.' She broke off, frowning down at her fingers, which she had been using to count off each promise, and then her brow cleared. 'Oh, yes, and I had to promise that I'd persuade Mr Banks to grant Daniel membership of the Horticultural Society of London.'

'Your husband had great confidence in your powers of persuasion,' Azhar observed.

'No, Daniel had great confidence in the results of his years of exhaustive research,' Julia replied. 'To be fair, his book is an excellent work, and his categorisation is innovative too. It is his legacy to the scientific world, and does deserve to be rec-

ognised. I don't expect to have any trouble per-
suading Mr Banks to grant his wishes.'

Julia pushed her hair back from her face, ad-
justing her position to face him more squarely.
'You know, I always thought that it was a love
of science that drove Daniel, wanting his work
to be recognised in the rarefied echelons of the
scientific and academic communities as one of
the definitive reference guides in its field. I respected him for that, but I wonder now if it was
fame he actually coveted, his name he wished to
be remembered.'

Azhar was forming his own, extremely uncom-
plimentary opinion of Julia's dead husband, but
he wisely chose not to share it. 'Does it make any
material difference?' he asked.

Julia pursed her lips, and then smiled. 'You
know, I don't think it does. Whatever his reasons, my task remains the same.'

'You have taken on a very heavy burden.'

'I thought so at first, and indeed there are as-
pects of it which—but actually, I have found the
experience of travel most liberating. I have not
been at all lonely you know. In fact I've very
much enjoyed my own company. And last night's
events aside, I have been quite captivated by the

beauty of Arabia. Besides,' she added, her smile becoming wry, 'I had no option. One cannot refuse a dying man's wishes.'

Azhar winced. Her words were so very nearly his exact thoughts on the summons that brought him here. Tomorrow—but he suddenly, desperately did not want to think of tomorrow. Not yet. 'So it is at your husband's command that you are here, alone?'

'You'll understand now why I found it somewhat ironic when you asked if I had his permission to travel,' Julia replied. 'Daniel is dictating my actions from beyond the grave just as effectively as he did before he passed away.' Her mouth tightened. 'But not for much longer. I'll finish his book, I'll make good on all those promises, and that will be an end of it. My whole life I have been doing another's bidding, drawing and painting to order. First for my father, then for Daniel. I have earned my right to freedom, and by heavens, I am going to enjoy it.'

Freedom. These last ten years Azhar had believed himself free, but from the moment he'd opened that summons he knew he'd been fooling himself. Freedom required the severing of all ties, all burdens, the honourable discharge of duty, just as Julia said. The last ten years had changed him for ever, shaped him into the man he was now, living the life he wanted to live. It was not the summons itself, with the unwelcome and completely unexpected news it contained, nor was it the command from beyond the grave that drove him here. It was this need for an absolute ending, for true freedom, which had driven him so many miles across the desert sands.

He and Julia sought the same thing. 'You crave your freedom. It would be churlish of me,' Azhar said, 'not to assist you in achieving that most desirable state of affairs.'

She beamed at him. 'You'll help me to find a guide, camels—and paints—will I be able to purchase paints?'

So little, she asked of him. She cared not for the dangers she had faced nor those to come, with her goal in sight. He, of all people, could understand that. He was forced to admire her. Her tenacity. Her fortitude. Her determination to make the best of an appalling lot. Not a tear had she shed. She had not theatrically thrown herself on his mercy, nor had she played the damsel in distress, though her situation would have been ample excuse to do so. She did not expect him to save her, she merely wished him to assist with providing her the means to save herself. She really was a most unusual female. 'I will help you,' Azhar said. 'I will take you to Al-Qaryma, and there you will find all you require.'

Her face lit up. 'Thank you, Azhar. Thank you so much.'

To his surprise, she grabbed his hand, pressing a kiss to his knuckles. Her mouth was warm on his skin. His body reacted instantly, sending blood coursing to his groin. Horrified, he snatched his hand away.

'I'm sorry. I did not mean—I didn't think—I...'

Her embarrassment fortunately masked his own discomfort. 'It has been a long and emotional day.' Azhar stirred the cooking pot. 'You must be hungry. Let us eat, and then you must rest. We will start for Al-Qaryma at dawn.'

They ate directly from the cooling cooking pot using their fingers. Julia, by now accustomed to the practice, and remembering to use only her right hand, ate with relish, not at all concerned at the lack of cutlery or the need to share.

Her confession had given her an appetite. She couldn't believe she had imparted all those intimate thoughts to this complete stranger. She had portrayed herself in a stark and very unflattering light. She was not at all proud of her feelings. She felt enormously guilty for even having them, never mind voicing them. Her resentment must have come over loud and clear, yet Azhar had not condemned her. On the contrary, he had seemed, from the little he had said, to be sympathetic to her stance.

Besides, it had felt good, finally, to articulate a little of what she was feeling. Daniel had reserved all his passion for his book, forcing her to bottle hers up. She had no idea if she was even capable of expressing it, for after that first time, the only time she'd ever dared to initiate any sort of intimacy and had been rejected, she had been careful not to alarm her husband with anything more than a tepid response to his own infrequent overtures. It seemed to satisfy him. Certainly he had never seemed dissatisfied, which was the same thing, wasn't it?

Recalling the way her stomach had lurched when she had kissed Azhar's hand, Julia wasn't so sure. It had felt like some sort of alchemical reaction between her skin and Azhar's. There had been a connection from his hand to her lips to her belly that set her blood tingling. And all she'd done was kiss his hand!

To her eternal embarrassment and his. What had possessed her? She slanted a look at him as he threw the remnants of their frugal meal towards his Saluki, and there was her explanation. Azhar was simply one of the most stunningly attractive men she had ever encountered.

One of the most intriguing too. He gave very little away. He was a rich trader. He was not married. He'd been away from this kingdom, his home, for ten years. That was the sum total of what she knew of him. The reason for his absence from home was definitely off the list of subjects he'd be willing to discuss however, and the last thing she wished to do was estrange him. Best if she stuck to more neutral topics.

'Thank you very much,' Julia said when he turned back to her, wiping his fingers on a large square of white lawn kerchief. 'I don't think I've ever eaten such a delicious hare.'

She was rewarded with a smile. 'Not even a fat English one?'

'Not even an enormous Cornish one,' Julia said, laughing. She leaned back to gaze up at the night sky. 'We had a telescope at our—my father's—

home in Marazion Bay, but the stars in the desert sky feel so close one almost doesn't need one. I have tried to paint it, but it's impossible to replicate such beauty.'

'You do not confine your art to botanical specimens, then?'

'I've had little time to paint anything else but—no, not wholly. When all this is over, I can paint what I like. And perhaps also what other people like too, since I'll have to find some way of earning my living.'

Azhar frowned. 'Your husband did not make provision for you?'

'What little we had will be consumed by this trip and the production of his book. Daniel assumed I would return to live with my father.'

'But you have other ideas?'

'I love Papa, but I do not intend to substitute one master for another,' Julia said wryly. 'I do not mean to imply that he is unkind or uncaring. My father is, as Daniel was, a sort of—oh, a sort of benevolent autocrat. Kind, and caring, but utterly selfish. Papa and Daniel both assumed my time theirs, their wishes mine. It never occurred to either of them that I might have wishes of my own. You see, a benevolent autocrat.'

'You have a peculiarly apt way of describing things.'

'But you understand? Your own father...'

'Is dead.'

Once again, his expression was blank. He hadn't moved, but she felt as if he had physically detached himself. It was an extremely effective method of closing down a subject, though it sent her curiosity soaring. Julia reminded herself of the need to keep him on her side. Silence stretched and became uncomfortable. She had to think of something to say. Anything.

'Are you familiar with the botanical gardens in Cairo, Azhar?'

A blank look was her answer.

'They were first established during Napoleon's occupation. A Monsieur Delile was the director then, a correspondent of my husband's. Monsieur Delile wrote the botanical chapters of *Travel in Lower and Upper Egypt*, you know.'

'No, I did not.'

'And you do not care to know,' she said, deflated. 'You would rather be alone.'

'No!' Not only Julia, but the Saluki hound flinched at this harsh exclamation. Azhar grimaced. 'Forgive me. This journey has been—

I have been—' He broke off, shaking his head. 'Please. Stay a while. Tell me—tell me a little more of your own journey. Did you stop in Cairo on your way to Damascus? It is a city I know well. One of my residences is on the outskirts.'

Julia eyed him warily. She was far more interested in what it was, precisely, about this journey that made him so—so edgy, yes that was it. But already, she knew him well enough not to pursue the subject. 'You have more than one residence, then? I assume that trade—whatever you trade in—is lucrative?'

'Silks and spices, mostly. I work hard but yes, it is lucrative. Though I travel a good deal, and have other residences in Damascus and Naples, I spend several months of the year in Egypt. I am well acquainted with Colonel Missett, your Consul-General, though apparently he is shortly to be replaced by a new man, Salt.'

'I didn't know that. Do you by any chance mean a Mr Henry Salt? It is such an unusual name, I wonder if it might be the same person.'

Azhar raised his brow. 'You know him?'

'A little. I have read his *Voyage to Abyssinia*, naturally.'

'Naturally?'

Julia grimaced. 'Naturally, because Mr Salt is—was—another of my husband's correspondents.'

'In fact, I too have read Mr Salt's account of his voyage to Abyssinia. It is a country with which I trade. I found his insights—interesting.'

'You mean they were in opposition to your own?'

'Our experiences of the country were very different.'

'You mean because your interest in the country is primarily commercial? From what I understand, a large part of Mr Salt's mission there was to promote trade too. Will you be cultivating his acquaintance in Cairo? Though I believe it is the Pasha who holds the real power there. Are you…?'

Azhar laughed. 'Yes, I am very well acquainted with him also. In my line of business it pays to be as well connected as possible. Permit me to tell you, madam—Julia—that you are a most singular female.'

'I don't know whether that is a compliment or an insult.'

'A compliment,' Azhar said, 'most assuredly, a compliment.'

In the firelight, his eyes seemed like molten gold. She knew she must be imagining the flicker of desire in them, it was the firelight reflected, but for a moment she allowed him to hold her gaze, to imagine what it would be like if he leaned over, closed the distance between them, touched his mouth to hers. Her stomach knotted, making her shiver.

Then reality intervened. Recalling the way he'd snatched his hand away from her earlier, Julia scrabbled to her feet, breaking the spell which could only have been one-sided. 'It is late, and I am very tired.'

Azhar too got to his feet, with a feline grace she could never hope to emulate. 'We will set out at dawn.'

'What about my things—the tent, my clothes…?'

He waved his hand dismissively. 'My mules can carry your personal effects. I will send someone for the remainder.'

Send someone! So he had family in this city they were visiting. Julia added this snippet to the very small list of things she knew of him. 'Thank you,' she said. 'For coming to my rescue today. For promising to help me when you have business of your own to attend to, and I'm sure the last thing you wish is to be encumbered with an inconvenient Englishwoman.'

'Cornish,' Azhar said softly. 'Goodnight, Julia.'

'You have not set up your tent.'

'Goodnight, Julia,' he said, firmly this time.

He meant to stand guard. And he wanted to be alone. And he didn't want her commenting on it either. She was getting rather good at understanding his silent communication method. 'Goodnight, Azhar.'

It had been a very long day. Clinging to the camel's hideously uncomfortable box seat behind Azhar, her bottom quite numb, Julia tried to ignore the increasing queasiness that assailed her as they swayed alarmingly atop the beast. The well-named ship of the desert was making her seasick. She would have given much to have been able to travel on one of the pack mules as had become her custom, but with her few remaining personal possessions to add to their existing burden, it had not been possible.

The initial excitement of sitting so intimately close to Azhar, their bodies perforce pressed together, had quite worn off. She was unbearably hot in her woollen skirt and jacket. The sheet which he had formed into a headdress for her provided much more protection from the sun than her hat, but her head was thumping all the same, her eyes were gritty with sand, and her skin damp with sweat. She had never in her life felt so unattractive.

In stark comparison, Azhar was even more good-looking in the daylight. His skin was burnished bronze, the colour of the sand dunes in the shade. His eyes gleamed, dark gold like the sun. His hair seemed almost blue-black, a sleek glossy cap when he took off his headdress to re-fold it. She couldn't see a single drop of perspiration on his brow, while in contrast her hair clung in lank tendrils to her forehead and her nape. It was so unfair, and really quite irritating, the way he seemed quite unaffected by the heat, drinking sparingly from his goatskin flask when they stopped, while she had to fight not to empty hers in one long, greedy gulp.

When the sun was at its zenith they had temporarily broken their journey, but Julia had the distinct impression this was for her benefit only. While she dozed fitfully in the shade, Azhar sat staring out at the desert wastes. The frown creasing his brow, the way his mouth was set, gave an austerity to his features today, making him more intimidating rather than handsome. She had a hundred questions to ask, not least of which was where she would spend the night, but with every mile they covered, he grew more distant and remote.

'Al-Qaryma.' Azhar brought the camel to a halt at the top of a sand dune, waking Julia from her I-am-not-going-to-be-sick trance, clicking his tongue to bring his camel to its knees and dismounting with annoyingly fluid ease, before helping her to scrabble awkwardly down.

One look at the view, however, and she forgot all about her nausea. The small city rose dramatically from the verdant green fields surrounding the large oasis, which shimmered in the late afternoon sun. Clusters of buildings hugged the contours, interspersed with the sparkle of fountains, connected by dusty grey ribbons which were the narrow winding roads. And above them all, sitting at the top of the low hill, was a huge palace, the domed roofs glittering white, the towers which fronted it trimmed with emerald and gold. 'It's beautiful,' Julia said, gazing entranced. 'It's like a magical city, rising up out of the desert. My goodness, how you must have missed it.

If this was my home, I don't know if I'd be able to tear myself away from it, never mind stay away for ten years.'

Azhar was staring at the view, his frown so deep it brought his brows together. 'It is undeniably beautiful, but a gilded cage is still a cage,' he said.

'What a strange thing to say. Whatever do you mean?'

'What I mean is that this city is no longer my home. This kingdom no longer forms the limits of my horizon,' Azhar said. 'I have no home. I have no people. I have no country. I answer to no one. My heart and my life belong to me alone.'

'You must lead a very lonely life.'

His smile was fleeting but unmistakably sensual. 'My determination never to burden myself with a wife does not preclude my enjoying the company of women.'

'I doubt you've enjoyed the company of this particular woman,' Julia responded tartly, because that smile was making her tingle. 'I've been nothing but an inconvenience.'

He shook his head. 'You underestimate yourself.'

Was he teasing her? He could not seriously

mean he enjoyed her company. His attention had turned back to the view of the city. His expression was almost impossible to read. 'Azhar, what *has* brought you back here? You have been away for so very long.'

'Not long enough. I never believed I would return. You know, the parallels of our situations struck me forcibly last night,' he said bleakly. 'In fact, you will be surprised to know that my reasons for this journey are very similar to yours. I too come in order to secure my freedom. I am also here at the behest of a dead man.'

'What can you mean? What dead man? Azhar…'

But he was already walking towards the camel. 'No more questions. Now is the time for action. All will become clear in due course.' He clicked his tongue and the ship of the desert once more dropped obediently to its knees.

Completely at a loss, Julia allowed him to lift her on to the camel. He mounted in front of her, and set the beast back on its feet. Their little caravan headed down into the valley, past the blue pool of the oasis, the vibrant green of the irrigated fields, and Julia, her head spinning with the onslaught of colour and scents, focused on staying upright in the saddle.

Questions jostled for room in her head, but there was no prospect of answers for the moment. On they went, through the winding streets, past piazzas with tinkling fountains, souks closed now for the day, the air still redolent with the cinnamon and mace, cardamom and cumin they had been selling. People were staring. In fact, a lot of people were staring, nudging each other, summoning yet more people. It was unusual for a woman to ride on the same camel as a man—that much Julia knew. Was that all it was? Perhaps their interest was exacerbated by her Western clothing. In all likelihood they had never seen a Western woman before. Yes, that was it. Though it was beginning to look as if the entire city was turning out to look at them as they passed.

Feeling extremely uncomfortable and extremely anxious, Julia was thankful to be able to hide behind her improvised veil. Azhar, she only then noticed, had not covered his face. Risking a glance back, she saw that they were being followed by a growing crowd. The nudges, the murmurings and mutterings were perfectly audible even above the hooves of the mules and camels, but Azhar looked resolutely straight ahead, his gaze unswerving. On they went, and the trail of people behind them turned into a procession, the mutterings and murmurings a sort of wailing— no, not wailing. It was not an unhappy sound. She could not see the women's faces, but the men were smiling, the children were laughing.

'Azhar,' Julia hissed, 'what is going on?'

Still he remained silent. Still they continued on. In front of their little caravan, the inhabitants of Al-Qaryma threw themselves down on to their knees. Someone had strewn rose petals in their path. Rose petals! Julia could hear singing from the human tide of people behind them. Bells began to peal. This was more, much more than mere hospitality. It was not Julia they were interested in either, but Azhar. Ten years he had been gone, yet all these people had come out of their houses to celebrate his return. Why? Who on earth was he?

She had the first inkling of an answer when he finally brought the camel to a halt at the palace. Two guards, armed with glittering scimitars, dressed in immaculate white, threw the gates wide and fell on to their knees in obeisance. More guards, two long lines of sentries, stood to stiff attention. From the high windows of the palace which looked out over the courtyard, Julia could see faces peering down. Behind them, the people crowded in. As Azhar clicked his usual command and the camel dropped obediently to its knees, the crowd fell silent.

Azhar dismounted. Julia slid down, her body drenched in cold, clammy sweat. 'Azhar?' she whispered, but his eyes were fixed on the huge portico, the formal entrance to the palace, where a man was emerging.

Dressed in a gold tunic, his headdress encrusted with precious jewels, the man made his way towards them. He was tall, would once have been considered handsome, but his body was running seriously to fat. Above the short, precisely trimmed beard, his cheeks were florid, his chin jowly. There was an air about him of entitlement, arrogance even, and a hint of petulance about his mouth. He was clearly privileged and in a position of power, and Julia suspected that he used both to his advantage. A man who demanded not only respect but subservience. A fraction of a second too late, late enough for this royal personage to notice, Julia dropped to her knees and bowed her head.

To her astonishment, Azhar remained standing. She watched from beneath her lashes as he approached. The man's smile was rigid. The barely disguised resentment in his expression made Julia shiver. The packed courtyard crackled with tension. He halted in front of Azhar and uttered one word. Julia's grasp of Arabic was basic in the extreme. Brother, she thought he had said, but that could not be. They were the antithesis of each other.

The slightest inclination of his head was all Azhar gave, but the royal person eased himself with difficulty to his knees and kissed Azhar's hand before getting up again, turning to the crowd, uttering the ritual words of welcome, and thanking God for Azhar's arrival.

Cheers erupted and cries of the traditional words of welcome rung out, over and over. Julia could restrain herself no longer. 'Azhar!' The sudden hush made Julia realise she had most likely broken every single protocol, if not committed treason, but it was too late now. 'Azhar,' she said, getting to her feet. 'Will you please tell me what on earth is going on?'

He turned towards her, and it felt as though every single person in the courtyard was holding their collective breath. 'Julia. Allow me to present to you my brother, Prince Kamal, Sheikh al-Farid. Kamal, this is Madam Julia Trevelyan. She will be our guest for a few days.'

Automatically, Julia dropped a curtsy, although the man completely ignored her, saying something over her head to Azhar. 'I don't understand,' she said, earning herself a shocked intake of breath from the crowd as she interrupted him, but she was beyond caring. 'If this is your brother then you...'

'I am Sheikh al-Farid, Crown Prince Azhar of Qaryma,' Azhar replied with a pronounced sneer. 'Welcome to my kingdom.'

Chapter Three

Azhar poured the last dregs of coffee from the pot. The thick, dark liquid, which he had always preferred without the customary sugar, seared its way into his stomach, adding to the edgy feeling which had kept him awake all night. His first night here in the palace for ten years. In the intervening period, he had not missed this place or this desert or this life, had taught himself never to think of any of it. Taught himself rather too well. Wrenched from his real life, returning so abruptly, it all threatened to overwhelm him. The allure of the desert itself was powerful. He had not forgotten its mystical beauty, but he had suppressed the memory of it. Yesterday, his first sighting of Al-Qaryma had stirred the depths of his soul. The world contained many other deserts, many other beautiful cities, but only here, in this kingdom, in this city, were his people.

His people?

No, they were not his people. Those crowds who had followed him through the streets yesterday, the people he refused to allow himself to acknowledge, they were not *his*. They were his father's people, and now they would be Kamal's.

As if on cue, a discreet tap on the door preceded a manservant, who announced Kamal's arrival. The dramatic change in his appearance struck Azhar afresh. Kamal had always been a greedy child, with a penchant for sweets and pastries that he made no attempt to curtail, but youth had protected him from the worst effects of over-indulgence. Now, at twenty-nine, two years younger than Azhar, his brother looked at least ten years older.

Taking care to mask his thoughts behind a benign countenance, Azhar got to his feet. 'At last. We did not have an opportunity to speak privately last night. It is very good to see you, Kamal. Get up, please, there is no need—you know I never did like to stand on ceremony.'

Avoiding the proffered embrace, his brother instead bowed over Azhar's hand. 'Things are very different now you are soon to be crowned. As King, ceremony is precisely what you are required to stand on.'

He had not imagined it last night, then, there was an appreciable edge to Kamal's tone. 'You must know I neither expected nor wanted this,' Azhar said, taking a seat on the divan by the window, and indicating that Kamal should join him. 'The summons I received came as a complete shock.'

'Our father's health had been in decline for some time. This past year, he was too frail to rule effectively. I was obliged to step in and assume control. With his blessing, I might add.'

'An obligation I'm sure you discharged with great skill.'

'One does one's humble best, however temporarily the responsibility rests on one's shoulders. The burden is yours now, my brother.'

Yes, his brother was definitely hostile. An understandable emotion in one who believed his powers were about to be wrested from him—and that was another thing he'd forgotten about Kamal, how much he enjoyed wielding even the most insignificant scrap of power and influence. It would be very easy to put his mind at rest, but Azhar's instincts told him to hold fire for the present. Though his intentions were set firm, though he had absolutely no doubt as to their validity, experience had taught him the benefits of keeping his own counsel until he was ready to act. Silence was a powerful ally. There was knowledge to be gleaned from keeping Kamal in blissful ignorance for the time being, and knowledge was even more powerful than silence. The time for Azhar to declare himself would come soon enough, but it was not now.

'When I said the summons came as a shock,' he said, choosing his words with care, 'I referred not only to our father's demise, but to the fact of my being named rightful heir.'

Kamal looked astonished. 'You jest! And it is a joke in poor taste, if I may say so. As if the King would ever have dreamed of disinheriting you.'

'I am being perfectly serious. I believed my departure to be final and irrevocable.'

'And yet you have returned none the less,' Kamal replied with a tight smile. 'I knew you would. I knew you would not be able to resist claiming your kingdom, even though you forfeited any right to it all those years ago.'

Azhar flinched inwardly at the barely disguised

animosity, though he kept his own expression neutral, reminding himself that his brother's feelings were perfectly natural. Kamal had always adored his royal status, had always resented his subordinate status as second son. As far as he was concerned, Azhar had returned to snatch what had become rightly his. His resentment was understandable, if disappointing to witness. 'You do me a disservice,' he said. 'I had no idea this kingdom was mine to claim. Our father...'

'Oh, please, let us be done with this pretence! You were always his favourite, and you know it, Azhar. Firstborn, favoured son—that was you. Nothing I did was ever good enough for him.'

His tone was horribly familiar. Azhar had forgotten how petulant Kamal could be when thwarted. One thing he had in common with their father, and another thing that had clearly not changed. As to his words, however...

'You know perfectly well that is preposterous,' Azhar said. 'When I left, he forbade me to return. "If you defy me and leave now, it must be for ever. The decision, once made, is irrevocable," were his actual words—not words that I am likely to forget.'

'What else could he say, in the face of your determination to disobey him?'

Azhar gritted his teeth. 'He made it impossible for me to do anything else. There is a world outside Qaryma. All I wanted was to see it. I have lost count of the number of times I begged him for permission to experience a little of what the wider world has to offer.'

'And the more you begged, the more determined he was to deny you, and the more determined you became to have your own way. You really were very alike in that sense,' Kamal said. 'Stubborn, determined to impose your will on everyone, able to listen to no other point of view. How ironic that the man who claims he never wished to be a king will now make a king in our father's image.'

Kamal was wrong. Azhar had never wanted the crown. He had come here with the express purpose of proving that. Although the words were said deliberately to rile him, they also provided the perfect opportunity to put Kamal out of his misery, but his brother's attitude set Azhar's resolve to wait. Unlike him, Kamal had acceded to their father's will, but from the sounds of it, not without a simmering sense of resentment. 'To return to my original point,' he said. 'The summons I received was a very great shock. When I left...'

'You know, I never did understand why you were so set on going anywhere, Azhar. Everything you could wish for is here, but you were always determined to shake the sands of Qaryma from your feet, weren't you?'

'It was never my intention to leave for good. If he had granted me permission to travel before I reached my majority, I would have honoured any conditions he set on my return. But he would not give me permission, forcing me to wait until I no longer required it, on my twenty-first birthday. He could not deny me the right to leave, but he could deny me the right to return, and that is what he did. When I left, our father made it clear that the price for my wanderlust would be permanent exile.'

Kamal snorted. 'He said that out of desperation to keep you here. He never gave up hope that you'd come crawling back on your hands and knees. You'd have thought that he'd be pleased to have a second son on hand to inherit, a son who, unlike his firstborn, was obedient and respectful and who actually wanted to rule, but, no—it was you he wanted. It was always you. All I was fit for was to send a summons to you upon his demise. He had Council witness it too. He could not have made his desire to exclude me clearer.'

'If that is true, why then did he insist the summons was sent after his death? He appointed you as Regent. Why not summon *me* to fulfil that role?'

'Ten years without a word from you, Azhar. Ten years!' Kamal said bitterly. 'Don't you think you'd made it very clear by then that you would never return while he was still alive?'

'He *knew* I didn't want this. He knew I have never wanted it. He could not bend me to his will while he was alive. That summons was his attempt to do so from beyond the grave.'

'A successful one too,' Kamal said with malicious relish. 'Our father could certainly be both capricious and vindictive. Perhaps by deliberately denying you the opportunity for any sort of reconciliation he was punishing you for turning your back on Qaryma and, more importantly, on him. Now it is too late to be forgiven, and you will have to live with that on your conscience. Poor Azhar.'

Anger warred with hurt at his brother's sarcastic tone. Pride kept both firmly under control. 'I have no desire for forgiveness, having committed no crime,' Azhar said curtly, getting to his feet. 'You overstep the mark, Brother.'

'Forgive me.' Kamal fell to his knees, and Azhar made no move to prevent him. 'It has been a somewhat difficult time, trying to protect your interests here, not knowing how long it would be before you returned.'

'I have been remiss, I should thank you for running the kingdom in the interim,' Azhar said, indicating that Kamal should rise.

'Yours will be the only thanks I receive,' his brother replied. 'You cannot have failed to notice yesterday how pleased the people are to see you.'

He had in fact tried very hard indeed to take no notice of anything on his arrival. Azhar waved his hand dismissively. 'A show of respect, nothing more.'

'They will be anxious to see you crowned.'

'Because a coronation requires to be celebrated, and most lavishly.' Azhar said wryly. 'The best things come to those who wait. I have only just returned.'

'But until you are crowned, there are certain

powers which you cannot exercise. The authority invested in me as Regent...'

'Can continue, I am sure, for the time being.'

'Of course, if that is your wish, but—but I assumed you would take immediate control.'

Kamal looked puzzled, as well he might. Azhar wasn't too sure himself what he meant, save to buy himself some time. He turned away to gaze out of the window, at one of the sixty-five palace fountains. He had counted them once. Odd, that such a useless fact should stick in his mind. His journey here had been fuelled by a sense of urgency, a need to finally sever the ties of duty that bound him to this place. But the urgency had dissipated with his arrival. He had no doubts about his course of action, but he needed to consider how best to implement it.

All he needed was a little time. Time to satisfy himself that Kamal was fit to govern or, if necessary, time to ensure that he could be moulded to be so. 'I require time,' Azhar said, turning back to his brother. 'Whether you believe it or not, my inheritance has come as a shock to me, and my absence has been a long one. The coronation must perforce wait. I require time to reacquaint myself with the kingdom. In the interim, you will continue to rule, while I decide how best to implement the handover of power.'

'How long do you envisage this interim period to be?'

He had no idea. 'I will inform you and the Council of my plans tomorrow.'

'And the woman?'

Julia. The thought of her was as refreshing as plunging into the cool, clear water of an oasis. Julia, his connection to the real world, his touchstone. Yesterday, reeling from the shock of his revelation, exhausted by the pace of the long day's travel, she had clung to his sleeve, begging him not forget her amid all the hubbub of his return. As if that was possible.

'Madam Trevelyan is an English botanist.' Cornish, Azhar corrected himself silently.

'What is she to you?'

'I found her alone at the Zazim Oasis. Her dragoman and his men had absconded in the night, taking everything with them.'

'Stupid foreigners, what do they expect! The desert is no place for a woman travelling alone. What was she thinking?'

Azhar's fists clenched. 'I am more concerned with your own thoughts. A nefarious deed was perpetrated at one of our biggest oases. Those thieving brigands should not have dared cross our borders, never mind dishonour our lands in such a way.'

Colour stained Kamal's cheeks. 'A kingdom without a king is weakened and open to abuse. How can I be expected to command respect without a crown?'

Earn it, Azhar thought bitterly. Respect cannot be demanded. But there was nothing to be gained by antagonising his brother still further. 'I could not leave Madam Trevelyan alone and without resources, so I brought her here. Any man of honour would have done the same.'

Kamal shrugged. 'As you pointed out, the Zazim Oasis is one of our biggest, and therefore a busy and popular stopping point. Someone else would have come along soon enough. As Crown Prince of Qaryma, I would have thought you had more pressing matters to occupy you.'

'As Crown Prince of Qaryma, I am responsible for the well-being and safety of everyone in this kingdom, whether citizen or visitor.' Suddenly weary of Kamal's company, Azhar clapped his hands loudly. The door opened instantly. 'Until tomorrow, Brother,' he said, leaving Kamal no option but to bow himself out. Azhar smiled inwardly. His privileged position was not without its advantages.

Having spent a blissfully comfortable night in the lavish quarters assigned to her, wallowing in the luxury of a hot bath before collapsing on to the huge divan, Julia had spent the morning anxiously waiting for some word from Azhar. She knew he would have weighty matters to attend to, but he had promised not to forget her. She was therefore both relieved and delighted when a servant arrived and silently bid her follow him. Perhaps he was to take her to the souk to purchase essential supplies. The sooner she began her work again the better.

She followed along behind as the servant led her through a series of marble-panelled corridors illuminated by glass skylights. The man walked quickly, forcing her to take a little running step every now and again in order to keep up. Through open archways she could hear the muted sound of voices. Silence emanated from other forbidding-looking, heavy doors where sentries stood in plain white robes, scimitars hanging from their leather-belted waists. What were they guarding—or who? How many lives were being lived out in this palace, in this city within a city? Where was this man taking her? And to meet whom? Completely disoriented, Julia followed him around another right-angled turn, to find the passage terminated in another of those huge, guarded doors.

'What is this place?' she asked, though she knew it was futile. Even if he understood her, the servant was the strong silent type. He was already backing away, and the guard at the door was ushering her forward with a face that seemed to Julia would brook no argument. Taking a deep breath, she stepped past him and entered the room.

Save that it was not a room. She was on a low terrace leading on to one of the most beautiful gardens she had ever seen. Cypress trees grew in shady groves. Mosaic walkways meandered through manicured beds ablaze with exotic flowers. Tall marble pillars stood at the head of a long pool full of brightly coloured fish. Water gushed from the mouths of the playful stone dolphins in the fountain at the far end. Her senses swam with the profusion of scents and sounds. In one corner another fountain fed an oasis-like space proliferating with cacti and other succulents, some of which Julia had never before encountered. Another sinuous pathway took her through a gate to a rose garden, the blooms, like the stars in the night sky, so much bigger and brighter than those on view at home. Beneath her feet, she could feel the gurgle of the complex subterranean irrigation system. Turning a corner at the edge of the garden, she found groves of orange, lemon and lime trees, more marble pillars and rustic bridges crossing the irrigation streams which had been allowed to bubble to the surface. Tucked away, almost hidden from view, was a small marble kiosk in the classical style, rather like a Greek temple, though on a much smaller scale. And standing at the entrance, looking very like he'd just stepped down from Mount Olympus, was Azhar.

He was dressed in loose trousers and a long dark-blue tunic fastened at the neck with black frogging. The simple lines of the tunic emphasised the breadth of his shoulders and chest. He wore no headdress, the sunlight making his night-dark hair shine like silk. He really was an extraordinarily good-looking man.

Prince. Not man, Prince. Crown Prince, no less. She would do well to remember that rather significant fact. She dropped a hasty curtsy. 'Your Highness.'

'Azhar is quite sufficient when we are alone, Julia.'

Emboldened by his smile, she gave in to the allure of the welcoming shade and the entrancing man, and joined him on the terrace of the kiosk. 'I've never seen such a wonderful garden. The sheer profusion of species quite takes my breath away. The irrigation system must be quite ingenious to allow such different varieties as roses and succulents to grow in the same soil, under this unforgiving sun. My father would be astonished, and most envious.'

'Ah, yes, I recall you said your father was a botanist, as well as a—how did you put it—a benevolent autocrat?'

'You must think me most disrespectful. I was somewhat overwrought.'

'You had just cause. In fact I can think of no woman I have ever met who would have been less overwrought, all things considered. Please, sit down and take some mint tea with me.'

'Thank you.' She did as he bade her, sinking gratefully on to a low, padded chair while fanning her face. 'I am honoured that you have found the time to grant me a personal audience.'

'You are not one of my subjects, Julia, this is not an audience. I have not forgotten my promise to help you.'

Because she had clung to his sleeve and begged him not to do so. Julia's toes curled and her cheeks heated at the memory. 'I embarrassed you in front of your subjects. When I awoke this morning, I was mortified to have behaved with so little decorum.'

'I should have given you some warning of what was to come. It was unfair of me.'

'A little,' she agreed, 'but honestly, Azhar, it was obvious that you were finding your return difficult enough, without having to explain yourself to a troublesome Englishwoman.'

'Cornish woman,' Azhar said with a small smile. 'You see, I do remember.'

And he was once again turning the subject. Julia hesitated, but she might never get another chance to talk to him alone. 'And I distinctly remember you saying that you had sworn never to return to Qaryma. And yet, here you are.'

Azhar shook his head. 'It is true, I am not here by choice. When I left Qaryma I thought it was for ever, but it appears my father had different ideas. Despite our many differences, he chose not to disinherit me when he died three months ago.'

'So that was what you meant yesterday, when you said you were here at the behest of a dead man.' Impulsively, Julia slid off her chair to kneel by his, taking his hand between hers. 'I'm so sorry,' she said. 'To return under such tragic circumstances must be very painful indeed.'

Stiffening, Azhar withdrew his hand. 'My father and I were estranged. I do not require your pity.'

Her cheeks flaming, Julia scrambled to her feet. 'It was not pity I offered, but sympathy. Whatever these many differences there were between you, this palace, this city, this whole kingdom must be full of memories. I would find it extremely painful, but I am a mere mortal. I expect princes are immune to such human emotions.'

She waited for inevitable rebuke, but when Azhar got to his feet he neither stalked off nor summarily ordered her to leave the garden. 'Yesterday, when we arrived, I half-expected my father to appear at the gates and forbid me entry,' he confessed. 'Last night, when they made me take his ceremonial place at dinner it felt—I had to stop myself looking over my shoulder. He was such a very powerful presence, it's difficult to believe that he's no longer here.' He caught her arm, turning her around to face him. 'Though he died three months ago, to me he has been dead for ten years, but the memories, the ghosts of the past, they linger. You were quite right about those. They are—I find them disconcerting.'

'Goodness! A prince who is neither infallible nor immune to feelings.'

Azhar smiled faintly. 'Only immune to certain feelings. Is it possible for you to ignore the fact that I am a prince?'

'You're not only a prince but a crown prince.' Julia wrinkled her brow. 'And a sheikh, you said. While your brother—he is also a prince and a sheikh? It is very confusing.'

'Not half so confusing or complicated as your British system is, as far as I understand it—or don't,' Azhar said. 'Sheikh is simply an honorary title given to a man of influence and high rank. As the King's sons Kamal and I are Princes. As the first born I am Crown Prince. And as the person my father chose to implement his will when he was no longer able, Kamal is also Regent.'

'So you wish me to forget that you are a sheikh

and a prince and a crown prince and soon to be King? That is a lot to forget,' Julia said ruefully. 'Will I be permitted to speak my mind without worrying about being cast in a dungeon?'

Azhar's smile broadened. 'I doubt even the threat of a dungeon would prevent you from speaking your mind. You are a most extraordinary woman.'

'Singular and now extraordinary. I am flattered.'

'To speak the truth is not flattery. I have never met anyone like you.'

'If you speak any more of these truths, I shall leave Qaryma with a swollen head.'

'For a woman who has travelled alone halfway across the world, who has taken on a task which would have sent almost anyone else—man or woman—running in the opposite direction, who has dealt with being robbed, and drugged, and carried off by a complete stranger to a remote kingdom she's never even heard of, you have a remarkably low opinion of yourself. Your husband has a lot to answer for since I suspect it was he who gave you your low expectations.'

'Don't you think that it is rather that my husband expected a lot of me?'

'Your husband certainly made a lot of assumptions. Whether he thought through the implications of what he demanded from you on his deathbed...'

'No, he didn't. That is very obvious to me now.' Julia rested her hands on the terrace parapet, gazing out into the garden. 'The other night, the things I said about Daniel—I hadn't given voice to them before. I hadn't even realised I'd harboured some of those thoughts. I must have sounded quite—uncaring. I'm not. I did care for Daniel. I respected him, and I did love him. I think he loved me too, in his own way, only not as much as he loved his work. His precious book. Which I do resent a little.' She grimaced. 'More than a little. I don't know why I'm telling you this.'

'Perhaps because we met under such unusual circumstances.'

'Perhaps. Certainly all of this, you, the palace, the city, it feels quite unreal. Perhaps it is because our paths have crossed only fleetingly.'

'Perhaps.' Azhar joined her at the parapet. 'Julia, are you quite set on returning to the desert to finish your task?'

'Of course I am. It's what I came here for,' she

replied, perplexed that he should have thought to ask such a question. 'Oh, are you concerned that I'll outstay my welcome? You need have no such fear. I know I behaved inappropriately last night, clinging to your sleeve and—and—but I very much appreciate that your time is precious. All I require are a few camels and a guide, and I'll be on my way. If you would be so good as to exchange some of my banknotes for local coin, I can purchase all that I need. My notes are for imperial pounds, obviously, but as a trader, I am sure it will be easy enough for you to reuse them in a business transaction. I will need drawing materials too, and watercolours. And some clothes. I am determined to purchase something more suitable to wear. But I am sure all of that can be done in a matter of a day, maybe two, so—' She broke off, for she was beginning to sound as if she protested far too much. 'So you see,' she concluded lamely, 'I won't be a burden to you for much longer.'

'You are not a burden to me, as you put it. I am not at all concerned that you will outstay your welcome. On the contrary, you are welcome to remain here in the palace for as long as necessary.'

'Thank you, but I really couldn't—my plants,

and drawings, and then there's the issue of my travel papers.'

'Your papers are hardly an issue. Obviously, I have the authority to grant you permission to remain here for as long as you require.'

'Obviously.' Julia rolled her eyes. 'I forgot.'

'You forgot,' Azhar repeated, an arrested look on his face. 'Good! I hope you can continue to forget my status. Can you do that, do you think? No, wait, don't answer yet. Come with me. I have a proposition for you.'

It was not at all what he'd had in mind when he summoned her to the garden, but the idea forming in his head made a great deal of sense. Azhar led Julia down from the terrace on to one of the winding paths through the lime grove. 'This is the largest of the palace gardens, but there are numerous others. In addition to the extraordinary irrigation system you mentioned, I am sure we have any number of plants unique to this part of the desert. I do not pretend to your expertise, but I could arrange for you to talk to our Head Gardener.'

'I don't speak Arabic, Azhar, and...'

He waved his hand dismissively. 'A translator could be arranged.'

They were at the boundary wall, looking hundreds of feet down to the swathe of green which was the Al-Qaryma oasis. The view was more stunning than Azhar remembered. He turned to see his own wonder reflected on Julia's face. Water almost turquoise blue, green so vibrant it was emerald, neat fields of crops, fruit trees, and then, as if someone had drawn an invisible wall, the sharp delineation which marked the start of the desert, the sands palest gold and silver in the late morning light, smooth and flat before giving way to rising dunes, rocky outposts.

'It is terrifyingly beautiful,' Julia said softly.

'Terrifying?'

'Nature at its most beautiful and most lethal. It is like standing on the edge of one of those lakes in Switzerland, so blue and so calm and so deep and so dangerous. You have the overwhelming urge to plunge in, even though you know the cold will kill you. This desert—your desert—it makes me want to walk into it and keep walking. You probably think I'm being ridiculously fanciful.'

'No. I would not have put it in those words, but

they are exactly how I feel about Qaryma. Ter-rifyingly beautiful.'

'You have missed it, haven't you? Despite what you said, I think you have missed it dreadfully.'

It was true that once upon a time this land and these people had been precious to him. He had loved this kingdom that he had been born and raised to rule, had never questioned his duty or his ultimate destiny. Until he had left, and taken his destiny into his own hands. He had turned his back and hardened his heart. It would be folly to let loose his hold on that hard-won protective shield, a shield which guarded his equally hard-won independence. 'No,' Azhar said firmly, 'I have not missed it.'

Julia looked sceptical. 'I find that very difficult to believe. Look at all this,' she said. 'It is utterly beautiful and all of it is yours.'

'I have been to many places in the world just as beautiful.'

'As have I, but only Cornwall is my home, Azhar. What is so wrong in admitting to an emo-tional attachment to the place you were born and raised, which is an integral part of you?'

Her words, echoing his own thoughts made

him uncomfortable. 'I have no home,' Azhar said stubbornly.

'You do now, Your Highness.'

It was her tone as much as her words that made his hackles rise. 'How dare you…?'

'…point out the truth to you, a prince?' Julia folded her arms and glowered at him. 'Go on, then, call the guards and have me charged with treason, though I should warn you that I shall have no hesitation in using your royal command to forget that you are a prince in my defence. Your case will be thrown out of court.'

Not for the first time, Azhar was startled into laughter. 'I doubt it somehow, since the court answers to me, but I must commend you most sincerely, madam, for so effectively implementing my royal command.'

Julia dropped a small curtsy. 'Thank you.'

She did not retract her words, and she did not apologise for them. Unpalatable as some of her thoughts might be, he could trust her to speak her mind, which was exactly what he needed from her. 'How long would it take you, do you think, to complete your work here?'

She shook her head, confused by the sudden change in subject. 'I don't know. I was almost finished. Perhaps a month, if I can locate the right specimens.'

A month. A month was more than sufficient to put any qualms he had to rest. Kamal lacked experience, perhaps judgement also. He was weak, he had always been weak, but that was because he had never been required to be strong. A month would give Azhar ample opportunity to assess the state of the kingdom, to address his brother's weaknesses and provide him with some guidance, thus ensuring that he could leave Qaryma in safe hands and with a clear conscience.

Though another month was a long time to be away from his business empire. He had left his agent to keep it ticking over, but he had never granted the man more than cursory authority. Azhar loved the cut and thrust of bargaining and barter. He loved the risks and the danger in some of the far-flung places he travelled to. He loved the thrill when a deal paid off, and he even relished the deals that did not, for the challenges they created. He loved it all, that life far from here, bounded only by his own ambition. He would miss it, but it would survive without him for another month. One more month, that was all it would take, he was sure of it. Then he would claim his freedom, escape this gilded cage, and in the process, help Julia to claim her freedom too. It was a most excellent plan.

'A month,' Azhar said, smiling at her. 'Excellent. We are agreed, then?'

'Agreed as to what?' she asked blankly.

Azhar was not a man given to indecision. One of the keys to his success in business was his ability to act quickly. Yet his instincts this morning had been *not* to act hastily and to buy himself some time. The relief of understanding why, and of coming up with a strategy to achieve it, was immense. Though in his excitement, he realised, he hadn't actually explained himself. 'That you will stay here as my honoured guest,' he elucidated. 'With unfettered access both to the gardens and the kingdom at large, you should be able to gather all the specimens you need. Further, that you will allow me to be your personal guide.'

Julia's jaw dropped. 'But how can you—I mean, won't you be far too busy being a prince? The people will expect…'

'I will leave Kamal in charge temporarily. Escorting you around Qaryma will allow me to become reacquainted with both my kingdom and my people, while at the same time allowing you to document our flora.'

'That is a very generous and, I have to say, most unexpected offer, Azhar. I can't imagine why you would wish to devote so much time to me when you have many much more important matters to occupy your time.'

She meant it, too. What kind of a man had her husband been, to be so unappreciative of his wife! 'It will be a very useful exercise, not to say educational experience, for me to view my—this kingdom through your eyes. All I ask in return is that you share your insights with me in your own inimitable way.'

'Even if they are not complimentary?'

'Especially if they are not complimentary.' She was frowning again. He wished she would not put quite so much effort into evaluating his words. There were some questions he would prefer she did not ask. 'What do you think, do we have a bargain, Julia?'

But Julia was not to be harried into agreeing anything. 'For a successful trader, it seems to me you are sealing a very one-sided bargain. As far as I can see, the profit would be all mine.'

'Not when one factors in the value of your de-lightful company.'

She laughed, but shook her head. 'I'm serious. You realise you are offering me far beyond what I could have achieved with only Hanif as a guide? To my knowledge, this desert is further south than any Western botanist has travelled. It will ensure Daniel's book is quite unique.'

Not an objective he had in mind, or even cared to achieve, but Azhar held his tongue. 'Then you will have discharged your pledge to him with added interest,' he said instead.

His reward was a beaming smile. 'You really do understand. Thank you, Azhar. Thank you very much.' Julia's smile turned mischievous. 'I am extremely grateful, and in return I promise that I will endeavour to be as rude, as critical, and as honestly disrespectful of this beautiful kingdom and its ruler as I can possibly manage. In my own particular way, of course.'

Chapter Four

Julia rubbed her eyes, pushed back the bedsheets and sat up. The divan was positioned on a central podium under an elaborate fretwork canopy supported by four intricately carved wooden pillars. Her bedchamber was ostentatiously decorated, the walls covered in embossed panels depicting delightful scenes of lush vegetation, colourful birds and other exotic animals. The stained-glass window set into the centre of the sloping roof filtered a soft, dappled light into the room, the colours dancing on the pale marble floor, which was deliciously cool under her feet. It was very early, but she was far too excited to sleep, for today she was to leave the palace with Azhar for the first time.

He had sent word last night, confirming what they had agreed two days ago in the garden. He must have briefed the body of elders he referred to as Council yesterday on his proposed plan of action. She found it somewhat baffling that someone as manifestly self-reliant as Azhar would permit another to make decisions on his behalf, even if the person concerned was his brother, who had apparently been in temporary power throughout the period of their father's illness. It seemed odd that the dying Sheikh had not sent for his heir sooner. They had been estranged, Azhar had said. Meaning, he could not—or would not—return to Qaryma while his father, the King, lived? He had expected to be disinherited, that much he had admitted. Had he then assumed that his brother would inherit? It was a reasonable enough assumption. She knew of many examples among the English aristocracy where second sons fell heir for all sorts of reasons. And Azhar's brother, would he too have assumed that he would become King? Julia knew nothing of the laws and customs of this kingdom, but it was likely, surely, that he would think so, especially since Azhar had been absent for so very long.

Ten years. So much would have changed in the intervening period. She supposed it did make sense for Azhar to take time to take stock before assuming power. It would also allow time for his brother to become accustomed to the idea of having to step down. Julia grimaced. It was unfair of her to judge, given she'd been in the man's company only a matter of moments, but she had taken an instant dislike to Kamal. He did not appear to her to be a man who would take kindly to being effectively deposed. The whole situation read like a fairy tale, the handsome Prince returning after ten years in the wilderness to oust his evil brother from the throne. Not that Kamal really was evil. Just a little repellent.

Julia smiled to herself. It wasn't like her to let her imagination run riot. But then again, she wasn't exactly in the habit of waking up in a private suite in a royal palace. She had never, in all her travels, nor even in books, seen anything so opulent. Or so beautiful. Padding across the bedchamber, she slid back the door which led to her sitting room. With triple aspect floor-to-ceiling windows, the glass panes set in delicate wrought-iron frames, light flooded in and made it the perfect place for her to work.

The sketch books, charcoals, pencils and watercolour paints which Azhar had miraculously sourced for her yesterday, were set on the table. It was extremely thoughtful of him to take the time to do so, when he had much more weighty matters to attend to. She had spent the whole morning sketching in the garden, retiring to this delightful salon to escape the worst of the afternoon heat and add splashes of colour to her outline drawings. She couldn't quite believe her good fortune. To have been rescued by a prince, taken to his magical castle and given her heart's desire! Julia smiled to herself. This might feel like a fairy tale, but she was hardly fairy-tale-princess material. Azhar however, was very much a prince. An extremely attractive, thoughtful prince, who might well think her unusual and extraordinary, but who was going to disappear from her life in a month's time. She had better not get too used to his charming company and his delightful smile and that way he had, of encouraging confidences from her that she would not normally give.

But on the other hand, provided she did remember this was a moment—or a month—out of time, it meant a whole month to enjoy all this. She curled her toes into the luxurious pile of the rug, woven in vibrant jewel-like colours, which covered the floor. An enormous three-sided couch sat in the conservatory-like windowed recess, strewn with cushions decorated with gold tassels, worked in the most intricate of silk embroidery. Further seating was provided by larger cushions and several low gilded chairs, which were set around the table. The windows were draped in long, pale voile curtains which protected the room from the heat, though the room itself faced north. Above her, the ceiling was also ornately worked, a lattice of cornicing in gold, crimson and emerald.

Pulling back the gauzy curtains, she gazed out at the view of the courtyard beyond, as enraptured today as she had been for each of the last three mornings. Unable to resist the allure of the early light, she opened the latch on one of the long windows and stepped outside.

The courtyard was enclosed by three walls, the fourth formed by the room from which she had entered it, and was thus completely private. It was hot already, though the air had that damp, salty taste of early morning. The sun was still low, the pale blue sky decorated with a few stray puffy pink clouds. A lemon tree grew in one corner, a wooden bench forming a crescent around its trunk. A long rectangular pool ran from the step down from the windows right up to the perimeter wall. Tall, precisely trained jasmine shrubs stood sentry-like in ceramic tubs on either side of the pool. The scent from the delicate white flowers was heady as Julia brushed her fingers along the dew-tipped leaves. Two steps led down into the pool, which was lined with iridescent turquoise tiles. Lifting the hem of her nightgown, Julia dabbed her toes in the cool water, shivering with pleasure as it lapped against her skin, up to her calves, then her knees as she went down the steps. She was about to give in to the temptation to immerse herself completely, when a noise from the terrace startled her.

Julia waded out of the pool, the hem of her nightgown flapping around her wet ankles. The maidservant bowed her head, though not quickly enough for Julia to miss the quickly suppressed smile. 'Good morning, Aisha,' Julia said in Arabic, clasping her hands and bowing in the customary greeting.

The maid smiled shyly, ushering her to the table, which had been set for breakfast.

'*Shukran,*' Julia said. 'Thank you, Aisha.' Seating herself on a large cushion, she forced herself to wait to be served, knowing that to help herself would be a huge breach of etiquette. The coffee poured from the tall silver pot into the delicate china cup was thick and dark and sweet. There were pastries filled with candied fruit and nuts, dusted with sugar powder; a thick yoghurt swirled with honey; and melon, peaches and fruit Julia had never seen before, delicately carved into flower shapes, served with orange water.

'Eat with gladness and health,' the girl said in Arabic, the phrase familiar to Julia as the one traditionally spoken before eating.

'Shukran,' she said again, feeling quite inadequate, making a mental note to improve her vocabulary with all speed. Crossing her legs awkwardly underneath her, she began to eat, closing her eyes as the buttery, flaky pastry melted on her tongue. The bittersweet coffee scalded its way down her throat, ridding her of the last vestiges of sleep. Sated, she was cleaning her fingers in a copper bowl of water scented with rose petals when Aisha returned, indicating that it was time for Julia to dress by holding open the connecting door to the bedroom.

The clothes laid out on the divan were not hers. Instead of thick brown wool and white cambric, these were a swathe of colours in the softest of fabrics. 'For me?' she asked, and Aisha nodded. Though it would be most improper of her to accept such a gift, Julia hesitated only a moment. Azhar would not have selected the clothes himself. She would recompense him, she would not wish to be beholden to him, nor accept his charity, but it would be churlish to refuse them.

The garments were not only practical but beautiful. The pale-green soft cotton shift, worn over pantaloons of the same material, had wide sleeves gathered into ruffles at her wrists. A wide sash of intertwined silks in shades of green was tied at her waist to hold the shift in place. Over this, the *abba* cloak was draped, the pretty beading embroidered around the hem keeping it in place. The *keffiyeh* which Aisha folded expertly before placing it on her head was made of the same cotton as her shift, held in place by another band of multi-coloured silks. The veil was of some filmy, incredibly light material that allowed Julia to breathe easily. Yellow ankle boots with pointed toes made of calfskin so soft that they felt like slippers completed her outfit. Julia gazed in wonder at the exotic creature in the long mirror looking back at her, astounded by the transformation. She could look like an Arabian princess after all!

'You like?' Aisha asked.

'I like very much indeed,' she replied, twirling around. Back in England, this clothing would be deemed indecent, despite the fact that she was showing almost no flesh at all, and she could understand why. The flimsy layers of material clung in soft folds to her body, emphasising her own clearly uncorseted curves. Aisha had expertly pleated her hair into one long thick braid which she had pulled over her shoulder. There was something decadent about that fiery red plait, something exotic about Julia's eyes flashing from above the flimsy veil. And something really quite delightful about the caress of the loose apparel on her skin too. She looked and felt utterly different. A sultry creature, fit for the desert.

Fit for a desert prince? What would Azhar think of this new Julia? Singular and extraordinary is how he'd described the old one. He'd said he thought her company delightful. Now, clad in her desert attire, for the first time in her life, Julia felt almost deserving of the description. She twirled around in front of the mirror again. Her headdress, her veil and her long plait of hair swirled sinuously in a wide arc. She felt decadent and daring, and, yes, she felt desirable too.

It was all a fantasy of course, a fanciful conceit, but a deliciously distracting one.

A month out of time, she had here in the magical city of Al-Qaryma before reality must again be embraced. For a month, she would allow herself to be this alluring creature. And for a whole month, she would enjoy the company of the man who had helped create her new persona. Whatever that entailed. In a month, the mirage would fade and she would be Julia again. But not now. Not yet.

Azhar was waiting for her in the main courtyard of the palace. A small circle of guards stood around him. He seemed, by the various gestures he made, to be issuing a complex string of commands. Aside from a scarlet headdress fastened with a band of gold silk, his dress was the same simple attire he had worn when she first encountered him at the oasis. Unlike Kamal, he had a natural air of command, and no need of ostentatious dress to artificially bolster it. The guards certainly gave him their full attention. A gentle breeze tugged his cloak out behind him, making the tunic underneath cling to his lean, muscular frame. The combination of austerity and beauty in his features took Julia's breath away anew. Suddenly shy in her new clothing, and uncertain as to whether he would expect to be treated as man or prince in the presence of others, she hovered in the lee of the portico waiting on him to notice her.

When he did, he dismissed the men curtly, and strode quickly over to her. 'Forgive me for keeping you waiting. I am concerned that the palace guard are not being used to the best of their abilities. Some of the practices I have discovered are incredibly inefficient and ridiculously wasteful. It seems my views are shared by several of the men too. I have implemented some changes now, but I will have to take a proper look at the detail later. Talking of which...' Azhar studied her appreciatively. 'My compliments, Julia. A quite remarkable transformation from English rose to desert flower.'

His lips brushed her fingertips, making her shiver. 'I certainly feel much cooler and more comfortable dressed like this,' she replied, feeling quite the opposite. 'I am much obliged to you for being so thoughtful. I will of course recompense you for the expense you have obviously gone to on my behalf, once I have exchanged my bank notes.'

'Of course you will.' Azhar spoke as coolly as she, but his eyes and his set expression told a different story.

'I mean it. It would not be proper for me to...'

Azhar stiffened. 'Julia, I rather think you left the boundaries of propriety behind when you headed out into the desert alone, but if it makes you happy, I will keep a tally of your expenses.'

'I didn't mean to insult you. I'm sorry.'

'No, it is I who must apologise. I sometimes forget that your customs are very different from ours.' Azhar's mouth softened again. 'You are my honoured guest, Julia. As your host, it is my duty to ensure that your every comfort is provided for, and you cannot deny that in those inappropriate English clothes you were very uncomfortable indeed.'

'I looked like a wrung-out dish rag, if truth be told. Thank you for being too much of a gentleman to point that out.'

Azhar laughed. 'I have no idea what that is, but I assure you, even if I did, nothing would be further from my thoughts. What I do know is that what you are wearing is an infinite improvement.

Now, if we are quite finished discussing fashion, we should ride out now while the sun is still low. Have you brought your drawing materials?'

'Yes. Another thing I must thank you for, and which should be added to my growing pile of expenses.'

'I assure you, my coffers can bear the strain. I don't know what other botanical equipment you will require, but if you provide me with a list I will have it delivered to your quarters. Now, let us commence.'

He led the way across the courtyard, where not one but two camels were waiting, and Julia's heart sank. After several futile attempts at mastering the art of mounting her own camel, horribly aware of Hanif and his men laughing behind their hands, she had chosen to ride one of the pack mules. With hindsight, this had been a mistake, an indication to the dragoman of her inexperience. She could not possibly ask Azhar to bring her a mule, but she wasn't at all sure she could get herself on to the high seat of the camel without help, never mind steer the beast.

Azhar, having stowed her drawing supplies away in the saddle bags of his own camel, took both sets of reins from the camel driver and dis-

missed the man. In response to the strange clicking sound, Azhar's mount dropped down and the
horrible groaning, growling noise which all camels made when forced to kneel began to emanate
from the beast.

'Do you wish me to help you?' he asked. 'There
is a knack to it.'

'I know,' Julia said grimly. Her palms sweating,
she approached her own camel and attempted to
imitate the clicking sound. What emerged reminded her embarrassingly of a slightly hysteri-
cal chicken. Screwing up her face for another
attempt, she must have managed by some small
miracle to produce something approximating the
correct noise, since her camel, albeit reluctantly,
dropped down with a loud groan of complaint.
She knew from bitter experience that she had
to get herself into the saddle quickly, before the
camel changed its mind, so threw herself at the
high box seat, scrambling on to it as the camel,
true to the form of every camel of her experience,
and regardless of Azhar's restraining foot on its
front leg, reared up alarmingly.

As the beast kicked its back legs out and Julia
lunged forward, she was aware of Azhar yank-

ing on the reins and calling out. She clung desperately to the pommel and managed to stay on board. Just. The invariable second attempt to dismount her had succeeded the last time, for she was not expecting it. This time however, when the camel immediately kicked its front legs out, instead of flying backwards in the saddle before tumbling over and landing on her behind, she leant quickly forward and clung on for dear life. Honour satisfied on both sides, the camel stood compliantly still and Julia, catching her breath, turned to Azhar with a triumphant smile, which quickly faded when she saw his grim expression.

'I assumed you knew what you were doing.'

'Well, in theory…'

He cursed under his breath. 'In theory? In practice you might have been killed.'

'Nonsense, I've fallen off several times before, and was only a little shaken up.'

Azhar cursed again. 'You could have fallen and broken your neck. I thought—I assumed that since you had spent over a month in the desert— did that scoundrel of a dragoman teach you nothing? How on earth did you manage?'

'I rode a mule,' Julia confessed, 'and before you

feel the need to point out to me that by doing so, I contributed to my own downfall by displaying inexperience, I have already worked that out for myself.'

She looked down. It seemed a long way down, and the cobblestones, unlike the soft desert sand, did look rather lethal. Julia shuddered. 'I'm sorry. I remember now, you said that the last thing you want on your hands is a dead Englishwoman,' she said, in a poor attempt at a joke.

She was rewarded with a poor attempt at a smile. 'Cornishwoman,' Azhar reminded her. 'But it is true, I would very much prefer if you managed not to kill yourself while you are under my protection. Can you manage to stay in the saddle if I lead your camel?'

Julia opened her mouth to demand the reins, and then thought better of it. 'I believe so.'

'If you think at any point that belief is unfounded, you will inform me of that fact,' Azhar said curtly. In a matter of moments he had mounted his own camel and drawn alongside her, surprising her by reaching across to press her hand reassuringly. 'My drawings look like tarantula tracks. It is not a weakness to admit to a lack of proficiency, Julia.'

* * *

The souks were already opening as they wended their way through the bustling streets of Al-Qaryma, the familiar scents of spices blending with the early morning freshness of the day. He could be in any city in the East, Azhar told himself, his *keffiyeh* fixed over his face, refusing to acknowledge the people who dropped to their knees as he passed, the little knot of children who ran after them. Yesterday, the Council had been shocked when he categorically refused to permit them to arrange the ceremonial audiences and formal celebrations which preceded any coronation. The people had been waiting three months already. Another month would make no material difference.

The Council had been even more taken aback by his refusal to take up his throne. But Kamal had been the custodian of Qaryma for more than a year as their father's illness increasingly sapped his strength. Kamal was more than capable of continuing to deputise, was he not? Azhar had demanded. The response to this question had not been unequivocal. Though some of the newer members of Council had indeed been enthusiastic, Azhar noticed that the elders were more restrained in their support for his brother, and even more reserved in their response to Azhar. Traditionalists, men who had been loyal to his father for almost as long as he had reigned, Azhar could not decide whether they judged him harshly for having left, or for having returned.

He sighed impatiently. It mattered not. They had no option but to do his bidding. He needed neither their acceptance nor their approval. When he chose to inform them of the real state of affairs, they would understand his actions—not that he required their understanding either. What mattered now, was to make the most of the time he had bought for himself. And in doing so, to enjoy the company of the unusual and extraordinary woman who accompanied him.

As they left the city and the oasis behind, along with the discomfiting attentions of the people who thought him their Crown Prince, Azhar brought Julia's camel alongside his. In her Eastern dress, she looked at the same time both exotic and yet unmistakably not of the East. The soft fabrics emphasised the slim lines and soft curves of her body. The bright colours highlighted the vivid green of her eyes, the burnished auburn of her hair. She had curled her legs around the pommel of the saddle. There was a tantalising glimpse of flesh above the top of her boot, below the gather of her pantaloons. Dragging his eyes away from it, he discovered she was watching him, trying to assess his mood. Behind his *keffiyeh*, he smiled. 'Would you like to attempt taking the reins yourself?'

Her eyes became wary. 'Azhar, I am a more-than-competent horsewoman, but I suspect I will never master the art of riding a camel. Nor will ever have cause to, since they are in rather short supply in England.'

'No doubt English camels, if they existed, would be twice the size of our scrawny desert ones.'

'Now you are mocking me.'

'Not mocking, merely gently teasing you,' Azhar said, bringing the camels to a halt. 'But I dislike the fact that you mock yourself by berating your inability to control a camel.'

'It is a stupid thing, not to be able to ride the ship of the desert when one has spent the last month travelling in that desert.'

'You are very harsh on yourself. Had your dragoman made an effort to teach you, I have no doubt you'd have mastered the art long before now.'

'I doubt Daniel would share your confidence.'

Azhar's hands tightened on the reins. 'Daniel is not here to disapprove.' The man was a fool. He evidently took every opportunity to point out his wife's inadequacies. But there was no point in castigating her for listening to such arrant nonsense. What she needed was encouragement. 'Would you like to take the reins, just for a short while, Julia?'

'What if it bolts?'

'It takes a great deal of effort to make a camel bolt. It takes a great deal of effort to get a camel to do anything, if truth be told. Its reputation for stubbornness is well earned.' Still, she looked unconvinced, eyeing the distance between the saddle and the sand dubiously. 'Julia, even if you do fall on your most delightful rear, the sand here is very soft. The courtyard was a different matter entirely.'

Above her veil, her eyes widened. 'You think my—my rear is delightful?'

Azhar laughed. 'Very.'

'How odd. No one has ever referred to it as delightful before.' Julia frowned. 'Actually, I don't think anyone has ever referred to it in any manner at all before.'

'Perhaps the men of your acquaintance are singularly unobservant,' Azhar responded. 'To say nothing of unappreciative.'

'Perhaps it is these clothes.'

'I was not admiring the clothes but the woman they adorn.'

She was close enough for him to see the flush on her cheeks beneath her filmy veil. Close enough for him to give in to the urge to run his fingers down the length of her silky plait of hair. Close enough for him to hear her sharp intake of breath as he did so. Close enough for his leg to brush against hers. For him to slide his fingers up her arm, over the soft billowing folds of her tunic, to rest on her shoulder. So close he saw the flame of desire he was feeling reflected in her eyes. So tantalisingly close he could almost touch his lips to hers.

But even as he shifted to close the final infinitesimal gap his camel bleated, and Julia's balance on the box seat wavered, and Azhar caught at the reins he had almost dropped. 'There is an old saying, that in the desert a camel is more useful than a kingdom,' he said ruefully, 'but as a location for lovemaking, it leaves a lot to be desired.'

Clutching the pommel of the saddle, Julia could think of nothing to say in response to this scandalous remark. How had they shifted from the subject of learning to ride a camel, to her rear— her *delightful* rear—to a kiss in the space of one conversation? How was it even possible that they had combined such disparate subjects? Her head whirled and her body thrummed. For once, she had no difficulty in reading Azhar's expression, for it exactly reflected her own feelings.

'Azhar…' Realising that she still hadn't a clue what she was going to say, she shrugged. 'I'd like to try taking the reins, please, provided you keep a close eye on my progress.'

'A most prudent suggestion,' he said, giving her a slightly crooked smile.

Julia laughed. 'I'm not sure that prudent is the word I'd use to describe what I'm about to do.'

'Perhaps not, but it is a great deal less dangerous than what I was in the process of attempting. And I am not referring to physical danger. I hope I did not offend you.'

'You must be perfectly well aware that you did

not. If you must know,' Julia said daringly, 'I've been wanting to kiss you.'

Once again, she surprised him into a laugh. 'I believe that is what they call serendipity,' he replied, 'because that is exactly what I too have been wishing to do. Though I could have chosen a more propitious moment.'

The way he was looking at her was making her feel not only daring, but decidedly decadent. 'Then I hope you choose better the next time,' Julia said, taking up the reins, and urging the camel into action.

It would have been a most dramatic gesture if it had worked. Sadly, the camel stayed firmly rooted to the spot. Julia tugged the reins tighter. The camel turned its long neck around and nonchalantly attempted to bite her. In her surprise, she loosened her hold on the reins, and to her astonishment the beast set off at a slow plod.

'I thought you said you understood the theory,' Azhar said, catching up with her on his own mount.

'Obviously I was wrong. What do I do to change direction?'

'If you will permit me to ride a little in front, your camel will naturally follow mine.'

'And to stop?'

Azhar laughed. 'Do exactly what you thought you should do to start. We have about an hour's ride to the oasis, do you think you can manage that?'

Julia risked a glance to the side. She was riding a camel, in the most beautiful desert, in the kingdom belonging to this most beautiful man. A man who thought she had the most delightful rear. A man who wanted to kiss her every bit as much as she wanted to kiss him. 'I know that I will regret saying this, but at this moment in time, I think I could manage anything.'

One hour later, she heartily regretted her words. Her rear felt not at all delightful, but quite numb. The relief she felt when Azhar's camel slowed in front of her was imhense. Bringing her own mount to a stuttering but effective halt, Julia dismounted by the simple process of sliding on to the sand, discovering to her cost that it lay in a very thin layer on top of crumbly red rock.

'Did you hurt yourself?'

Dazed, she shook her head, allowing Azhar to pull her to her feet. Having discovered that the best way to avoid seasickness from the swaying saddle was to concentrate only on the view in front of her, Julia's vision had been focused entirely on Azhar's back. Now, she took stock of her surroundings and gasped with surprise. 'What is this place?'

Azhar spoke the name in Arabic. 'It means Oasis of the Red Rock and the Tumbling Waterfall,' he elaborated. 'Rather more prosaic in translation.'

'There is nothing at all prosaic about this place, it is absolutely breathtaking.'

The oasis was small, a hollow protected by a semi-circular rock formation about thirty feet high. The waterfall tumbled down from the centre of the rocks into a deep pool. Years of pounding water had carved out fantastical shapes on the rock face. Behind the cascade, a species of silvery-green moss grew in long fronds. Trees the same strange colour of silvery-green grew on either side, almost as tall as the rocks, their reflections shimmering on the ruffled surface of the water. The air was refreshingly cool and damp, the shadow cast by the rock formation a welcome relief from the heat, which was already searing, though it could not be much more than ten in the morning.

The low stone houses, constructed of the same red rock, clung to the perimeter of the water on the shaded side, blending in so well with their surroundings, that Julia didn't notice them at first. 'It is so quiet,' she said. 'Does no one live here?'

'At this time of day, the men will be at work,' Azhar replied. 'There is a diamond mine two hours' travel from here. Only the women will be at home.'

'And I suppose they will not reveal themselves to a stranger. Though—you know, it has only just occurred to me, when we arrived in Al-Qaryma you were recognised almost instantly, even though you have been away ten years.'

Azhar finished hobbling the camels. 'I was a grown man when I left, Julia, and I did not spend all of my formative years closeted behind the palace walls.'

Curious as to how he had spent his days, she was distracted by a cry of welcome coming from the largest of the village houses. An old woman stood in the doorway, her lined face unveiled, her arms extended in welcome. When he saw her, Azhar's face lit up. 'Johara,' he said to Julia. 'She is a herbalist. I was afraid—but I should have known she would still be here. I think she will live for ever. Come, let me introduce you.'

He got to Johara's side in time to prevent the woman from falling to her knees, pulling her into an embrace and speaking gently to her in his own language.

'Madam Julia Trevelyan,' Azhar said, introducing her.

The woman's face was heavily lined, her tiny frame bent and frail, but her eyes, under their drooping lids, were a bright and fiercely inquisitive blue. Herbalist, wise woman, fey wife, healer or witch, depending on which culture they inhabited, Julia had encountered Johara's kind several times on her travels, and knew that they commanded respect as well as fear. She dropped to her knees, bending over the woman's gnarled hand, and muttered the traditional words of greeting in her halting Arabic.

After helping her back to her feet, she was rewarded with a nod of approval from Azhar, and a look she could only term quizzical from the old woman, who then broke into a torrent of Arabic, accompanied by many gestures. Standing to one side, Julia watched as the doors to the other houses in the village opened, and women of all shapes, sizes and ages began to emerge, two, three sometimes as many as four from each. They were all heavily veiled. One by one, they came forward, bowed over, eyes to the ground, forming two lines in front of the herbalist and their Crown Prince.

Feeling awkward, Julia shuffled to one side. Azhar, his back to the women, deep in conversation with Johara, seemed not to have noticed their arrival. Julia tugged on his sleeve to get his attention, motioning over his shoulder. He turned, most reluctantly, it seemed to her. Had he been ignoring them? She caught what looked like a momentary flash of annoyance, or embarrassment in his eyes, before he said some sort of formal greeting and indicated that they should rise. They did so slowly, their eyes above their veils quite patently expecting more from him, but Azhar spoke under his breath to Johara and turned away.

'We are invited to take tea,' he said to Julia, taking her arm, compelling her into the wise woman's house without a backward glance.

'That was a little rude, if I may say so.' Julia shook herself free. 'Those women wished only to show their respect to their future King, and you as good as turned your back on them.'

Azhar's mouth tightened. 'I do not deserve—' He broke off abruptly. When he spoke again, it was through gritted teeth. 'I am not yet their King. I have not yet been crowned.'

There was a faint flush on his cheeks. 'That is sophistry. Does it embarrass you, their adulation?' Julia asked, confused by the strength of his reaction, recalling now, Azhar's refusal to acknowledge the crowds which had followed them through the city on their arrival. 'It does seem a little strange to me, the bowing and scraping I mean, but then I come from a country which has locked one King up, and put an overweight, over-indulged and frankly over-excitable popinjay on the throne in his place.' The similarities between the two Regents, Prince George and Prince Kamal, struck Julia suddenly. Now it was her turn to blush. 'I did not mean to compare the two, of course. It is the merest—I mean I am sure that your brother is not a...' *Libertine? Rake?* 'Profligate.'

'Are you? You seem very certain about everything else, for one who has spent less than fifteen minutes in his company.'

Azhar gave her one of his haughty looks. Instead of inhibiting her, it made Julia's hackles rise. 'I am a most astute interpreter of character,' she said.

'So astute, that you employed a thief as your dragoman.'

'Oh! That was most—' Once again, she broke off. 'You are quite correct, of course. It is I who have been unfair, leaping to judge a man I do not know. Not that I am acquainted with Prince George either, but his habits are well established, and—and anyway, Azhar, we have strayed very far from the point. Even if it does make you uncomfortable, all the women were doing was showing you the respect due to their Prince.'

'Even a prince must earn respect, Julia.' Azhar took off his headdress, refolded it and replaced it. 'It was not my intention to be rude. I—'

A woman bearing a huge tray of tea things interrupted him. She was followed by Johara, who ushered them both to take their places on the cushions by the low table. As the sweet mint tea was poured with due ceremony, Azhar asked Johara to explain her craft for Julia's benefit, translating the old woman's words and Julia's eager questions. Though she had encountered some of the plants mentioned, many were strange to her, either due to their local names, or simply because she had never encountered them before. Questions, more questions and yet more, Julia threw at Johara via Azhar, as the encyclopaedic extent of the woman's knowledge became apparent. Finally, Johara clapped her hands and summoned one of her daughters.

The book which was reverently laid on the table was folio-sized, bound in dark-red leather, and clearly ancient. 'You are privileged indeed,' Azhar said. 'This book has been passed from mother to daughter in Johara's family for more than two centuries.'

The illustrations were so beautiful that Julia gasped. Plants, flowers, trees and roots, one species to a page, below which were what she assumed to be recipes for medicinal potions, documented in minute Arabic script. Julia carefully turned the pages, tracing the delicate paintings with her fingers. 'These are wonderful. Please tell Johara that I am extremely honoured, that I have never seen anything quite so exquisite. *Shukran*,' she said, putting her hands together. 'Please tell her that I am very, very grateful.'

'Johara says that you are welcome to copy the

drawings if you wish, but you must not transcribe the recipes, or a curse will befall you and your family,' Azhar said. 'It is a warning I would not ignore lightly. But I thought you may prefer to take the likenesses of some of the specimens in their natural habitat. Many of them grow here at the oasis. Johara's daughter will show you where, if you wish.'

'If I wish! When may we start? Oh, I did not mean to be rude, but…'

'But you are anxious to begin your task,' Azhar said, smiling. 'We have about four hours before we must leave.'

'Thank you. Oh, thank you so much, but what about you, what will you do while I am working?'

'I have ten years of history to uncover, Julia. I shall not lack occupation.'

As Azhar waited for Johara to summon the women of the village, he watched Julia heading off to the other end of the oasis with mixed feelings. The honesty he had requested of her came at a price. She saw too much. More, he suspected, than she chose to share with him. He suspected too, that he would prefer her to keep those thoughts to herself.

Her perception discomfited him, surprising him into confidences he would rather not make, forcing him to confront facts he would prefer to ignore. His people's unwarranted adulation, for example. Did they not realise that he had abandoned them? He had expected resentment at his return, sullen acceptance at best. If only his brother had made more of an effort to endear himself to the people. He'd had ten years to prove himself worthy. But then, hadn't Kamal always held the belief that birthright alone was sufficient? Recalling Julia's comparison of his brother and the English—what did she call him?—popinjay Prince, Azhar snorted in amusement. It was apt, there was no denying that. He wasn't quite sure what a popinjay was, but he could imagine.

Yes, Julia saw too much, but Julia had not the full picture. If she did, she would understand—Azhar caught himself short. He needed her honesty, but not her understanding. He had no need to explain himself to Julia. Even if she was correct about the adulation. It was odd, he had no compunction in misleading Kamal and his Council, he had been most careful to tell no lies, even when he revealed only part of the truth. But it sat very ill with him to be misleading the people.

Outside, the women had gathered. What he intended to do was for their own good. And his. It was the only possible outcome. But in the meantime, as Julia had pointed out, coronation or not, he owed those who thought themselves his subjects some respect. Picking up his *keffiyeh*, refolding it carefully, Azhar headed outside to demonstrate that fact.

Chapter Five

It was early evening by the time they returned to the palace. Azhar escorted Julia to her quarters, carrying her drawing materials, which he now set down on the table in her sitting room.

'Thank you so much for this opportunity, Azhar. I have completed more drawings in one afternoon than I have previously managed in two or three days in the open desert. I only wish I could speak your language more fluently, I have a thousand questions I'd have liked to have asked Johara. She is one of the most knowledgeable herbalists I have ever met.'

'And you have encountered many such women on your travels?' he asked.

'Several. They have proved to be of immense help in compiling Daniel's book.' Julia smothered a yawn. 'I beg your pardon, it has been a very long day, though a most productive one—at least from my point of view. I am afraid I was not of much assistance to you.' She slanted him a look. He had pulled off his headdress, and was standing at the window, staring out at her little courtyard. 'To be honest, I'm not exactly sure what you expect of me.'

'To speak your mind, as you did today,' Azhar replied ruefully. 'It was not my intention to offend the village women, but I did. You quite rightly pointed it out to me, for which I am most grateful.'

'But the important thing is that you took steps to remedy the situation,' Julia said. 'I saw you talking to them.' She went over to stand next to him, pulling open one of the long windows to let in the faint evening breeze. 'You do care, no matter how much you deny it.'

Azhar stepped out on to the terrace, indicating that she should follow. 'It is incumbent upon me, Julia, to behave honourably, that is all.'

'As a prince of royal blood, you mean?'

'Yes, but also as a man.'

'That, I would never doubt. You could easily have left me at the oasis, but your conscience would not let you, and for that I will always be eternally grateful. To the man, not the Prince.'

It was dusk, and though they were in the middle of a palace, in the middle of a city, it was that time of the evening when a stillness, a silence fell over everything like a cloak. Azhar slid his arms around her, pulling her towards him. There were only a few layers of cotton and silk between them. His hand slid down to rest on the small of her back. 'Julia?'

Her stomach knotted. She ran her fingers through the short, soft silk of his hair. 'Azhar?'

'We are not on a camel now.'

'No, we are most certainly not on a camel.'

'So I wondered if it might be possible that the moment might be...'

'Propitious?'

'Precisely,' Azhar said, dipping his head towards her 'Very, very propitious. And very well chosen, in my humble opinion.'

Her eyes drifted shut as his lips caressed hers, sending shivers of delight over her skin. He kissed her slowly, flattening his hand on her back to mould her to him as his lips shaped themselves to hers. He kissed her as if he was tasting her, as if he was savouring her. The combination of the twilight, the pent-up heat of the desert sun glowing on her skin, the alluring desert man holding her tightly against him, the seductive shimmer of her desert clothes, the persistent flicker of desire that had lingered all day waiting to be ignited, made her stomach flutter, and it made the blood sparkle in her veins. She ran her fingers up his back, relishing the sensation of fine silk rippling against the knot of his spine, and their kiss deepened. His tongue touched hers, and Julia let out an odd little sigh of delight. And then, as slowly as it had begun, the kiss ended, fluttering to a stop.

Opening her eyes, Julia blinked. Was that the searing kiss she had speculated about when they were alone in the desert? She certainly felt hot, but perhaps there were different degrees of kisses. 'I am even more glad than usual that we are not on a camel,' she said. 'I have never been kissed like that before. Thank you very much.'

'Julia, you are most welcome. It was a pleasure, in every sense of the word.' Azhar pressed his lips to her brow. 'I must leave you. I am expected to dine with my brother, and then tomorrow I have urgent business which will keep me fully occupied for the next few days.'

'The palace guards to sort out.'

'Amongst other things. I discovered, from talking to the women at the oasis today, that there have been problems with the importing of some necessary supplies which need investigating, and there is an issue with certain traders at the souk which—but you will not be interested in these matters.'

'I thought that you were leaving these matters to Kamal?'

Azhar shrugged. 'Trade is my business. It is simpler for me to take care of them.'

Julia hid a smile. Impossible for him not to, more like. She wondered how long it would be before he wrested control from his brother. Definitely less than a month. 'Do not worry about me,' she said. 'Between your beautiful garden and the oasis today, I have enough material to keep me busy for at least a week. Please don't feel obliged to spend time with me.'

'It is a pleasure, not an obligation, but if you are content to get on with your cataloguing, then we will agree to meet in the garden in three days' time. I will have your maid bring you water to bathe.'

'Thank you, after so long on that saddle that will be most welcome.'

'Hot water can be most soothing for tired limbs and bodies.' Azhar's smile was wicked as he ran his hands down her back. As his fingers curled into her bottom, he let out a soft moan, and his smile faded as his lips found hers once more.

She was left in no doubt this time. The kiss they shared was not only searing but carnal. There was no gentle introduction, no softness, this kiss was hard and dark and wild. His tongue tangled with hers. She bent back, opened her mouth to him, dug her fingers into his shoulders to steady herself as he pulled her tight against him. There could be no mistaking his arousal. The feel of him, rigid between her thighs, elicited an answering throb between hers. She curled her leg around him, surrendering to the urge to press herself closer and he groaned, kissing her harder, deeper, until she was forced to drag her mouth away in order to breathe.

His breathing too was ragged. For a long moment they stared, dazed, into eyes dark with desire. The strength of her passion took her aback. All of a sudden, she remembered Daniel's horrified look that night, under another foreign sky.

Mortified, Julia started to disentangle herself. 'I'm sorry,' she said, 'I've never—I did not mean to—I don't know what came over me.'

'The same feeling which came over me, I hope.' Azhar caught her as she turned away, forcing her to face him. 'Passion. In my culture it is recognised as a perfectly natural and healthy appetite, and has been for millennia. There is nothing to apologise for or reproach yourself about, Julia.'

'There's not? Only I thought that—I thought that a woman—such a lack of restraint, it was…'

'It was quite intoxicating.'

'You mean you're not shocked?'

'Shocked! In the name of all that is sacred, what kind of a man was your husband? No, do not answer that, I have already a very good idea.' Azhar smoothed her hair back from her brow. 'There is nothing more effective in igniting a man's desire than a woman's passion. To see the fire in your eyes, to feel the fire in your blood as you touch me, it sets me on fire too. Do you imagine I would prefer to kiss a woman who responds only with—with compliance? No, I would not. No red-blooded man would. Never apologise for passion. Restraint, Julia, has no place in lovemaking.' Azhar kissed her briefly once more on the mouth. 'I am now officially late. Enjoy your bath. My only regret is that I cannot share it with you.'

'Azhar!'

He laughed. 'My English rose. So easily shocked. There is much you might learn of the East before you leave. You have only to ask. I am not without expertise in this field.'

'Cornish,' she called after him, 'I'm a Cornish rose if I'm any kind of rose.' But he merely laughed again, grabbing his headdress from the couch before closing the door to her apartment softly behind him.

Not without expertise. The meaning was far beyond Julia's ken, but that did not prevent a shiver of longing to course through her. The notion of herself as pupil to Azhar in the arts of love was a sinfully delicious one. It seemed this new Julia was brazen as well as different.

Two days later, Julia set down her brush with a sigh of satisfaction and stretched out her arms. She had almost finished the specimens she had taken from the Oasis of the Red Rock and the Tumbling Waterfall. She wished she could remember how to pronounce the name in Arabic, but though she could hear the word in her head as Azhar had said it, she could not reproduce it.

Setting this last painting aside to dry, she made for the terrace where Aisha had left a jug of lemon sherbet, careful to push the curtains back in place to protect her precious drawings from the destructive rays of the sun. Tomorrow morning she would see Azhar again for the first time since they had kissed. As she remembered those kisses her stomach knotted. She very much wanted to acquire more of the knowledge he had hinted at, though she wasn't sure she'd have the courage to ask. It seemed impossible to imagine such a conversation in the cold light of day. A practical demonstration under cover of darkness now—but, no, she couldn't even bring herself to imagine that.

She took a sip of the refreshing citrus drink, wandering restlessly over to the seat under the lemon tree. Restraint, Azhar had said, had no place in lovemaking, yet restraint was all Julia knew. No man wants a woman to respond with compliance, he'd said. Yet again, compliance was all Julia had ever offered. It was all Daniel had expected—or wanted? Did that make her husband less of a man or Julia less of a woman?

Leaning her head back against the bark of the tree, she closed her eyes, trying to remember how it had been, making love with Daniel. Awkward, because she knew nothing of the matter, her mother having died when she was eight and the only other woman in their household being Papa's housekeeper, a dour Cornishwoman who had never married. So, yes, it had been awkward at first, because Julia hadn't known what to expect and Daniel—but had Daniel been any more experienced than she?

She sat up, startled by this thought, which had never before occurred to her. Why not? Julia furrowed her brow. Was it possible that she had simply assumed that, because he was a man, he must know better than her, or because he was Daniel, and even before they were married she had acquired the habit of accepting that Daniel always knew best? Julia cringed. That made her sound awfully weak-willed. Even rather pathetic. But was it true?

She considered this carefully, staring down at the sugary dregs of ice in her glass. Upon reflection, it was highly unlikely that Daniel had been intimate with any woman before their wedding night unless it was one of the rough women who walked the streets around the tin-mining ports of Portreath or Hayle—but, no, she could not countenance that he would be so inclined. 'Good grief,' Julia muttered, half-appalled and half uncomfortably amused, 'I do believe poor Daniel was as innocent as I.'

They had progressed, after those first attempts, to the point where Daniel achieved satisfaction, but Julia had never felt more than the faintest of stirrings in response to her husband's touch. She had learned through trial and error how to arouse herself, but she had never dared share that knowledge with Daniel, knowing that she would be mortified, and convinced that he would think it sordid. Had she, by keeping it to herself, deprived them both of pleasure? And had her *restrained* response restrained her husband?

With a sinking feeling, Julia was forced to admit that it was very possible. For the first time in weeks, she surrendered to that familiar feeling, a combination of helplessness at having wasted so many years of her life, and profound regret that she had not had the courage to try to alter it for the better while Daniel was alive. How she resented Daniel—and to a lesser degree, her father—for creating that Julia. And how she despised herself for remaining that version of Julia for so long.

It was her own fault.

'No.' She jumped to her feet, waving her arms about, as if by doing so she could disperse these destructive thoughts. She was done with this self-indulgent way of thinking. She had left that Julia behind when she had set out on her travels. She was a new Julia now, and when she had fulfilled all of her deathbed promises, the new Julia would be free.

'And in the meantime, I should remember that I was not the only one who was *restrained* during our lovemaking,' she told the lemon tree. 'Daniel wasn't interested in my pleasure. Quite the contrary. Daniel positively *quenched* my pleasure the one and only time I attempted to display it.'

Julia returned to the terrace, putting her glass down on the tray with a decided thump. 'Well, Daniel,' she said, gazing up at the celestial blue sky, 'I am done with having my pleasure quenched. And now, I would very much like to discover what it's like to have it sated.'

Julia spent a fitful night full of tedious and endless dreams in which she was required to chase after complete strangers with notes she had forgotten, messages she could not remember. Waking as the sun came up, she threw back the damp, tangled sheets and with it her mood, determined to waste no more time on what might or might not have existed in the past, and concentrate on the task which would allow her to put it behind her for ever.

Opening the lacquered cabinet which contained her new clothes, she allowed herself a moment of sheer sensual pleasure, running her hands through the swathes of silky, filmy materials, admiring the bright profusion of colours. She would never have chosen such colours herself, her practical streak leaning her towards brown, black or grey. As an artist, it wasn't that she lacked an eye for colour, but she'd never applied it to herself. It was Aisha who was responsible for this selection of garments, enough to allow her enough variety of choice for the month she was to remain here, but neither too opulent nor too numerous to make Julia feel embarrassed, for she knew, no matter what Azhar claimed, that he would not allow her to pay for them. His attention to detail extended beyond business. He was a very thoughtful man. Who would be out of her life in a month's time,

her conscience reminded her. But Julia dismissed
her conscience. She had better things to do than
count the days.

She selected a pair of dark-blue pantaloons
trimmed at the pleated ankles with black beading, and tied at the waist with a black silk sash.
The turquoise tunic was weighted with the same
beading along the hem and the wide flowing
sleeves. Her hair was glossy from the oils with
which Aisha had treated it before washing, and
scented from the rosewater in which it had been
rinsed. Julia had always disliked her hair, thinking the flamboyant colour detracted from her serious nature, and the serious nature of her work
too. Another thing that had changed here in the
desert. She liked the idea of herself as fiery, even
if it was merely a conceit. She left it loose over
her shoulders, pulled on a pair of turquoise slippers, and a swathe of turquoise silk to cover her
hair and face while she made her way through
the palace and would be on public view. Picking
up her drawing materials, Julia left her quarters
and headed for the garden.

Azhar poured himself a cup of the coffee which
he'd had sent out to the kiosk. Hearing footsteps,

he got to his feet expecting Julia, but it was his brother who appeared, and judging by the expression on Kamal's face, he had not come here to admire the garden. Azhar's heart sank.

'You've been spying on me,' Kamal exclaimed, as soon as he got close enough to the kiosk to be heard.

'Good morning, Brother. Will you take a cup of coffee with me?'

Kamal ignored him, panting as he climbed the shallow steps to the terrace to throw himself without ceremony on to one of the low chairs. 'What do you mean by it, going out to the mines and questioning the workers?'

'You have been misinformed. I went to the village, not the mines,' Azhar said, his voice hardening. 'It sounds to me as if you have been spying on me, rather than the other way round. And your spy, if I might be offered an opinion, is singularly inept.'

'I am acting as temporary ruler at your express request, I would remind you. Naturally, I expect to be informed of anything untoward.'

'Naturally. But I wonder why my paying a visit to one of my own villages would be viewed as untoward,' Azhar asked coolly.

Folding his hands over the taut mound of his ample stomach, Kamal shifted uncomfortably. 'You gave them no warning. The normal protocol is to send advance notice of an impending royal visit to allow an appropriate welcome to be prepared.'

'And to prevent any surprises, presumably. In any event, it was not a formal visit. I took Madam Trevelyan to meet the herbalist, Johara.'

Kamal sneered. 'To indulge her bizarre obsession with our plant life. How very thoughtful of you. It might be better in future if you brief me more specifically on your intentions when abroad in the kingdom.'

'Better for whom, Kamal?'

His brother shrugged. 'I merely wish to avoid any unfortunate misunderstandings.'

Azhar eyed him over the rim of his coffee cup, wondering what misunderstandings, unfortunate or otherwise, Kamal was referring to. He had left the village on good terms with the women, and Johara had been so impressed by Julia that she had insisted Azhar bring her for a return visit. Yet Kamal was uncomfortable. Was he hiding something or perhaps his nose was simply out of joint? 'I made my intentions clear when I addressed Council,' he said. 'During this interim period I shall be taking the opportunity to become reacquainted with Qaryma.'

'If you intend to visit other villages, other mines...'

Azhar stiffened. 'I will go where I choose, speak to whom I choose when I choose. You may be acting Regent, but I am not accountable to you.'

Kamal's eyes flashed with temper. 'No, but I am accountable for this kingdom.' He heaved himself to his feet. 'Things have changed, Azhar.'

'Which is precisely why I have decided that in this interim period...'

'*You* have decided!' Kamal hissed a vicious curse. 'Ten years you have been gone, and you think you can pick up the reins as if you had been gone ten minutes, making changes here and changes there to things that have been functioning perfectly well without you. Ten years you have been out in the world making your fortune, caring nothing for what happens back here, but still expecting me to protect your inheritance. Ten years I have been here, supporting our father through his illness, taking up his responsibilities when he was too weak—and what have you been doing? You have no right to criticise me, certainly no right to judge me.'

'Kamal...'

'You do not deserve this kingdom or its riches. You never wanted them. They should be mine!'

'Kamal!' But his brother threw off his restraining hand and stormed down the steps of the kiosk. 'You speak in anger but you are absolutely right,' Azhar muttered wearily under his breath. 'I have never wanted to rule, and I do not deserve to own any of it.'

As Julia turned the corner and took the path leading to the kiosk, Kamal came barrelling towards her, pushing her violently from the path as he passed, his face scarlet, creased with rage. Stooping down to retrieve her headdress and her scattered drawing materials, she stared at the departing Sheikh in astonishment.

'Are you hurt? Let me help you.' Azhar, who had obviously come after his brother, bent down to help.

'I'm fine, thank you. What on earth happened to make him so angry?'

Azhar shook his head, leading the way to the terrace and pouring them both a cup of the bitter dark coffee he preferred unsweetened, and which Julia was learning to enjoy. She waited while he sipped, drummed his fingers on the table, sipped again, staring out at the garden. He was dressed today in dark-blue trousers under a striped blue tunic. Shadows smudged the skin under his eyes. A pulse beat in his throat and the fact he flexed the fingers of his left hand compulsively were the only signs that his temper was not completely under control.

Finally becoming aware of her scrutiny, he looked up. 'As a parting shot he called me the illegitimate son of a donkey, which may sound ludicrous to you, but in our language is a great insult. Treasonous in fact, when directed at a future king.'

'A fact which I am sure will give him a sleepless night worrying about the consequences, once his temper cools.'

'Kamal knows perfectly well that I would not punish him for something said in the heat of the moment, and in private.'

'Does he? Then I hope he is duly grateful. Were the cases reversed, I doubt you would find him so forgiving.'

'No, no, you mistake the matter,' Azhar said.

'When all is said and done, Kamal is my only brother.'

Julia opened her mouth to tell Azhar exactly what she thought of Kamal, then thought the better of it, recalling her other, most unfortunate comparison to Prince George. 'Obviously, you know him much better than I,' she said, in what she hoped was a neutral tone.

Her hopes were unfounded. 'Equally obviously, you do not actually believe that,' Azhar said. 'Please enlighten me.'

The pulse was still quite visible in his neck. 'No,' Julia said.

'No, you do not agree with me, or, no, you will not enlighten me.'

She managed to stop herself from folding her arms defensively just in time. 'No, I will not be intimidated into saying something which will make you even angrier than you already are,' she said.

'I am not angry with you.'

'Yes, you are,' Julia said, 'because for some reason, you are reluctant to be angry with your brother.'

The flexing fingers stopped. Azhar pushed his coffee cup aside and got to his feet, staring out over the garden. 'I am angry with Kamal, but it is unfair of me to be so. He resents my return, quite understandably so, when he has been custodian of the kingdom for so long. He perceives my enquiries into the well-being of the kingdom as criticism of his judgement. Again, understandably.'

Azhar did not sound at all convinced, Julia thought as she finished her own coffee and joined him. It was the first time he had admitted to any concern over his brother's abilities, that his travels out into the kingdom were not merely to allow him to become reacquainted with it, but to ascertain its state of health, but she decided not to draw attention to this fact. 'If your brother had nothing to hide,' she said instead, 'he would have no need to be defensive.'

'I might be defensive myself, if the situation was reversed,' Azhar replied. 'Kamal—oh, I don't know. Things here have changed, Kamal told me so himself. No doubt he is anxious for my approval, nothing more.'

He gave himself a little shake. 'Enough of Kamal. This is one change that I heartily approve of,' he said, pushing her hair back from her face. 'From the first moment I saw you, I wanted to see it like this.' He smoothed her hair down her back, his fingers feathering down her spine. 'A river of fire.'

His touch was certainly setting her alight. She suspected he was using her as a distraction, but at this moment Julia was more than happy to be distracted. She stepped into his embrace, setting her hands on his shoulders, feeling the ripple of his muscles beneath the soft cotton of his tunic. 'Is there such a thing as a river of fire?'

Azhar slid his hands up her sides to rest just under her breasts. 'A river of fire is what you have kindled in me,' he said softly.

He must be able to feel her heart hammering. He must be able to feel the heat of her skin through her tunic. Julia flattened her own hands on to his back, smoothing down the ridge of his spine to the taut curve of his buttocks. His pupils were dark. His breathing was just very slightly ragged.

Azhar cupped her breasts. She bit back a moan as he began to circle her nipples with his thumbs. The thin layer of silk grazed her acutely sensitive skin. His touch sent ripples of sensation down her body, making her belly clench, making her insides throb. He leaned closer, his mouth on her ear, nipping at her lobe.

Her body was clamouring for her to throw herself at him, to beg him wildly to take her, words that she had never spoken in her life. She was a mass of pulse points. Her nipples ached. She curled her fingers into his buttocks simply to stop them wandering, and felt him tense at her touch, saw the flare of heat in his eyes. He kissed his way along her jaw. He licked his way along her bottom lip, all the time his hands cupping and stroking, stoking the fires which blazed under her skin, running a path from her nipples to her belly to the raw ache building between her thighs.

And then he kissed her. A dark kiss, like melting chocolate, like warm honey, sweet and heady, it clogged her brain and added to the clamouring of her body. His tongue touched hers, stroked hers, making her languorous and setting her alight at the same time. When he broke the kiss she moaned in protest, until he covered her nipple with his mouth, sucking through the silk of her tunic, and Julia let out a strange little mewl of pleasure. She shifted restlessly against the low parapet, her hands roaming up and down Azhar's back, feeling the flex and tense of his muscles, wanting to do more, but without any idea of what to do, hesitant about getting it wrong. And distracted. Very distracted. By his mouth, on her other nipple now. And then on her lips again, in a kiss that she could drown in.

And his hands. His hands, dear heavens, his hands. On her bottom. Pulling her into him, pressing the hard ridge of his arousal between her legs. And then his hands again. Unfastening the sash that held her pantaloons together, slipping between her thighs, sliding inside her.

Julia's stifled moan had a rough edge to it. He slid his fingers higher, and began to stroke her. She was so hot. And she was so tight. Yet he slid so easily inside her, over her, and...

'Oh, yes, that,' she cried out before she could stop herself. 'I mean—I didn't mean...'

'This?' Azhar said, doing it again. 'You mean this? Do not be shy Julia, how am I to learn what pleases you, if you don't share it with me?'

'Everything you've done pleases me.'

'Then let me please you some more,' he said. He kissed her and he stroked her, tongue and fingers entering her in unison, arousing her in unison, making her tighten around him, making her moan against him, making her arch her body so that he could thrust higher. She could hear herself pleading and moaning, and she couldn't stop herself. She clung on, not wanting it to end, afraid that it would not end, but then Azhar urged her to let go, and he did something new and magical and she had no choice but to let go, with a shuddering cry, to cling on to him as her climax ripped through her, hot and wild as the desert just behind them, rippling like the soft sands of that desert, leaving her as alive, as bright and vivid as the desert sky above them, as if all that colour and all that exotic beauty had been infused into her veins.

'Goodness.' Julia blushed. 'I mean—goodness.'

Her utter delight, and the fact that she made no attempt to disguise it, was refreshing as well as arousing. Not that Azhar needed to be further aroused. 'Surely you are not at a loss for words?' he teased.

The hectic flush on her cheeks deepened. 'I am not in the habit of talking after such events. Or during. Not that such events are—oh, you know what I mean.'

He pushed her hair back from her face. 'The

pleasure of such events, as you call them, can be enhanced by communication.'

'It was certainly pleasurable for me,' Julia said. 'But you...'

'We have a saying, Julia. Any journey has many destinations. That was merely the first stage along the way. And sufficient for now.' She looked unconvinced. Truth be told, he would give a great deal for a welcome release, especially looking at her now, hair wild, her tunic in disarray, her nipples still clearly defined through the silk. 'Part of my pleasure is watching you learn to enjoy yours, Julia. To help you learn, if you wish me to, though I suspect that, freed from constraint, you may help me learn too.'

'I can't imagine how that would be possible. I don't know what you want, and even if I did...'

'Julia, when the time comes, I promise you will know.'

She smiled uncertainly. 'I hope the time comes soon. I can't believe I've already been here nearly a week. Only three more, and I will be heading back to England.'

She had not meant it, but her words were as effective as a dousing of icy cold water. In three weeks, he too would be claiming his freedom.

Though it was all he longed for, it was a frighteningly small amount of time to achieve all that was required. It also meant that he had only another three weeks to spend with Julia, and oddly, for he was not at all in the habit of spending any significant time with a woman, that also seemed too brief. He liked her. He'd better be careful not to like her too much. 'You are certain that another three weeks will be sufficient for your purposes?' Azhar asked.

'Oh, yes,' Julia replied blithely. 'There are more than sufficient plants even within the small part of this lovely kingdom I have already visited to complete Daniel's book in that time. Besides, in three weeks' time I am sure you will be more than ready to take your rightful place as the King of Qaryma, and anxious to do so.'

Honesty, he had asked of her, yet he had not been honest with her in return, and looking down into her frank green eyes, Azhar realised that he did not want to lie to her. Though he had known her only a few days, all his instincts told him he could trust her. 'Julia, I won't be taking the crown from Kamal in three weeks.'

'You need more time?'

'I won't be taking the crown from Kamal at

all,' Azhar said. 'My father did us both a great disservice by his refusal to change the line of inheritance. When I left ten years ago, it was for ever. I have not come here to take up my crown, Julia, I have come to hand it over. In three weeks' time, I intend to abdicate.'

Chapter Six

'Enter,' Julia called out brightly in Arabic, in response to the tap on the door of her suite, assuming it was her maid come to clear away the breakfast dishes. She finished rolling the last of the dried plant roots she had collected two days ago in protective cotton before placing them carefully in the replacement specimen trunk. She looked up, smiling. 'See how perfect a home it is for my growing collection of specimens,' she said.

But it was not the maid who stood watching her, it was Azhar. 'Your return visit to the village at the oasis was productive, then?' he asked.

'Oh! I was expecting Aisha. Yes, very productive. Johara and I managed to communicate passably well, between my limited vocabulary and a lot of gesticulating.'

Azhar was clad in bottle-green today, his trousers and tunic both made of silk. 'I am sorry that I could not stay to act as your translator.'

'You had your own business to attend to at the diamond mine. I hope your day was equally as productive.'

'Not particularly. The mine itself is apparently not as productive as it once was but I was unable to get a clear explanation as to why.'

'Perhaps the reserves are simply running out.'

'Perhaps, but it is a source of concern none the less.' Azhar rubbed his eyes wearily. 'The trade in diamonds provides Qaryma with one of its main sources of wealth. The impact of the decrease in output is starkly reflected in the Treasury accounts which I spent yesterday reviewing—much to my brother's chagrin, needless to say.'

'You surely don't suspect him of fraud?' Julia exclaimed.

Azhar shrugged. 'I have no reason to suspect him of anything. I wish merely to ensure that everything is in order.'

'Before you hand full control over to him, you mean.' Julia closed the lid of her new specimen trunk and pushed it to one side. 'We have barely had a chance to talk since you told me of your intention to abdicate power.'

'Were you shocked?'

'Very at first, and then I recalled what you said to me that day, when we were approaching the city for the first time. That you were here at the behest of a dead man to claim your freedom.' Julia smiled faintly. 'I didn't understand what you meant at the time but I can now see you meant to be free of the crown. If that is the case, Azhar, if you are truly resolved to leave here, I can't understand what you need me for?'

'That has not changed. It is extremely important to me to leave in the firm knowledge that Qaryma is in safe hands. There is a real danger that I may see only what I want to see. A fresh perspective is what I need, and you are the ideal person to provide it. Someone dispassionate, with no emotional attachment to Qaryma.'

Exactly as he had described himself, Julia thought but did not say. 'Why haven't you told Kamal of your plans? You intend to trust him with your kingdom, yet you don't trust him with the knowledge that it will be his. Unless—is this some sort of test period? To allow you to assess him—but then, if he fails...'

'He won't fail. He cannot be allowed to fail. It is impossible for me to remain here, Julia. My freedom has been very hard won.'

'Until you actually abdicate, your freedom has not been won at all,' she replied tartly.

Azhar's laugh was bitter. 'You are quite correct. For the last ten years, the freedom I thought I had claimed was a mirage.'

'You really did think your father had disinherited you?'

'I had every reason to.'

'It must have been a terrible shock to discover he had not. You said you received a summons to tell you your father was dead, I think?'

'The summons was from my father, though he instructed that it be sent only on the occasion of his death. He clearly had no desire to be reconciled with me, our estrangement was every bit as final as I believed it to be. Unlike your husband, my father could not control my actions while he was alive, but—'

'By refusing to disinherit you, he was forcing you to return against your will. He was trying to control you from beyond the grave,' Julia interrupted, her eyes wide. 'Just exactly like Daniel!'

'Precisely. I knew you of all people would understand.'

'I do. I must say, though, that you must be in a tiny minority of men who would willingly renounce such a powerful and privileged position.'

'Most men do not understand all that being in a position of power entails. Power comes with great responsibility attached. As a king, I would be constrained by my duty to my kingdom, bound to it by my crown. That is not freedom.'

Julia shuddered. 'No, indeed, but as the eldest son you must have grown up knowing Qaryma would one day be yours.'

'And railing against that fate, though I never believed I could avoid it. I never wanted to rule, whereas Kamal—it is one of the things that made him so angry the other day in the garden. He has always desperately wanted to rule. Even when we were children, it was a bone of contention. He wanted it but could not have it. I had no interest in it but was burdened with it. The irony has always eaten away at him.'

Julia rolled her eyes. 'I can imagine. Were you never close? I know almost nothing of your past.'

'That is because I have put it behind me,' Azhar said. Julia drew him a sceptical look, forcing him to throw his hands up. 'By the time I leave here, it will be behind me for ever.'

'Context is all,' Julia retorted. 'To understand a plant, one must understand its environment.'

His lip twitched. 'I am not a rare species to be documented and categorised.'

'No, you are not rare, you are quite unique, which is why I'd like to understand you a little more.'

'You flatter me.'

'To speak the truth is not flattery,' Julia said, quoting his own words back at him.

'You are a very devious woman, Julia Trevelyan.'

'I don't think I'll add that to my list of compliments. Has my deviousness paid off?'

Azhar laughed. 'Yes, but you must not assume you have set a precedent. We will take a tour of the palace. You want to know more about my past. The palace both contains and defines my past. Can you be ready in half an hour?'

'The palace is formed around four courts. The First Court functions merely as an entrance courtyard, with access to the stables, the guards' quarters, the kitchens and stores. Anyone may enter the First Court. We are currently in the Second Court, which is the first inner courtyard, and the first to which entry is strictly controlled. You will observe too, that it is surrounded by a much higher wall than the First Court.'

Julia gazed around the huge open space, where five distinct paths formed by box hedges bordered by cypress and plane trees, radiated out at angles from the gated entry. She had passed through the space before, and had been much taken by the carefully tended formal gardens, which were laid out in the classical style around a huge central pentagon shape. She had noticed the high wall only to remark to herself on the quality of the shade it provided. Now it made her shiver. 'It is like a castle keep.'

'That is because it was originally built as a fortress. These walls form the oldest part of the palace, which dates back almost five hundred years.'

'Are there still wars?'

'Not for at least a century.'

'Then the walls and the gate...'

'Serve tradition. Symbolise the majesty of the King. Act as a reminder of his strength and his power. The walls demonstrate the gulf that lies between a king and his people.'

'A gulf that you must have breached. You know the desert, Azhar, and the little I've seen of the people—they know you.'

'That is true.' Azhar agreed. 'Even as a child, I hated the confines of these walls. I always yearned to know what was happening outside them.'

'But your father preferred you to remain inside?'

'He preferred that my trips into the kingdom were formalised.' Azhar led the way along the middle of the five paths. 'My father believed that a king must be seen to rule, that he must be a presence to his people, but that presence must be orchestrated. Processions. Feasts. Ceremonies. Always, the line between the King, his family and his subjects must be drawn firmly in the sand. And always, from my earliest days, as soon as I was old enough to think for myself, I disagreed with him. I wanted to see for myself, hear for myself and experience life for myself.'

'Then as now,' Julia said.

Azhar smiled grimly. 'Then as now, as you say. If I make mistakes, they are my own. A king can never make mistakes.'

'Never admit to them, at any rate. That is one

royal trait that Daniel had in abundance,' Julia interjected. 'He hated to be in the wrong. There was a time in South America, when our barge—' She broke off abruptly, shocked by the bitterness in her voice.

'Your barge?'

Azhar raised an enquiring brow, but she shook her head. 'It doesn't matter. He blamed me, and though it was ludicrous I allowed him to blame me because it was easier than arguing with him. It is mortifying, on reflection, how much I permitted his opinions to rule me.'

'And to give you a very low opinion of yourself,' Azhar said gently.

'Yes, you've said that several times, and I'm beginning to think you're right, which is why I've resolved to try not to dwell on the past. I am not incapable of making mistakes—my dragoman being an obvious example—but nor am I inept. I have travelled alone halfway across the world. I have been robbed, and drugged and carried off by a complete stranger to a remote kingdom I had no idea existed until a week ago, and yet here I am, still alive and kicking. You see,' Julia said, smiling, 'I do listen.'

'I am glad to hear it.'

Azhar's smile made her belly clench. His mouth distracted her. It reminded her of the kisses they had exchanged in the garden. It made her want more of them. She shouldn't be thinking about kisses. 'We are supposed to be talking about your past, not mine,' Julia said.

She dragged her eyes away from the beguiling man to the almost-as-beguiling surroundings. It was cool in the shade of the tall trees. At the centre of the pentagon, on either side of their path, were a pair of matching fountains, their bases formed in a star shape, patterned with gold mosaic, the inside tiled in the traditional turquoise. In the centre of each, water spouted from a huge urn. Julia sat down on the edge of the nearest fountain, trailing her hand in the water. 'It is very quiet here. I would have thought a court like this would be full of people coming and going—for it is a sort of waiting room, isn't it?'

'Yes,' Azhar said, with one of his fleeting smiles, 'a waiting room. An empty one.' He sat down beside her, leaning back on the edge of the fountain to gaze up at the inner wall, visible above the cypress trees. 'My father was always very wary of foreign traders,' he said. 'He believed that Qaryma should be self-sufficient, that the wealth we had should be protected. He knew this desert like the back of his hand, but he rarely ventured beyond the boundaries of his domain, save on official visits.'

'My own father never leaves Cornwall. He says that everything he needs is there, and in a way it is,' Julia said. 'He has his home, and he has his gardens, and he has his society meetings—men of science like Papa, who meet once a month to discuss the latest discoveries.' She made a face. 'Actually, what they mostly do is regurgitate their own work.'

Azhar laughed. 'You make it sound as if they chew over their papers and spit them out.'

'That is more or less exactly what they do,' Julia replied. 'In Cornwall, Papa is respected and admired, an established expert. Celebrated, in a way. Botanists travel from all over England to see his gardens, you know.' She chewed her lip. 'His fame in his field is well deserved, but it is a small field. He disapproved of Daniel's book. He said it was far too wide in scope—that the best works concentrated on a narrow field of study.'

Azhar caught a small darting fish in his hand, its tiny scales flashing gold and green. 'Then I assume he disapproves of your finishing it?'

'Actually, he doesn't know that's what I'm doing,' Julia confessed.

Azhar placed the wildly flapping fish gently back in the water. 'Then what does he think you're doing here in Arabia?'

'He doesn't know that either. He thinks I'm on a Hebridean island—that is in Scotland, the most remote part of Britain I could think of. I told him that I needed solitude to recover from Daniel's death.' Azhar looked so astonished that Julia laughed. 'I wanted to surprise him with with the book when I had finished.'

'I think you will do rather more than that.'

'You think he'll be angry?'

Azhar shook his hand dry. 'In my experience men like your father do not like to be upstaged, especially by their own children.'

'Do you think your father was afraid that you'd make a better king than he?'

Azhar snorted with derision. 'My father thought no one would make a better king than he. What he was afraid of was that I wouldn't make any sort of king, which is why he refused to allow me any sort of freedom.'

'That is a recipe for disaster. He must have known a child with such an adventurous spirit as

I imagine you would have been, would grow into a man who wanted to explore the wider world. If only he had permitted you to travel when you were younger, to satisfy your natural wander-lust…'

'It was not so simple,' Azhar said with a sigh. 'It was not only my desire to experience a world beyond Qaryma, Julia, it was the fact that for me, Qaryma was…'

'…a gilded cage,' she finished for him with a smile. 'A very beautiful one, and one that no longer contains your father.'

'If I remained here, it would contain me though, for the rest of my life.'

'Surely you exaggerate?'

Shaking his head, Azhar got to his feet, taking her hand to help her up. 'Come, we can continue our tour later. I have ordered refreshments to be brought to us.'

'This is the reception room for the Divan next door,' Azhar said, stepping aside to let Julia enter in front of him. 'The Divan is the room used for meetings of the Council, where foreign visitors are received, and for ceremonies such as weddings and coronations.'

'So it's a throne room?'

'That is one use. I will show it to you after we have eaten.'

He sank on to one of the velvet cushions scattered beside the low marble table, but Julia continued to examine the room. As one of the first chambers which visitors encountered, it was opulent, designed to both intimidate and impress, but Julia, Azhar noticed with amusement, was rather entranced than awed, running her fingers along the ornate mosaic patterning on the walls, gazing for almost a full minute, her neck craned, at the stained glass of the domed ceiling, circling around the twelve pillars which formed the portico to the Divan itself, trailing her fingers through the fountain in the centre of the of the room before finally joining him at the table, occupying the cushion beside him and eyeing the fruit and pastries with undisguised relish.

'I'm ravenous,' she said. 'I have never eaten such delicious food in my life as has been served to me here. I shall go back to Cornwall with a huge tummy.'

She patted her patently concave belly, and bit into a pastry. 'Almonds, of course, there are always almonds. And raisins. And—chicken?'

'Guinea fowl.' There was a stray flake of pastry on the corner of her mouth. Azhar watched, fascinated, as she licked it before popping the remainder of the pastry into her mouth, closing her eyes so as to savour it.

He shifted uncomfortably on the cushion. Did she know what she did to him? She plucked another sweetmeat from the platter, a pastry tube coated in sugar and cinnamon. Azhar's shaft stiffened. She could have no possible idea of the visions she was conjuring, he doubted she had ever even caressed a male member. He poured himself a cooling glass of sherbet and took a long drink.

'Delicious!' Julia said, quite oblivious of the effect she was having. 'May I have some sherbet? I'm hot.'

And he was on fire. 'Let me cool you down,' Azhar said, taking a small lump of ice from the silver chafing dish and sliding it into her mouth. Her lips formed into a perfect 'oh' of surprise, and Azhar surrendered to the impulse to cover them with his own.

Cold ice, the warmth of her lips, the softness of her tongue, the heat from his body, made him shiver with delight. Though he longed to devour her, he savoured her, holding himself rigid, restricting the contact to their lips and their tongues. She smelled of jasmine. The ice melted, and he reached blindly for another piece. Julia opened her mouth, her eyes slumberous, her cheeks flushed, and when he covered her lips with his, kissed him back with a fierceness that threatened to overpower the fragile grip he had on his self-control.

The next lump of ice, he trailed down the column of her throat, easing her back on the cushions, unfastening her tunic buttons to push the garment aside. Her skin was milky white. Her nipples were pale-pink peaks. He let the ice melt on them, watching her shudder, aware of those big beguiling eyes of hers fixed on him, then he took one of the icy cold buds in his mouth and sucked hard.

Her moan made his groin tighten. The second nipple, delightfully hard, swapped ice for fire as he enveloped it with his lips. Still she watched him, her eyes glittering, her hair, free from her headscarf, glinting fire in the dappled light from the stained-glass ceiling. He knew that she longed to touch him, but he knew that she would not, without a cue. She learned quickly. And she was untutored. The combination of voluptuary and innocent was intoxicating. That they were indulging in such carnal pleasure here, right next to the Divan, added an extra *frisson* to Azhar's enjoyment.

He opened the last of the buttons which held her tunic together. Another lump of ice, teasing down her body, pooling in the dip of her naval. He licked it dry. He undid the sash of her pantaloons.

'Azhar, someone might come.'

He laughed. 'That is not a possibility, Julia, it is a certainty,' he said, tilting her bottom up to swiftly remove the garment.

'Azhar!'

'Julia, we will not be disturbed. No one dares enter without my permission.' He took one final piece of ice from the dish.

'What are you going to do with that?'

She had no idea. The knowledge that he would be the one to initiate her only heightened his desire. Smiling wickedly, Azhar put the ice on his tongue, knelt between her legs, and slid his tongue inside her.

She arched up under him. He lifted her higher, his hands cupping her rear. The ice had already melted, but it had served its purpose. She was wet, hot and already swollen. The last time he had lingered, this time he brought her to a climax swiftly, licking over her and into her and then over her, the sweet rush of her orgasm making him pulse in response, his tongue sweeping over her as her climax ebbed, bringing another rush, and then a final one. Her hands were digging into his shoulders. The soft flesh at the top of her thighs was damp. She lay sprawled on the scarlet cushions, her hair spread like a halo around her, her breasts heaving delightfully, her face suffused with colour. And her eyes, cloudy with sated passion, still fixed on him.

It was a primal response, this surge of male pride that he had given her such pleasure, but he relished it. His shaft jutted painfully in the constraints of his trousers. He could not remember ever feeling so aroused. Five, six strokes inside the slick heat of her, would be all it would take. But Azhar wanted much more than five or six strokes. He could wait, even if it meant tipping the last of the ice down his front. He looked at Julia, all creamy flesh and pink nipples and dark auburn curls between her legs, and he realised what he needed most was to stop looking at her.

He got to his feet, reaching for her hand to pull her upright. 'I will leave you to—to rearrange yourself,' he said.

'But what about you?'

'I too need to rearrange myself,' Azhar said wryly.

'No, I meant...'

'I know what you meant. This was simply another staging post on our journey of discovery, Julia. Not one I had planned, but I promise you, a most delightful way station for me as well as you.'

Julia was eyeing the pastries with intent when Azhar returned, his hair wet, the flush faded from his skin. It was foolish to feel shy but she did, and even more foolish to be embarrassed by the appetite their lovemaking had given her, but she was.

'Eat, please,' Azhar said, when she turned resolutely away from the table. 'But avoid the cinnamon-and-sugar ones, for the sake of my sanity.'

She studied him from under her lashes as she took sustenance. Would anyone be able to tell what they had just shared, by looking at them? Azhar, staring off into space, his plate of food all but untouched, looked his usual remote self, while she felt as if the wild, sensual creature she had become must still surely be etched on her face, even if she had rearranged her clothing and subdued her hair under her scarf.

She nibbled on a sugared almond and poured herself another glass of sherbet. Fifteen minutes ago Azhar had been flushed with passion. Not long before that, his face had been set, his eyes dark with anger. Though it still seemed incomprehensible to her that he could walk away from all this, she did understand his desire for freedom. Bad enough being wed to Daniel, but to marry a kingdom…

Bad enough! Julia set down her sherbet glass carefully. Her marriage was not bad. She had not been unhappy, and she knew of worse, far worse marriages. But she had not been happy either. Azhar had likened Qaryma to a gilded cage. Julia smiled at the notion of describing her marriage in such a way, yet there was no doubt she had felt confined by it. The promises she had made to Daniel constrained her still, though in a way, they had also helped her grasp her freedom. Without the impetus of completing his book she would not have come here, would not have tested her resourcefulness, would never have discovered the sensual side of her nature which had been subdued for so long. Would never have met Azhar.

Looking at him, recalling what had passed between them right here less than an hour before, she felt the most delightful shiver. She was not yet free, but the process of claiming her freedom was proving far more enjoyable than she could ever have imagined.

Azhar ushered her through the marble pillars. 'Why are there no guards?' Julia asked.

'Because I had them stand down while we are here.'

'Oh. What about the Second Court, did you have that cleared too?'

'Not cleared, it is the main thoroughfare through the palace, but I asked that only those with urgent business be allowed to pass through.'

'Asked or commanded?'

Azhar shrugged. 'To most here it amounts to the same thing.' He lifted the heavy iron bar that held the double doors together, and threw them wide. 'The Divan.'

The room was about fifty feet long with a domed roof crowned by a gold crescent in the very centre. Gold constellations were painted on the ceiling, and the floor was worked in an intricate pattern of turquoise-and-gold mosaic. In contrast, the walls were stark white relieved only by a thin band of gold and turquoise. Aside from the huge carved chair upholstered with cloth of gold, the vast space was completely empty.

'My brother and I used to play in here as children,' Azhar said. 'We used to race with our wooden horses, stage mock fights with our wooden scimitars.'

'So you were close when you were younger, then?'

'There are only two years between us,' Azhar replied. 'Our mother died in childbirth two years after Kamal was born, and our father never took another wife.'

'Is that unusual?' Julia asked in surprise. 'Wasn't he lonely?'

'My father married as all kings of Qaryma marry, for the sake of an heir. Since my mother provided him with two, he did not feel the need to take another wife. As to whether he was lonely—if you mean did he take lovers then the answer is yes. He enjoyed the company of women in that way. It is one of the few things we have in common.'

'Two things,' Julia said, before she could stop herself. 'You both take lovers, but neither of you offers love.'

The look he drew her was measured. 'As you say. And what about you, Julia?'

'What do you mean?'

'Do you still have room in your heart for love?'

'If by that, do you mean will I ever marry again, the answer is an unequivocal no. My freedom is not quite so hard-earned as yours, but it is every bit as precious,' Julia said. 'But we are not here to talk about me. Tell me more of the Council meetings that take place here.'

'Under my father they convened three times a week, though Kamal has reduced it to once. Membership is hereditary, representing the oldest families in the kingdom, although the King also has the authority to invest a man with specialist knowledge or skills. The Chief Overseer in charge of the diamond mines, for example.'

'So the Council which meets now is the one your father selected?'

'Kamal has nominated a number of younger men. A number of my father's associates have stepped down.'

Azhar was pinching the bridge of his nose. It

was a habit he had when he was unhappy about something, Julia had noticed. 'That may be a good thing. Younger men often have a more progressive outlook,' she suggested.

'Or they may be more easily swayed. Although the King of Qaryma wields absolute power, it is easier to rule with the Council on your side. My brother has always been overly fond of getting his own way. He does not take well to having his will thwarted, but nor is he particularly strong-willed.' Azhar grimaced. 'A compliant Council is an ideal solution.'

An ideal solution for a weak ruler. Julia braced herself, for she understood now how very much he did not want to hear her question. 'Are you quite certain that you wish to hand over your kingdom to such a man? Can you trust Kamal?'

'Have you seen enough?' Azhar walked away, holding open double doors at the other end of the Divan. 'These will take us out to the Third Court. I am not ignoring your question, Julia,' he said, as she passed him. 'I am considering how best to answer it.'

The Third Court was about half the size of the Second, and a very different space. Two large pavilions sat adjacent to each other. There was a fountain in each corner, a low, precisely trimmed maze, and more mosaic paths. 'This court is reserved for the royal family,' Azhar said. 'Those gates in the wall lead to what was once the old-style harem complete with concubines and eunuchs. My mother had it opened up, and turned into what is simply the women's quarters. Some of her former maidservants still reside there along with Kamal's wife.'

'I'm surprised that someone as obviously greedy as your brother has only one.'

'He may have his faults but he is still my brother. I would appreciate it if you kept such thoughts to yourself. Apart from anything else if overheard they might be considered treasonous.'

'My apologies, it was a poor attempt at humour,' Julia said contritely. 'Where are we now?'

'This building is the library,' Azhar said, opening the door of the largest pavilion which on closer inspection was cruciform in shape. 'We will be comfortable in there.'

The door to the library was panelled in bronze. Glass-fronted bookcases lined the walls of each of the arms of the cruciform, while light poured in through the windows set into the domed roof at the centre, where a huge round couch was placed.

Azhar sat down here, indicating that Julia should join him.

He stretched his long legs out in front of him and folded his arms. 'You asked if Kamal and I were close. You would imagine that we would be so, with only two years between us, no mother, no other siblings, but we were not. I was a typical boy in many ways. I liked to ride—horses and camels—I liked to fight with my sword and my fists, I liked to swim and to run. Kamal—well, Kamal has always been indolent. Unfortunately, our father was a man who valued what he called masculine prowess. In my father's eyes, Kamal was less of a boy because he did not shine as I did at such things. I never—how do you say it—rubbed his face in it?'

'Nose.'

'Nose. Well, I never did that, but it didn't matter. Kamal was jealous. I think there was a part of him that wished to emulate me. And he relied on me too, to play the big brother, even though he would rather he was the elder brother, you know? He was always outreaching himself, relying on me to bail him out when he came unstuck. Like the occasion when he took liberties with the sister of one of our friends, and her brothers set upon him.'

'He must have resented you,' Julia said.

'That has not changed,' Azhar said wearily.

'It must have been difficult for him to stomach,' she added, thinking that that had not changed either. 'Taller, stronger, faster.' *Much more attractive.*

'And my worst crime of all. Older.'

'The heir, by accident of birth. A heinous crime indeed,' Julia agreed wryly.

'I know, but I believe Kamal really does believe it is my fault.'

'You don't like him much, do you?'

Azhar winced. 'I try not to let it show, but he is not stupid. Weak and petty and indolent, but far from stupid. I am not blinded by my determination to abdicate, Julia. All Kamal needs is the incentive to improve. Once he knows that Qaryma is his, that I truly am out of his life for ever, then he will prove himself.'

But she was beginning to suspect that Azhar was blinded. Like her, he craved his freedom, but there the similarities ended. Daniel was dead. Azhar's love of his kingdom had merely been buried. He was an honourable man with a strong sense of duty. This notion he had, that he could set Qaryma to rights and Kamal too, it was a most laudable intention, but it was impossible.

Julia's toes curled inside her slippers, but honesty was what Azhar had requested of her, and true to herself was what she had resolved to be. 'You have set yourself a herculean task if you plan to remedy things in just three short weeks, and—and I think you should ask yourself why,' she said carefully. 'No matter how much you deny it, you care for your kingdom, and you know in your heart that your brother is not fit to rule—will never be half the man that you are. You may quell your conscience by shoring things up, by remedying whatever problems you uncover. That may permit you to enjoy your freedom for a few more years, but it will be what it has always been—a mirage. You will be obliged to come back eventually. I am so sorry, Azhar, but whether you like it or not, the one thing you cannot abdicate from is your conscience.'

Azhar got to his feet. He was angry, she could see the pulse beating in his throat, but he was making a huge effort not to show it. 'I will not permit you to condemn me to a lifetime of captivity until you understand what that would entail. And the price I have to pay. Come with me.'

'Where are we going?'

He strode out of the library, across the Third Court to yet another set of iron gates, which he opened with a huge key, ushering her through a passageway to a door, which he then heaved open. 'The Fourth Court,' Azhar declared.

It was a square formed by three high walls and one low parapet. In the centre was a kiosk, but it was the gardens which drew Julia's attention, for they were laid out not at all in the formal style of the Third Court, but in a riot of colour, more in the style of an English cottage garden than the garden of an Arabian king.

The space was surprisingly intimate. Aromatic herbs planted at the edges of the winding mosaic paths scented the air as her tunic brushed against them. The parapet looked out over Al-Qaryma to the oasis and the desert beyond, the same view as the large garden, but from a higher viewpoint. That wall there must form the boundary between the two. Rushing from one path to the next, she found a tantalising mixture of flowers and shrubs, some exotic, some quintessentially English, all jostling for space, and living happily together in a way she would not have given any credence to had she not seen it for herself.

'It is as if someone has commanded the East to merge with the West,' Julia exclaimed. 'A secret garden, whose is it?'

'The Fourth Court is exclusively for the use of the King of Qaryma.'

Julia's eyes widened. 'Your father's private quarters?' While she had been running from path to path, Azhar had remained quite still at the door of the Court. This was no magical garden for him. It was his father's inner sanctum. 'I'm sorry,' she said. 'I should not have allowed myself to get so carried away.'

Azhar shrugged. 'I had forgotten,' he said. 'I don't remember it being so—' He broke off making a vague gesture. 'Seeing it through your eyes, I can see it is—I can understand your surprise.'

'Who tends to it?'

Another shrug. 'The palace has an army of gardeners. There is an entrance door in the connecting wall to the main garden where you have been working.'

Julia hadn't noticed a door, and she had spent

hours and hours in the other garden, but now was hardly the time to ask if it was possible to...

'I'll have someone give you the key,' Azhar said, as if he had read her mind. 'If you really want to paint this, that is. I doubt there are any new species for you to catalogue.'

'It is the unexpectedness of it that appeals to me. I had not thought—that is, I thought your father—all this, it does not really equate with the man I imagined.'

'No?'

Azhar's expression was unreadable, but there were tiny lines of tension around his eyes, and the pulse still throbbed at his throat, a sure sign that he was discomfited. She touched his arm lightly but he turned away towards the building which stood in the centre of the Court. 'This is the Royal Kiosk,' he said.

The kiosk had two storeys, the broad roof overhanging to form an arcade which surrounded the building. A huge gilded dome emerged from the centre of the roof, with a small minaret sitting incongruously beside it. The marbled exterior was, like the kiosk in the main garden, alabaster white, throwing the brilliant colours of the tall stained-glass windows, six on each storey on the façade alone, into stark relief.

Azhar opened the double door with another key and stepped aside for Julia to enter. The room was breathtaking in its beauty and of staggering size, for it was double height, taking up the entire length of the kiosk, the ceiling arching up into the gilded dome at the centre of the roof giving it a cathedral-like ambiance. Light streamed in, vivid rays of emerald, red and blue, dancing over the intricate mosaic floor. The walls were tiled to the first-floor level, in rich glazed colours that gleamed, as if they had been polished. From the dome hung the biggest chandelier Julia had ever seen, on a very long chain, set over the marble table chased with gold which stood in the very centre of the room. At the furthest end, set into a window embrasure, was an enormous divan. There was no other furniture in the huge space.

'Another throne room,' Julia said, her voice hushed.

'This is where my father conducted his private audiences. He signed his official papers and royal decrees at that table. This is the room from which he ruled and wielded power.'

Julia turned in circle, her head back, gazing

up at the dome. 'When you said this was your father's private quarters, I imagined something more intimate.'

Azhar's smile was twisted. 'There are some anterooms at the rear of the kiosk, it is bigger than it looks from the outside, but this room is where my father spent most of his time.'

Julia shuddered. It was an intimidating space for one man to occupy, but then she supposed that was the point. 'Well, now I can at least understand the garden,' she said. 'Of course it is a very clever design trick,' she added, when Azhar looked at her questioningly, 'It seems so wild, uncontrolled, so natural and yet that can only be achieved by meticulous planning.'

Azhar was prowling restlessly around the room, stopping every now and then, his eyes drawn to the divan. Judging from his stormy expression, his memories were extremely unpleasant. 'My father liked to control everything, even nature,' he said bitterly. 'It was in this very room that I last saw him. It was here that he informed me that if I left I would never be welcomed back. Growing up, my father tried to shape me and cultivate me like that garden out there. Tame any wildness, impose order. As I grew older the constraints became unbearable, but the more I protested, the more repressive he became. I am a man of action, have always been a man of action, yet he would not let me *do* anything. He wanted to control every minute of every hour of my time. Growing up here as heir, Julia, my life was not my own.'

He spoke with such passion, she couldn't help but empathise. Her marriage bonds were as nothing to the bonds a king-in-waiting must bear. 'I can see now why you felt you had no option but to leave.'

'He gave me no option. I was desperate to go earlier, but until I was twenty-one I could not do so without his permission. At the time, all I wanted was the taste of freedom, not to leave Qaryma for ever, but to be free to leave for a period and then return. He would not grant me even temporary freedom.'

'Perhaps because he knew that once you tasted freedom you wouldn't come back,' Julia said.

Azhar shrugged. 'It is impossible now to know whether that was true. If I had left at sixteen or seventeen or even twenty, with my father's good wishes, without the need to make my own way, to pay my own way, I would not have started my business. I would not have sown the seeds of the life which I have grown for myself outside Qaryma. I would in all likelihood have returned, but I cannot be certain.'

'Your father was a fool, if you ask me,' Julia said. 'I'm sorry if that is treasonous, but it's true. He should have known that trying to keep you in Qaryma was a recipe for disaster. There is nothing more tempting than forbidden fruit. His behaviour more or less guaranteed your departure.'

Azhar laughed dryly. 'As the date of my birthday drew nearer, I began to dread that my father would be taken ill. That he might die before I could escape was one of my greatest fears.'

'But you did escape.'

'On the very morning I achieved my majority. "I am twenty-one," I said to him, "you can't stop me from leaving."'

'"But I can prevent you from returning," he said to me. And so, in a way, he granted me my freedom. Freedom, Julia.' Azhar grinned. 'For the first time, to be free to do what I wanted when I wanted, to go where I wanted—to answer to no one. You cannot imagine how good that felt.'

'I can,' she said warmly.

'Of course you can.' He pressed her hand. 'We

want the same thing, after all. As time passed, as I began to establish my business, to make a life for myself, I quickly realised that I would never return. That my father had actually done me a favour by exiling me.'

'And allowing you to become a man of action.'

'With every action my own. I had escaped. I was no longer a King-in-waiting defined by my kingdom, I was my own man defined by my own success—and in the early days, my failures too. I love my business, Julia. It is a—an integral part of me. If I remained here, as King, I would have to give it up. I won't do that,' Azhar continued, his tone harsh. 'I left my father with a son who valued what I did not, a son he could have moulded into his image as he had tried to mould me. Kamal is much more malleable. But my father...'

'You think that your father was blind to Kamal's weaknesses?'

'I doubt it. But I don't understand why he didn't take steps to remedy them.'

'Perhaps, despite your conviction to the contrary, it was because your father secretly hoped you might return.'

'No! I am here as a punishment, not a reward.

Kamal will rule, Julia, because I will not surrender my life to wed myself to Qaryma.'

'Is it really such an onerous task?' she asked hesitantly. 'Couldn't you appoint agents to run your business? I'm sorry, Azhar, but if being a king is truly so awful, then frankly I don't understand why a weak man like your brother would be so happy to take it on.' She flinched at Azhar's thunderous expression, but she had gone too far to stop now. 'I know your brother only through what you have told me of him, and what you've told me has led me to surmise that he is selfish, that he is lazy and that self-sacrifice is anathema to him.'

Azhar said nothing, but his eyes were flinty. He didn't like what she was saying. She hated saying it, but she owed it to them both to continue. 'The people of Qaryma love you, Azhar. They respect you. They *want* you and not your brother. I know you think that it's undeserved.' She paused, but still he said nothing. 'You think that because Kamal remained by your father's side, that he deserves it more,' she forced herself to continue, 'but—but you are the legal heir, you are the heir your father wanted, not Kamal. What's more, with every sleepless night you spend trying to make this kingdom safe for your brother's rule, you prove that you love it. How can you see this as a prison sentence, when it is so obviously what you are destined to do?'

She felt quite sick with dread, for she knew how painful her words were to him, but beneath it all she was proud of herself for having had the gumption to speak. Azhar slowly unclenched his fists. When he whirled around, she thought he was going to leave her, but instead he strode over to the divan and sat down.

'I am Sheikh al-Farid, King Azhar of Qaryma,' he declaimed. 'I am the source of all power, all wisdom, all happiness. I am the infallible one. I make the laws and I enact the laws. None can question me. None can harm me.'

Her jaw dropped.

'These are the words I would speak at my coronation, and his father before him. You may think those words ridiculous, mere ceremony, but it is what many people here in Qaryma believe. As King, I would wield absolute power, Julia. That is how Qaryma has always been ruled. There is no other way to rule, except not to rule.'

He pushed off his headdress to run his fingers through his hair, then held out his hand for her to join him. 'Such power comes at a high price. It is extremely hard work to appear infallible,' he said wryly. 'My life would not be mine to command, it would belong to my people. Those words, the promises I would make if I took the crown, would require me to put this kingdom and these people first, before everything else.'

'As you did, I imagine, over the last ten years, while building your trading empire.'

His smile became a grimace. 'Exactly like that, which is part of the problem. Unlike my brother, I am incapable of doing things by half-measures. In ten years, I have never been satisfied with my achievements, have always been driven to conquer one more summit and one more. Can you imagine how I would be, when placed in charge of a kingdom?'

'Selfless,' Julia said.

She meant it as a compliment, but Azhar shook his head grimly. 'No, for that implies that I would not resent it, and I would.' He took her hand, lacing his fingers between hers. 'You ask if I could appoint agents to run the business I have grown from nothing, the business which it the only thing I have of my own. The answer is that, yes, I could, if all I cared about was the money, but I don't.'

'No,' Julia said with a smile. 'It is the doing that you care about, isn't it?'

'Yes. The doing,' Azhar repeated, pressing her hand. 'And the travel—or at least—it is not so much wanderlust, that craving has been satisfied in the last ten years, but there is a difference between knowing that I can go wherever I choose, and knowing I can go only where my kingdom requires me to go, do you see?'

She nodded once more. She was beginning to see very clearly. Azhar's reference to Qaryma as a gilded cage seemed now an appalling understatement. 'You would be wedded to your kingdom.'

'And expected to wed for the kingdom,' Azhar said dryly, 'a fitting bride taken for the sole purpose of producing an heir, whose sole purpose would be to inherit all this. And so it would go on. I won't do it, Julia.'

She pressed his hand to her cheek. 'The problem is, Azhar, that you are so honourable, and so incapable of giving anything less than your all, that you would do it, if you had to. You could not be half a king, could you?'

'No. Now do you understand why I cannot be one at all?'

Julia bit her lip. 'Yes,' she said. It was not a lie. She understood perfectly why he would not, and why he must leave, but she could not imagine how he was going to salve his conscience afterwards.

Chapter Seven

Action, Azhar resolved, action was what was required to demonstrate to Julia that he was right and she was quite wrong. Yes, three weeks was ambitious, but where there was a will, anything could be achieved, and he had a will of iron. Curse Julia and her doubts and her endless questions.

He stopped his furious pacing and gazed out of the window. He was not thinking straight. Her assertion that his conscience would not allow him to stay away from Qaryma was of course nonsense, but there was no harm in admitting, just to himself, that he did care for the kingdom where he had been born and raised. He did care for the people too. He wished for them only the king they deserved, a king who wanted to reign, and who was fit to reign. Not a king who saw his kingdom as a millstone around his neck. Not a king who had abandoned them ten years ago. And who would leave again in three weeks' time, for ever.

He pushed open the window that led on to his private terrace, taking his coffee with him. As far as Kamal was concerned though, he should be viewing the points Julia raised in a positive light. Shortcomings which could be addressed, not fatal flaws which could not.

Actions. Azhar knew exactly what actions he would take. Summoning a servant, he rattled off a series of commands. The fresh perspective which he'd asked Julia to provide was already paying dividends.

Having spent the morning writing up her notes, one of her least favourite and most neglected tasks, Julia had eaten some fruit for lunch and fallen asleep on the couch in her sitting room. When Aisha shook her gently awake she was confused, the beginnings of a headache niggling behind her eyes from the sun streaming through the curtains she had left open. It took her a good five minutes to understand that Azhar required her presence in a room whose

name she couldn't translate but which was located in the Second Court.

At Aisha's insistence, she changed her crumpled clothing for a matching tunic and pantaloons
in navy blue, a sky-blue scarf fastened over her
face as she made her way through the palace. By
the time she arrived at the Second Court, hurry-
ing after the huge sentry, Julia was beginning to
wonder if Azhar had decided he'd had enough
of the honesty he'd demanded from her, and was
having her expelled from Qaryma.

The huge door slammed shut behind her and
the scene before her convinced Julia that she was
right. Though the chamber was much smaller
than the Divan, and in a way more ornate, the
air was oppressive with authority. The walls were
panelled and painted, the ceiling vaulted and
tiled, the floor marble. In the centre, the throne
was more like a low chair with clawed feet covered in gold leaf. And on the throne sat Azhar in
a white-silk tunic and cloak. His headdress was
also white, though the headband which kept it in
place seemed to be made of golden rope.

Hovering in the doorway, Julia pushed back her
veil. 'You look extremely regal,' she said. 'What
is this place? Ought I to kneel?'

Azhar got to his feet, extending his hand in welcome. 'It is the Hall of Pleas, and of course you should not kneel.'

'You mean it is a court room. Am I on trial?'

'Have you committed a crime?'

She returned his smile uncertainly. 'Some of the things I said to you yesterday about your brother were treasonable.'

'But some of them were valid,' Azhar said, 'and as such, needed acting upon. This morning I had a formal audience with Kamal here. I have started to put measures into place to address your legitimate concerns.'

Julia surveyed the room, the throne, the Prince in front of her. 'You dressed up to give your brother a dressing down.'

Azhar smiled faintly. 'I thought a show of authority was in order to remind my brother that my word is final, my orders brook no challenge.'

'The first time I saw you, you were sitting on a camel dressed in the clothes of a nomad, yet there was something about you that made me think— oh, I don't know,' Julia said. 'I suppose what I mean is, you don't require clothes or a throne to intimidate or exude natural authority, Azhar.'

'Julia, you have singularly failed to be intimidated by me regardless of my attire, for which I profoundly thank you. Now, I do not have much time. I have summoned Council to assemble in an hour. The first of my actions, of which I hope you will approve.'

Approve! Azhar had never asked for her approval before. He had probably used the word inadvertently.

'I have ordered Kamal to resume the thrice-weekly meetings,' Azhar was saying now. 'A weak ruler—and you notice I do not deny that my brother is weak—needs a strong Council to bolster his reign. I intend to review the membership before I leave too, to ensure that he has the wisest and most trusted advisers possible.'

'Excellent decision,' Julia said, because Azhar seemed to require something from her.

It seemed to be sufficient, for he smiled. 'Then there is the matter of re-establishing the security of the border,' Azhar continued. 'The actions to be taken will be as follows.'

He proceeded to list a good many. Julia marvelled at his eye for detail and his memory for tasks. It was almost as if Azhar was putting measures in place to prevent his own return.

'The issue of the falling diamond yield still

troubles me. There is something I am missing, I am sure of it. I have resolved to visit the other mines. I hope you will accompany me. We will go further east, where the terrain is very different—you should find some new species worthy of your attention, and I would value your insights into—whatever we may uncover.'

'I will do what I can, though my lack of Arabic...'

'As an artist, you have an eye for detail, Julia, that much is apparent in those beautiful paintings you produce.'

'Thank you, but I am really only a competent draughtsman, nothing more.'

'You call yourself a draughtsman, but you are a true artist. I thought you were resolved to refrain from demeaning yourself and your talents.'

'Very well, I am an artist,' Julia said, 'and my artistic eye is at your disposal. How far are the mines from Al-Qaryma?'

'Far enough to require that we spend two nights away from the palace. We will camp in the desert.'

'Shall we be travelling—you will no doubt be expected to travel with a large caravan?'

'This is not a royal procession. We will be travelling unaccompanied.'

Two nights under the stars. Alone with Azhar. The prospect was both thrilling and slightly scary. What if their journey led to their other intimate journey progressing? To what undiscovered and magical places might that lead them? With Azhar as her guide the voyage was bound to be as exciting as the destination.

She shivered, then remembered the real point of their trip. 'I am flattered, Azhar. I appreciate the honour you have done me by confiding in me. Can you rely on Kamal to implement your instructions while you are temporarily absent?'

Azhar's frown was back in place. 'He was naturally defensive, he certainly was inclined to view my suggestions as criticisms, but he did not refuse to co-operate.'

'Kamal has no option but to co-operate,' Julia said. 'As far as Kamal is concerned, you are his future King.' Azhar drew her one of his intimidating looks, but she simply glared back at him. 'Wasn't that the point of dressing up, of choosing this court room for the audience?'

'What matters is his co-operation. I have achieved that,' Azhar said stiffly.

And all at once, Julia saw the fundamental flaw in his logic. It was so simple, so obvious, she couldn't believe she had not spotted it before. Azhar thought his brother weak, but he did not doubt his good faith. Or he would not doubt it. When Azhar left, Kamal would be King. A weak man who was also an honest man would be grateful for the checks and balances and props that Azhar had put in place. But a corrupt man would set about dismantling them in an instant.

Julia's heart sank. Azhar claimed to value his freedom more than anything, but first and foremost he was a man of honour. He would surrender his kingdom to a weak ruler, but he would never leave it in the hands of a corrupt one. She hoped most fervently that their trip into the desert would prove that Kamal was the former, otherwise Azhar would be sealing his own fate.

'May I take your silence for agreement?' Azhar asked her.

Julia hesitated only fractionally before nodding. She was rewarded with a smile in which she was certain she detected an element of relief. 'I must leave you now,' Azhar said, 'I do not wish to arrive late to Council. Contrary to the opinion of some, I have found that tardiness serves not to enhance one's sense of importance, but rather gives the impression that one does not value the importance of others. Have your maid pack for you. We leave at dawn.'

A brief smile and Azhar was gone, leaving Julia with her second unwelcome insight of the day. It was not a reluctance to contradict him which kept her silent, but a reluctance to hurt him. She was beginning to care about this man, and she would be a fool to allow herself to care more. Whether he remained in Qaryma or not, wed to his kingdom or wed to his business, his future lay a world apart from hers. She had her own future to think of, her own freedom to finalise. This next trip into the desert would move her much closer to completing her collection of species.

Time was running out for her here in this fantastical world. But in the meantime, she resolved to make the most of it. Alone in the desert under the stars, there would surely be the opportunity for another stage of the journey she and Azhar had set out on. A journey she would embrace, not shy away from.

The sky was a spectacular deep fuchsia pink when they set out at dawn the next day. As the sun climbed slowly above the horizon, it lightened from pink to orange and then suffused gold. Julia had managed to mount her camel fluidly in the Bedouin manner, stepping lightly on its neck, giving her that vital few seconds extra to seat herself before it reared up. Still slightly smug from this success, and concentrating hard on mirroring the swaying rhythm of the beast she rode, for it did not come naturally by any manner of means, she did not notice that she and Azhar had no pack mules with them until they were well clear of the city.

'We don't have any tents. And my clothes…'

'It is taken care of,' Azhar replied.

'How? In what way is taken care of?'

He glanced over at her. 'In the way of a surprise, Julia, nothing more sinister. A series of small treats, to show my gratitude.'

'Treats? What sort of treats?'

Above the flutter of silk that covered his face, Azhar's eyes crinkled into a smile. 'All will be revealed in due course. On any journey patience is a virtue, and enhances the experience. I hope to have the opportunity to demonstrate that to you.'

There was no disguising his meaning. Julia reminded herself that this was not shocking since it was not real, it was fantasy. The world would be real again soon enough. She resolved once again to embrace whatever was to come. She wasn't shocked, she was excited.

The sky settled into newly minted blue, the sun to pale gold. The desert stretched before them, a vast swathe of undulating sands. Like the sky, the air was newly minted, not yet too bright nor too hot, though it would certainly be both very soon. Julia would never be able to acclimatise herself to the heat in the way the true people of the desert did. She still wilted like a water-starved plant in the blaze of the afternoon sun, and her head still ached if she was foolish enough to stay out in it too long, but she loved the tingle on her skin, that particular combination of dry air and sand that was the essence of the desert. She loved sunrise and sunset. She loved the oddly salty taste of the air as dark descended and the wondrous night sky lit up. She loved the way the landscape shifted and changed before her eyes. And she loved the contrasts, the sifting golden sands and the soft red rocks, the vivid greens of the oases and the exotic variety of crops that grew there. The colours of the clothes and the scents of the markets. She had even come to terms with the distressing variety of noises emitted from her camel, the sour huff and puff of its breath as it carried her, the groaning when she forced it on to its knees, the bleating sound it made when communing with other beasts.

She curled her leg around the pommel, shifted in a vain effort to get more comfortable on the box seat, and looked around her with a contentment so all-consuming she felt she might burst. This was her favourite time of day, when the morning sparkled with promise. Of new places and new experiences. Of new people. Perhaps even new plants.

And beside her, Azhar. Looking at him, she felt her contentment turn to a fizz of excitement. His tunic had pale-blue-and-white stripes today, the boots which clad his long legs dark-blue leather. His cloak was plain white silk, billowing out in the gentle breeze around his muscular frame. His *keffiyeh* was also white silk, tied with a scarf of dark blue. He sat on the camel with that graceful ease, that unconscious air of command that Julia had noticed from their very first meeting. Azhar did not need a huge caravan to follow him, he did not require a posse of servants or even cloth of gold to proclaim his status. He looked every inch the sovereign.

Despite the fact that his desert clothes covered all but his hands and the top half of his face, he still managed to look quite devastatingly attractive too. Beneath her veil, a smile tugged at Julia's mouth. This man, this powerful, honourable, quite beautiful man, found her attractive. It astounded her, but she no longer doubted it, and the knowledge thrilled her, imbuing her with a confidence she had never possessed before. So far, this so-called journey of physical exploration of theirs had been focused entirely on her. She had been content—more than content—to allow Azhar to direct it, and to define each destination. Looking at him now, Julia decided to surprise him. She wanted to see him naked. She wanted to see him out of control. The small issue of her utter lack of expertise in such matters momentarily deflated her, but not for long. Instinct, she told herself, would take over, fed by passion. It was the most natural thing in the world, what occurred between a man and a woman. She simply had to let nature—her nature, previously dormant—run its course.

* * *

It took three hours to reach the village, by which time Julia's mind was far from the night to come, with all its potential excitement, and focused only on keeping her numb bottom securely perched on the boxed saddle. Above them, the sky was now azure blue dotted with white clouds. A mountain range loomed on the far horizon, the jagged rock streaked pink and purple by the sun's rays. The terrain had become progressively rougher over the last hour, the soft sand giving way to hard-packed mud and coarse gravel. The houses formed from adobe were built into the foothills, a cluster of domed roofs, arched windows and doorways which huddled together for protection. Three palm trees loomed high somewhere behind the houses, their green fronds vivid against the mud brown of the buildings, indicating that there must be an underground well nearby.

They were expected. As Azhar dismounted, Julia was surprised to see a servant wearing the palace colours emerge from the shade to take the reins. She followed suit, managing with relative grace, and the servant took her reins too.

'This is another of our diamond-mining villages,' Azhar said, pushing back his headdress to reveal his face.

'Where is everyone?' Julia asked, puzzled. 'Surely you don't send women and children down the mines?'

Azhar laughed, holding out his arm. 'This way,' he said.

She followed him through an archway that she'd taken for a doorway, then stopped short with a gasp of surprise. The village was formed in the shape of a circle. In the centre were the palm trees and the small turquoise pool of the well. A huge silk canopy had been stretched across the space under the palm trees and anchored to the roofs of some of the houses, forming a vast open-sided tent, under which tables laden with food and drink were heaped. The villagers themselves were formed into two rows, men and women and children, in the classic pose of obeisance.

Azhar stepped forward, making the traditional greeting and asking them all to rise. Still standing under the archway, Julia watched as the villagers did as he bid them with some alacrity, rushing forward to surround him in a babble of excited exclamations. She understood almost nothing of what was being said, but it was clear from the odd combination of deference and excitement that Azhar was no stranger to this village—or he had not been in the past. He was smiling, relaxed and at ease, showing none of the discomfort that had been apparent when faced with the huge show of adulation the first day they had arrived in Al-Qaryma, and again, on the first occasion they had visited Johara. Though now she thought about it, on the second visit to that oasis, Azhar had been as he was here, quickly discouraging the formal greetings and encouraging his people to approach him.

His people. They clearly were his people, whether he wanted to admit it or not, and he was every inch the ruler of those people too, whether or not he wanted to admit that either. Such obvious affection and respect did not stem from what was due but what had been earned.

Unsure of her reception, unwilling to detract attention from Azhar, and embarrassed once more by her limited Arabic, Julia would have happily remained in the background, but he seemed to have other ideas, indicating that she join him. Though her veil was firmly in place, her bright plait of hair and pale skin betrayed her foreign origins. She kept her eyes down, feeling absurdly shy, raising them only when a little ripple of applause broke out in response to Azhar's introduction.

'I told them that you are a famous English botanist, come to study our plants and to tell the world of the beauty of our desert,' Azhar told her. 'This is Fatima, a friend of Johara and also a noted herbalist,' he added, introducing the older woman. 'She says she has some plants which may interest you. Do you wish me to come with you, to translate?'

'No, no,' Julia replied hastily, 'I would not deprive all these people who are clearly eager for your company after so long.'

'This was a favourite place of mine, back in the—when I was—before. One of our best swordsman is a native of this village. He is the Chief of the Guards at the palace, and taught me how to fight with a dagger as well as a scimitar. Fatima is his sister. Go with her, I can see she is eager to impart her knowledge,' Azhar said, translating his words into his own language for the sake of the other woman, and receiving a beaming nod in return.

* * *

She was gone a full hour, and could have spent another three in Fatima's company. Compared to the other oases Julia had visited, this village was arid, so the small selection of hardy species which clung to life here was quite different from anything she had so far collected and documented. She took no samples, for the numbers of plants were sparse and she had no wish to disturb this fragile habitat, but her pencils flew over the paper as she took likeness after likeness, managing at the same time to extract sufficient information as to life cycles and usage with a combination of simple words and gestures.

Returning to the canopied tent in the centre of the village, she wholly expected Azhar to be waiting impatiently for her to leave, but instead found him seated on a large cushion surrounded by a cluster of men and women, all of whom seemed to be talking at once. Mindful of her allotted role as objective observer, though she could not imagine what it was she would be expected to observe, Julia helped herself to a small plate of food and sat down on the periphery. The mood of the villagers seemed to be indignant. There was much shaking of heads and vehement denials of something. Whatever Azhar was saying, the villagers didn't like it, to the extent where their indignation threatened to overcome their innate respect for their Prince. One man actually jumped to his feet, gesticulating wildly. Another said something that sounded inflammatory. The response was a shocked and suspenseful silence as they waited for Azhar to respond. As the silence stretched so long as to make the tension palpable, the man shuffled his feet, colour darkening his face, but when Azhar finally spoke his tone was mild, bidding the man to sit back down, and to explain the source of his anger, as far as Julia could understand.

A small hand tugging at her cloak distracted her. She looked up to find not one but three children staring at her, and smiled. They needed no further encouragement, dropping on to the carpets which had been spread over the dusty ground, staring up with wide-eyed fascination at this unfamiliar and exotic stranger. On impulse, Julia opened her notebook at a fresh page and began to sketch. The simple line drawing of a camel was a resounding success. She tore out the page to be passed around and then drew a horse, which was met with the same reception.

Morwenna, her father's fat cat smiling malevolently at a mouse drew gales of laughter, encouraging Julia to abandon reality for the creatures who inhabited the Cornish tales she had loved as a child: a fantastical sea creature rearing out of the waves; a mermaid on a rock combing her fingers through her seaweed hair; and a wispy, wraith-like siren rising from the marshes. The smallest children fought to sit on her lap as she drew, watching entranced as her pencil flew over the paper. Fascinated fingers tugged at her long plait of red hair. Each drawing was greeted with bursts of laughter, awed exclamations, and cries for more and yet more. Only when a pair of much larger hands relieved her of her latest sketch did Julia become conscious of the time that had passed.

Azhar crouched down to examine the drawing of an absurdly beautiful fairy with gossamer wings, while the most curious of the children, a fairy-like creature herself named Amira, peered over his shoulder. 'What is it?' he asked.

'A Bucca,' Julia replied. 'They live in the tin mines and in the caves in Cornwall. If you see one, then you can be sure a storm is coming.'

Azhar handed the drawing to the little girl and

helped Julia to her feet. 'I fear that a storm of a different nature may well be coming here,' he said grimly.

'Some of the villagers certainly seemed agitated.'

'I thought at first that they resented my enquiries,' Azhar said. 'Like you, I saw the anger, but I assumed it was directed against me—my absence. It seems, however, that I insulted them when I asked why the yields from the mine had decreased so radically. They thought I was accusing them of idleness when they insist they work as hard and as productively as ever.'

'So this mine too is not performing as well as you expected,' Julia asked.

'According to the accounts, and to the Chief Overseer of the diamond mines, who sits on the Council. He is a man of considerable experience, he inherited the position from his father before him. But his accounts do not tally with the word of these miners.'

'What about the other mine that you visited?'

Azhar shook his head. 'I spoke only in general terms regarding working conditions to the miners there. I had no reason to question the yields quoted by the Chief Overseer. The mines are very old, it is not inconceivable that over time...'

He broke off, rubbing the bridge of his nose. 'I have a horrible feeling that with each question I ask, I dig another shovelful of sand from my own grave.'

His tone was rueful, but his eyes were troubled. 'You could always refrain from digging any deeper,' Julia said, knowing that the suggestion was impossible.

'Unfortunately, my instincts insist that I dig deeper. If the Chief Overseer has been systematically defrauding the Treasury, then it is best that I uncover it now, and resolve the issue on Kamal's behalf.' Azhar shook his head. 'It is time we left, we have another two hours ride before we reach our camp for the night. Was your time spent with Fatima profitable?'

'Extremely.'

'And you have made a number of new friends, I can see,' Azhar said, smiling down at the children. 'Though their demands seem to have prevented you from enjoying your food.'

'I forgot all about it,' Julia said, looking at her almost full plate in surprise. 'Will you catch us a hare for dinner?'

'I think I may be able to do slightly better than that,' Azhar said intriguingly. 'Shall we go?'

He was silent and pensive as they journeyed further east, brooding over what he had learned. His remark about digging his own grave had been intended to be flippant, but in truth the situation was both serious and concerning. To accuse such a senior figure as the Chief Overseer of dishonesty was unprecedented. The very nature of the role and the sums involved demanded unimpeachable probity. The holder of the post must enjoy the complete trust of the King. That the man was also a member of Council—Azhar would have to have incontrovertible proof. Punishment for such a crime would be grave, but the dishonour it would bring not only to the perpetrator, but to his whole family was almost worse. He had to be very sure of his facts, for the consequences were so dire for all concerned, including him. Such an accusation had not been made in living memory.

Yet if it was true, the light it cast on Kamal's judgement was also extremely worrying. If the man proved to be corrupt, it would reflect very poorly indeed upon his brother's astuteness. It was one thing to prop Kamal up, quite another to expose him as gullible, though how such a heinous offence could be kept quiet, even if it was for the good of the kingdom—but here Azhar drew his thoughts to an abrupt halt. If the matter proved to be as grave as it seemed, Kamal must deal with the consequences. Azhar could identify the issues, he could even assist with putting a strategy in place to deal with them, but the longer-term implications were his brother's problem.

Azhar had his own business to return to. A business which he had created, nurtured and expanded, and which must be suffering from his prolonged absence, no matter how diligent his agent might be. Freedom. It was tantalisingly close. He must keep that goal as clearly in sight as Julia did. In a little over two weeks, freedom would be his, secured at an even greater cost than he had anticipated when he first arrived. Every passing day brought new concerns to the surface. Every question he asked begat only more questions. He was weary of it.

A little over two weeks was all the time he had left with Julia. He didn't want to think about that either. Tonight, he would forget all of it. Today he had played the Prince, tonight he would be simply a man alone with a desirable woman in the middle of the desert.

The camp was set up on the edge of the small oasis, which was little more than a deep round pool and a stand of palm trees. The two tents sat at right angles to each other, their tastefully striped coverings and decorative golden tassels a far cry from the simple construction that Julia had last camped in. A thick rug was spread on the sand in the awning of the larger tent of the two. A fire was set ready to be kindled. Lamps were hung from the awnings, ready to be lit. The sun was already setting behind them as they arrived, casting a golden glow over everything.

'What do you think?' Azhar asked.

Julia stared at the scene in wonder. 'Is this real? It looks quite fantastical. How on earth did all of this get out here in the middle of the desert?'

'I ordered that it be so.'

'And here, as if by magic, it is. Is this one of the treats you promised me?'

'I wanted your lasting memory of the Qaryma desert to be much more pleasant than your last experience,' Azhar said, helping her from the saddle.

'Drugged, robbed and left for dead. Until you came along and saved me, that is.' She undid her veil and pulled off her headdress, shaking out her heavy plait of hair. 'When I am back in Cornwall, my memories of Qaryma will not be of the desert, magical and beautiful though it is, they will be of you and our fleeting time together.'

'Then we must make the most of what little time we have left,' Azhar said.

The sun was disappearing fast from the horizon. The air was cooling rapidly. The thick silence which heralded the transition from day to night descended. Julia caught his gaze. 'And what, pray, does making the most of it involve?'

Azhar's smile was sensual. 'That very much depends on you.'

'Actually,' Julia said, pushing his headdress back to run her fingers through his hair, 'I too have resolved to make the most of our precious time together.'

'And what, pray, does that entail?'

She rested her hands on his shoulders and stood on her tiptoes to brush her lips against his ear. 'That very much depends on you,' she whispered.

His hands tightened on her arms. Julia nipped the lobe of his ear. She was nervous. What if he rejected her? What if he thought her overtures foolish, or naïve or simply unexciting? She knew that such thoughts were self-destructive, but they crept in, hovering at the edge of consciousness as she pressed a kiss to his jaw. It was rough with the day's growth. Her own skin was gritty with the sand that permeated everywhere. She felt hot and damp and singularly ill suited for seduction. Defeated, she stepped back. 'I think I'd like to freshen up.'

But as she turned away, Azhar pulled her back into his arms. 'In a moment.' He tilted her face up, to look into her eyes. 'Julia, whatever you are thinking, be assured that you are wrong.'

'You can't possible know what I'm thinking.'

He stroked her cheek, trailing his fingers down her throat. 'Have you forgotten what I told you, that there is nothing more effective in igniting a man's desire than a woman's passion? To see the fire in your eyes, to feel the fire in your blood as you touch me, it sets me on fire too. Do you remember?'

'I hadn't forgotten, but...'

'You are the most desirable woman I have ever

met, Julia.' Azhar kissed her eyelids. 'I look at you, and I am aflame.' He kissed the tip of her nose. 'I want you as I have never wanted another woman.' He pulled her tight against him. 'You can do nothing that will quell that passion. Everything you do ignites it. Do not be afraid, Julia.'

'I'm not afraid.'

'Then forget what has happened in the past. You are not that person. Not now, not here.'

She nodded. She closed her eyes. She twined her arms tightly around his neck. And when she put her lips on his, she discovered it was very easy indeed to do exactly what he asked of her.

He tasted of salt and sand and heat. His mouth was warm, his lips soft, his hands feather light on her shoulders, her back, her sides, setting her pulses racing, setting her skin tingling. Did her touch do the same to him? He said so, and he wouldn't lie, but...

'Julia?'

She dragged open her eyes.

'Stop thinking.'

'I can't.'

'Why not? You had no problem switching that clever mind off the last time,' Azhar said.

Her insides clenched in anticipation, but she

shook her head. 'The last time it was—you were—it was for me. I want to reciprocate, only—only I am not sure what to do or how to do it,' Julia finished on an embarrassed whisper.

'You do not have to—I told you, I take my pleasure from yours, Julia.'

'I know.' She risked looking at him, and discovered that his eyes were dark with desire. It gave her courage. 'I want to know if it's the same,' she said with a small smile. 'Whether I can take my pleasure from yours. Will you help me find out?'

His laugh was deep, throaty and intensely arousing. 'You are the most surprising woman I have ever met. Has any man ever been asked such an irresistible question?'

'Does that mean you will?'

He caught her roughly to him, kissing her deeply. 'Yes,' he said. 'It means that I will. With pleasure. In fact with what I am certain will be mutual pleasure.'

Chapter Eight

Julia's kisses had aroused him beyond belief. Her shy, delightful plea to be permitted to pleasure him stirred Azhar's blood. Patience, he told himself, but what he really needed was control, and he wasn't sure how much of that he could muster.

He left her briefly to prepare the bathing tent. The bath stood ready, as he had ordered, scented with rosewater. The candles set on the low table where the oils and soaps had been set out were quickly lit. Soft drying cloths were laid in a neat stack. At the rear of the tent, the trunk containing Julia's clothing lay open. In the space at the front, around the bath, were thick rugs, velvet cushions, a table set with her brushes and combs. He had thought only of her comfort when ordering it to be set out like this, but being surrounded by familiar personal possessions would serve equally well to relax her.

Holding back the tent flap, Azhar beckoned to her, relishing the look of wonder on her face as she took in the unashamedly luxurious tent. 'If ever I had any doubts that you were a prince,' she said, her eyes gleaming, 'they are well and truly dispelled. No mere mortal could conjure such wonders from thin air. It must have taken an army of servants to set the camp up. Where are they?'

'I have made them disappear. I am not a prince, I am a magician,' Azhar said.

She laughed. 'Whichever you are, you have certainly worked your magic. Thank you. This is completely indulgent and wholly unnecessary but...'

'I like to indulge you. Take your time. There is no rush.'

He turned to go, but Julia called him back. 'A bath such as this is most soothing after a day spent on a camel,' she said. 'You told me so once, and I discovered you were right.'

She was nervous, but she was also—there was a look in her eyes that made his heart race. 'I remember,' Azhar said.

"And—and if I remember correctly, you also told me that a massage was of great benefit to tired limbs and bodies.'

'That is true.'

'We have both been on a camel all day. I presume your limbs and body are as tired as mine?'

She was blushing wildly, but she was looking straight at him. Her courage staggered him, even as her daring made the blood thunder in his ears. 'Julia, you do not have to…' He stopped short, realising how easy it would be for her to misinterpret his words. 'If you are asking me to share your bath with you then I would like that,' he said. 'I would like that very, very much.'

Her smile was his reward, partly relieved, partly nervous, but mostly pleased. It touched him, that smile. He had no doubts of her ability to arouse him—she only had to look at him to do that—but he wanted very much to prove it to her. He wanted her to see how much she aroused him, and by doing so, to be assured of her own potent attraction. The line between encouragement and direction was a fine one, but he was determined to tread it.

'If we are to bathe we must first remove our

clothes. All of them,' he said, slipping off his cloak before unfastening hers.

Julia hesitated only briefly before pushing her headdress off, unfastening the buttons of his tunic with shaky fingers. He kicked off his boots. She did the same. He unfastened the belt which held his trousers in place. She undid the buttons of her own tunic. He stepped out his trousers. Julia untied the sash at her waist and stepped out of her wide pantaloons. Her breasts rose and fell quickly beneath her tunic, the only item of clothing she still had on. He wanted to tear it from her but forced himself to wait, not wanting to rush her, more importantly not wanting to wrest control from her.

Her eyes fixed on his, she lifted the tunic over her head and dropped it to the floor. Her arms fluttered up to cover her breasts, but she stilled them, standing proudly naked under his gaze. 'Julia,' was all he could manage. His whole body ached with desire. He could not resist touching her. Taking her long braid of hair in his hands, he undid the ribbon and began to untangle it, running his fingers through the fiery river of red, letting it ripple out over her shoulders, down her back, over the creamy mounds of her breasts. Her nipples were dark-pink peaks. The silky curls between her legs were dark auburn. He could count her ribs, she was so slender, and yet the flare of her hips from her narrow waist was delightful.

'Julia,' he said, touching her carefully, reverently, her arms, her waist, the curve of her bottom and her breasts. His breath was ragged. Hers was shallow. He wanted to kiss her. He wanted to sink his shaft deep inside her. But he waited, because that was what she wanted.

'Now you,' she said.

He lifted his tunic over his head and dropped it to the floor, horribly conscious of his engorged shaft jutting proudly from his body. He knew women found his body desirable. He had never been self-conscious about his flesh. But he could not recall ever standing like this, flamboyantly aroused, being blatantly examined by a woman he was absolutely certain had never so blatantly examined a man in such a way before. He found himself hoping he pleased her, something he had never before doubted to be true.

She touched him lightly, mirroring the way he had touched her. Her fingers on his shoulders, fluttering over his chest, his nipples, stopping at his hips. She bit her lip, her eyes on his shaft, and then fluttering up to meet his, the question in them clear. He took her hand, curling it around him, and at the same time kissing her deeply. She kissed him back. Her breasts pressed against his chest, the hard peaks of her nipples a delicious *frisson* of pressure on his skin.

Then she broke the kiss, her eyes drawn down again, running her hand experimentally along his length. Azhar shuddered, his eyes closing momentarily. She did it again, the pads of her fingers lightly caressing the sensitive skin at the tip, and Azhar had to bite back a moan, had to clench his fists in an effort to hold on to some element of control.

'You don't like that?' Julia said.

'I like it,' he said through gritted teeth, 'but if we are going to bathe, then you will have to unhand me.'

Julia smiled, tightening her hand just a fraction around him. 'I don't want to unhand you. I'm not ready to bathe yet,' she said, stroking him this time, all the way up, all the way down.

His breath expelled in a rush. He had thought he couldn't get any harder, but he had been wrong.

'Lie down,' Julia commanded. She gave him a

little encouraging shove. 'Lie down, Azhar,' she said, this time with a great deal more confidence.

He lay down on the cushions. Julia dropped to her knees between his legs. Her hair fell over her shoulders, brushing his belly. He shuddered. She gathered a handful of her hair in her hand and brushed it over his chest. 'Do you like that?' she asked him.

'Yes.'

She stroked his nipples with the hair. Satin soft, yet it positively ached. 'Do you like that, Azhar?'

'Julia,' he said with a tight smile, remembering her own words, 'Everything you do pleases me.'

Her laughter was husky. She trailed her hair down his belly, brushing it lightly over his skin. He could see tantalising glimpses of her nipples. Her knees brushed the inside of his thighs. His heart was hammering so hard he was surprised he could still breathe. The anticipation of what she would do next was almost as arousing as what she did. Satin-soft hair on his shaft now, and Azhar let out a deep moan. She trailed it down his length then back up again. The sensation was so intense, his fists clenched.

'You like that, Azhar,' Julia said, and this time it was not a question.

She leaned forward to kiss him, and her breasts pressed against his chest again. He could feel the soft brush of her sex on his shaft, and in response, he could feel, horribly close, too close, his climax gathering. Her mouth was achingly sweet. He arched under her, pressing himself unashamedly against her, and she gave a soft, feral cry. The urge to take her then, to feel her hot, sweet, wet flesh tight around him, was almost overpowering. He dug his fingers into the cushions at his side. Julia's tongue touched his, and he cried out again.

'Julia...'

'Azhar,' she said, deliberately teasing him with the brush of her nipples over his chest, 'I do believe you like that too.'

It was there in her eyes, the gleam of satisfaction he had wished for her to discover, arousal enhanced by the power to arouse. 'Julia, I like that so much that if you do it again...'

She did it again. And she laughed as he groaned, a laugh of sheer delight that was curtailed as he pulled her to him, ravaging her mouth, his hands curved around her rear, praying for one more second, two more seconds, five more seconds of control even as her mouth and her tongue and the weight of her flesh pressing down on his body made exerting that control agonising.

'Julia,' he said, quite desperate now.

And she understood. She sat up. She knelt back between his legs. She took his shaft between her hands, and she stroked. Inexpert as her touch was, it was all he needed, all he wanted. Too gentle, but more than enough. With a hoarse cry, Azhar climaxed, grabbing a drying cloth just in time, feeling as if the seed he spilled had been torn from deep inside him and when he thought he was done spilling more, as Julia stroked him again, and then again.

Julia surveyed the man lying beneath her with wonder. He lay sprawled, his eyes closed, his lashes thick on his cheek, his arms spread, and his male part still thick and hard in her hand. She felt an odd flush of triumph, knowing that she had done this, that she had taken him to such heights, that she had forced him to lose control. But it was most certainly not the only triumph she felt. She knew now what Azhar meant. His pleasure had most decidedly been her pleasure. Her nipples ached. She cupped her breasts, shuddering as the brush of her palm connected with the sensitive skin. Closing her eyes, she risked the tiniest brush of her thumbs over the peaks, remembering how Azhar had touched her like this, and had to bite back a moan.

Opening her eyes again, she found he was looking at her. Hastily, she dropped her hands, but Azhar shook his head. 'No, don't stop.'

She shook her head, mortified.

'I like it, Julia,' he said with a slow smile. 'Every bit as much as you do. Do it again.'

He liked it? Unconvinced, but almost too aroused to care, Julia touched herself again, cupping her breasts, running her thumbs over her nipples. Her back arched. Her eyes drifted closed. Deep inside, her muscles clenched.

Azhar pulled her on top of him, his mouth claiming hers briefly. 'No,' she said, 'this was for you.'

He rolled her on to her back. 'And this is for both of us,' he said. He kissed her. Then his lips were on her breast, licking her nipple, his hand teasing the other. Then he eased her legs open, and his mouth was on her belly. And then lower. Julia arched up, thrusting unashamedly as he licked into her. She had had no idea she was so close, so ready, so tight. To try to hold back would be futile, and she did not want to hold back. A lick, a thrust, she did not know what he was doing nor did she care, save that it was exactly what she wanted. Her climax ripped through her, wave upon wave of hot, heady pleasure, and she cried out with a wild abandon that she did not know herself capable of.

The water in the bathing tub was refreshingly cool as Julia sank into it—alone, after all—some time later. Her body felt heavy, her skin glowed. She lay back, closing her eyes, drifting into a languid state, sated and satisfied in a way she had never been before. The image of Azhar, also sated and satisfied, lying beneath her, made her shudder. She could not possibly be aroused again so quickly, yet she was. Was this normal? Was her body, deprived of such carnal pleasure, now becoming addicted?

She sighed, lying back in the water, enjoying the lap of it over her skin. They had not even made proper love. Though her experience of making proper love was far too proper for her new decadent self. There would be nothing proper about making love with Azhar. It would be as improper as she could possibly imagine, and more, since she actually couldn't imagine—though she wanted to. She wanted to know what she had been missing all these years.

Julia sat up, splashing water everywhere. Initially, the month she had agreed to stay had seemed to stretch out like an eternity, and yet already more than half of it was gone. When she set out from Cornwall, this trip had merely been the first step on her path to freedom. Her desire to fulfil her promises and claim that freedom was every bit as fervent as before, but the sense of urgency was no longer there. The desert was not simply a means to an end, an exotic habitat that she must traverse in order to complete a task, it had an allure all of its own. She would happily linger here another month, or even three.

'And just how, exactly, would you manage that, Julia Trevelyan?' she asked herself sternly as she stepped out of the bath and wrapped herself in one of the huge drying cloths. She had just about sufficient funds to get herself back to England. There could be no question of her extending her trip here. 'And no real desire to do so, without Azhar,' she muttered ruefully. For she had spoken the truth earlier. Alluring though the desert was, it was Azhar who had bewitched her.

She finished drying herself and selected a loose cotton tunic to wear. Even if their idyll was by some magic extended for another month, it would still have to end, because that was the nature of idylls. They were not real.

In the real world, she and Azhar could be nothing to each other. Aside from the problem of geography, there was the matter of the freedom they both valued so highly. Azhar did not want a wife. Julia did not want a husband, and she most certainly did not want another husband who was already married to something else. 'I refuse to come second-best ever again, whether that be to a scientific treatise or even an Arabian kingdom,' she muttered to herself.

She shuddered. 'Never, never, never again.' Picking up a comb, Julia set about pulling it ruthlessly through her damp and tangled hair.

The gold mines were located deep into the mountains, an arduous morning's trek over terrain that was treacherously steep and stony. Though her camel seemed to be quite untroubled by this, the box saddle on which she balanced swayed so much that Julia felt as if she was sitting in a dinghy in a storm without either sail or rudder. Aware of Azhar's watchful eye, determined not to add to his troubles by breaking her neck, she clung on for dear life.

He had retreated into himself today. Sheikh, trader, Prince, he looked any or all of those as he rode, sitting straight and tall in the saddle with an ease that was even more impressive now that Julia herself knew how very difficult it was. She marvelled that this intimidating man, made more mysterious by his cloak and headdress, could be the same man who had lain naked and aroused beneath her, had unravelled at her touch, and who had brought her to a peak of pleasure she had not known existed. Looking at him now, she felt as if she barely knew him. Was he thinking the same of her?

No, he was not thinking of her at all. He was thinking about the meeting to come with the Overseer of the gold mine they were to visit, which he had discussed with her over dinner last night.

'The entrance to the mine is just there,' Azhar said, in confirmation a few moments later.

It looked to Julia like a cave, but as they drew closer she could see that it was in reality the entrance of an extremely steep tunnel cut into the red rock of the mountain. A wide wooden ladder was affixed to the ground, dropping at a sharp angle into the black hole that was the mine shaft. 'How far underground does it go?' she asked, peering over the edge.

'It is not so much deep as long,' Azhar replied. 'The tunnels spread for miles through the mountain. There is silver as well as gold here.'

'How many men work below ground?'

'There are two teams of fifteen. The conditions here are difficult as you can see, almost no plant life to interest you I am afraid. The men work for five days, then return to their village for five days to rest. Their oasis is almost another half-day's travel from here. While they are here, they shelter in these huts,' Azhar said pointing to a huddle of adobe shelters about a hundred yards away. 'Come, I have arranged for us to meet the Overseer there.'

It was dusk once again, the end of a very long day as they neared the end of their return journey. 'Is it the custom for men and women to take tea together as we did?' Julia asked. 'It was very hospitable of the Overseer's wife to make the trip from her village simply to serve it. When you suggested she sit with us, she looked quite shocked, it made me wonder whether my presence at your side has been causing all manner of outrage.'

'As a foreigner and my guest, I hope you feel you have been treated with the utmost respect throughout.'

'And with a great deal of kindness too, but...'

'But that does not answer your question,' Azhar said. 'It is not unusual, but in some households it is not common practice. I have not previously met the Overseer. By asking his wife to sit with us I was demonstrating that I respected and trusted him.'

'And do you?' Julia asked.

Azhar nodded slowly. 'What did you think?'

'You said yourself that the yields from that gold mine are not an issue. In fact you said they had increased slightly in the last two years,' Julia said. 'I could only partially follow the conversation, but it seemed to me that when you mentioned the diamond mines, he looked quite uncomfortable.'

'It could be because he knows that they are not so productive and does not wish to be seen to triumph.'

'Yes, but it is more likely that he knows there

is something wrong and is either afraid to mention it, or unwilling to voice unsubstantiated suspicions,' Julia said.

'Either way, it would be unfair of me to force the issue—and besides, rumour is not evidence.'

'And you are now certain that you will find tangible evidence?'

Azhar sighed heavily. 'I fear so. The conflicting accounts of the Chief Overseer and the diamond miners do not square.'

'What if it is the men who are stealing the diamonds?'

'Not possible. They are searched as they leave the mine every night. No, it is the Chief Overseer, I am certain of it, but I have to be careful how I go about proving it. I don't want to alert his suspicions.'

Julia worried at her bottom lip. If Azhar truly thought that the Chief Overseer of the diamond mines was corrupt, then it would be an ideal opportunity for Kamal to demonstrate his authority. But what if the Chief Overseer was not the source of corruption, what if it went higher? That could only mean one thing.

Her heart contracted. She couldn't bear to think of what that would do to Azhar. While he had been out speaking to the returning gold miners this afternoon, the Overseer's wife had managed to ask Julia rather diffidently when she planned to return to England, and if the Crown Prince intended to escort her. She seemed inexplicably relieved to hear of Julia's plans to return so soon and alone. Thinking that the woman had mistakenly assumed her a possible bride for Azhar, she had gone to great pains to contradict her, and had been even more confused by the woman's amusement. Now she wondered if what was as the root of her questions was simpler—a fear that their Prince, having been absent for ten years, might desert them again. Leaving another prince to be crowned, one whom they neither wanted nor respected.

She knew she ought to tell Azhar of this conversation. She also knew it would be one more shovel full of sand dug from his grave, as he put it. Azhar had already had the benefit of her objective viewpoint in confirming one piece of bad news, she couldn't bear to give him another. Besides, she could be wrong, couldn't she? Her few words, their many hand gestures, she could have completely misinterpreted the whole thing.

When the time came—if the subject came up—

then she would come clean, she promised herself. But right now, what Azhar needed, and she wanted desperately, was for him to forget he was a prince, and to remember that he was a man.

A man who could conjure this magical encampment into existence. Tonight, the lamps had been lit to welcome them. The fire had been re-laid. Julia pushed back her veil and slid down from her camel with a sigh of relief.

'Azhar, I cannot tell you how much I appreciate this enchanting place,' she said. 'Knowing we are coming back to such luxurious comfort at the end of a long day makes all the difference. It was very thoughtful of you.'

'Julia, if I'm being complete honest my motivation was not entirely selfless,' he replied. 'I did not wish to share your company with anyone else.'

'If that is the case, then I am afraid I am very selfish too,' she replied, 'since I feel exactly the same way.'

'Are you fatigued, Julia?'

'No, I...'

'Sore from the saddle, perhaps?' Azhar asked. 'Tired, in limbs and body?'

His smile was sinful. His sinfulness was infectious. 'I think perhaps I am,' Julia said.

'Then go into the bathing tent, remove all of your clothes, and we will do something to remedy that.'

She assumed he intended for them to bathe together, since they had not done so the previous night, having become more than a little distracted. In the bathing tent, Julia lit the candles and hurriedly prepared herself, then equally hurriedly grabbed a clean drying cloth to cover her nudity. It was silly of her to be embarrassed, but she couldn't bring herself to wait for him without any covering at all. Should she get into the water? He hadn't said so, and she was under no obligation to do only what he asked, but—but she was most curious as to what he would request of her, so she gathered the thick cotton around her and sat on a velvet cushion.

She did not have to wait for long. Azhar's eyes lit up when he entered the tent and saw her, but he made no move to touch her, instead he threw off his cloak and headdress and hurriedly pulled off his boots before arranging several of the huge cushions together into a makeshift divan. 'You look like the most delightful gift, waiting to be unwrapped. In a way, that is exactly what you are—a gift from the gods. May I unwrap you?' he asked, leading her over to the mound of cushions.

Blushing, she allowed him to remove the cloth, and was rewarded by Azhar's sharp intake of breath. 'You are quite, quite lovely,' he said, running his hand slowly down her body, from her shoulder to her bottom. 'Such delicate skin,' he said, 'like alabaster.'

Azhar kissed her. She kissed him back. The touch of her tongue on his brought an instant response, making his member stir against her. It thrilled her, that instant response. Julia leaned in closer, brushing her breasts against his chest, and kissed him again.

'Not yet,' Azhar said, dragging his mouth away, turning her away from him, easing her on to the cushions. 'Before we sate our desire, we must ease your aches and pains.'

Julia lay on her tummy feeling extremely exposed and not a little confused. A rustling behind her told her that Azhar had removed his tunic. He moved her plait over her shoulder. Then he knelt down behind her and began to knead her shoulders. His hands were oiled. His touch was expert. The perfume in the oil began to suffuse the room as it was warmed by contact with her skin. Julia closed her eyes in ecstasy as he worked on the knots and tensions in her muscles that she hadn't even been aware of. Her shoulders felt as if they were being unfurled. Her spine felt as if it was being loosened. She felt heavy and floaty at the same time. His thumbs worked into the knot at the base of her spine. More oil trickled on to her back, and then he began to work on her buttocks, building a very different kind of tension.

He was kneeling between her legs. She could feel the roughness of his thighs against hers, the whisper of his warm breath on her neck, the press of his erection, and all the time his hands sliding and slickly kneading her bottom, her flanks, the inside of her thighs, her bottom again. She was a mass of sensations, at the same time helpless to move and unwilling to move. He pulled her forward, tilting her upwards, and his hands slide between her legs, then inside her. The oil made her slippery, his fingers slid over her, into her, over her. She arched up against him, wanting more than his fingers this time, and he slid his hands up her sides then moved them underneath her to cup her breasts.

Julia moaned. Azhar kissed her neck. She slithered against him, her back to his chest, her buttocks on his thighs, the thick girth of his member sliding over her, though not inside her. She moaned again. 'Azhar, please.'

His fingers deliciously tugging on her nipples roused her to an agony of wanting. His mouth on her ear, he whispered, 'Are you sure, Julia?'

'Desperately.'

He pulled her toward him, lifting her on to her knees before entering her. The combination of perfumed oil and her arousal made her slick, drawing him deep inside in one delightful, delicious movement. She clenched around him, holding him, wanting him deeper, fighting a primal urge to move.

He eased her further on to her knees and pushed higher inside her. Julia clenched and held him, shuddered as he eased himself slowly out, and then thrust again. Higher this time, and she held him again for agonising seconds. He was so thick. So hard. Another thrust. Another hold. Her climax was too close. She clenched everything.

'Slower?' Azhar said.

'Slower,' Julia agreed, though she had no idea how…

He lifted her on to his knees. She had no idea how he did that either, but she didn't care. He was still inside her. Her bottom was pressed into his belly. His hands were on her breasts. She arched her back in response, and he buried his face in her neck. Her nipples tingled, ached, pulsed. She moaned in protest when he took his hands away to rest them on her waist.

'Slowly,' he whispered in her ear, moving fractionally inside her, encouraging her to lift herself just the merest amount. Pulsing. Slow, delightful pulsing. And then slow, delightful thrusting. His arm around her waist to hold her, his mouth on her neck, and inside her, throb and thrust, throb and thrust, until she could feel it, the tension, the growing sense of spiralling out of control, and Azhar slid his hand over her, adding a sliding, stroking finger to his thick, thrusting member, and Julia came so violently and so suddenly that she would have fallen forward if he had not held her, still stroking and sliding and thrusting, until he groaned deeply, his own climax taking him, lifting her free just in time to spend himself safely.

* * *

Later, they sat by the fire under the awning of the sleeping tent to dine. Above them the moon formed a hazy crescent, the brightness of the stars dimmed by a film of dust from a distant subsiding sandstorm that turned the sky grey-blue. The food was delicious, but Azhar had little appetite for it. The day had brought him no solace, indeed had only added further to his disquiet. Yesterday, he had been appalled by the idea that a man who held such a senior position of trust as the Chief Overseer did, a man whose very title commanded respect, could be corrupt. Today, even without the hard evidence he required, he had moved from suspicion to certainty. But his disquiet did not stop there. It was almost impossible to imagine that corruption of this magnitude could go undetected.

Unless it was condoned, by the only man with higher rank than a member of the Council. Azhar knew that. And Julia knew that too, though she had refrained from saying so. Which made Azhar feel rather sick. Julia was never slow to speak her mind, regardless of how it would be received by him and yet on this occasion she had bitten her tongue. He suspected it was not because she feared his reaction but because she felt sorry for him. Perhaps even pitied him.

He hoped against hope that his brother was not implicated. Even if it were true, technically the diamonds belonged to the crown, and the crown belonged to Kamal. Azhar pushed his plate to one side with a sigh of irritation. He was going around in circles to no avail. When he had firm proof, he would deal with it, but not until then.

'Aren't you hungry?' Julia, dressed in a simple green robe tied at the waist, had finished her plate of food and was looking at him with some concern.

Azhar shook his head.

'There is no point in worrying about it,' she said, displaying that annoying habit she had of seeing too far inside his head. 'You will find evidence or you won't, but there is nothing you can do about it tonight, save allow it to keep you awake.'

Her skin was flushed from the fire. The fire in his belly rekindled as he remembered their earlier lovemaking. 'I have no intentions of sleeping,' Azhar replied.

Julia smiled, a sinuous, feline smile. 'I do have

intentions,' she said. 'They don't involve sleeping, but they do involve you.'

'I hope they're not good intentions.'

She laughed, pushing him on to his back and rolling on top of him. 'Good or bad, you must decide for yourself.'

Chapter Nine

Five days spent in a flurry of activity including implementing stricter border controls and poring over detailed financial ledgers, conspired to make the two nights he had spent in the desert with Julia seem like a fleeting dream to Azhar. The news that a prince from a neighbouring kingdom had called without notice meant he had to cut short the latest in a long series of Council meetings, but the man waiting in the Divan was a very different visitor than the one he was expecting.

'Kadar! This is indeed a surprise.' Azhar strode across the room to greet his old friend. The two men embraced warmly. 'You look well,' Azhar said, and indeed the years had been kind to Kadar, whose scholarly habits and fierce intelligence had always seemed at such odds with his rangy, athletic appearance. They looked much more like brothers now than he and Kamal did.

'A welcome surprise, I hope,' Kadar said. 'When I heard you had returned, yet you did not contact me...'

'A most welcome one, how can you doubt it?'

Kadar eyed him quizzically. 'Ten years, with not a word from you?'

'Kadar, I...'

'I did not come to berate you, nor to demand explanations for your silence. Allow me to say only that you have been missed. I am glad you are back, although the circumstances that bring you here are to be regretted. My heartfelt condolences on the death of your father. I know you did not see eye to eye with him but he was unquestionably a fine ruler of Qaryma. As you will be, my friend.'

Azhar smiled uncomfortably. 'Forgive me for receiving you so formally here in the Divan. I was in session with my Council. When they informed me the Prince of Murimon had arrived, I naturally assumed it was your brother. Come, let us retire to my private quarters and we can catch up. We have much to discuss. As you say, ten years is a long time. A lot has happened.'

'More, obviously, than you realise, Azhar. My brother, Prince Butrus, died some months ago in a riding accident. He was thrown from his horse and struck his head on a rock. I assumed you would have heard.'

'Dead!' Azhar came to an abrupt halt. 'My deepest condolences. But—' He broke off, only now realising the significance of what his friend had said. 'You mean you are now—that Murimon is now your responsibility?'

'It would appear so,' Kadar said with a wry smile. 'I can't quite believe it myself.'

'But what will you do?' Azhar asked, aghast.

'Try to make a better prince than my illustrious and much-loved elder brother? Do not ask me how that is to be done, for I have no idea. This has all been a tremendous shock to me. It was always simply a matter of time for you, but for me—it simply never occurred to me that I would find myself thrust into the public eye.'

Azhar shook his head vehemently. 'You are wrong, I never expected to inherit either.'

Kadar looked startled. 'I know that you were always at loggerheads with your father, but you are the first born, how could you have expected anything else?'

Azhar ushered his friend into his sitting room, ordering refreshments to be brought. It was not in his nature to lie, but while he did not doubt Kadar's discretion, he found himself reluctant to confide in him. 'For a man whose life has changed for ever, you seem remarkably sanguine,' he said.

'It is not in my nature to rail against the fates,' Kadar replied. 'What will be, will be.'

'But in the past, you cared for nothing save your precious books. You will find you have little time for scholarly pursuits, now you have a kingdom to rule.'

'No less than you will have for foreign travel, now that you too have a kingdom to rule,' Kadar retorted with a flash of anger that was quickly suppressed. 'At least I know I can rely on you as a staunch ally. We will be able to visit each other as often as our fathers did back in the old days.'

'Peace and politics aside, our friendship is one of the most valuable things to emerge from those state visits,' Azhar said warmly. 'I remember the first time I saw you on a horse, a wild stallion from my father's stable, I thought it would be sure to throw you in less than ten seconds.'

'I believe it took all of forty,' Kadar said, laughing.

'You lasted twenty more than I would have done, and even at the age of eleven, I considered myself something of an expert horseman. Until that day, I had taken Butrus's word for your devotion to your books and little else. You were an abject lesson to me not to make assumptions, and I confess, the excuse I needed to avoid your brother's company on future visits. I know that your people worshipped him, thought him a perfect paragon of a prince, but I'm afraid he was also a terrible bore.'

Kadar laughed. 'Exactly what Butrus himself said of me.' His smile faded quickly. 'All the same, he was an excellent prince, while I— but there, enough of that. I am glad that you are back, Azhar. I am glad that we will once again be friends as well as allies.'

Azhar smiled uncomfortably. The situation was extremely awkward. Kadar had more than sufficient cares of his own to deal with, without being privy to his. Time enough for him to learn that his ally would not be Azhar, but Kamal. Though now he thought about it, Kamal had always been disparaging of this bookish second son of Muri-mon. So perhaps not such a staunch ally after all.

The servant brought them refreshments, and for a while the talk turned to old times, but Kadar too seemed to be aware of how much the inter-vening years had changed both of them. 'Much as I'd like to, I cannot linger,' he said. 'My broth-er's untimely passing bequeathed me not only a kingdom, but also his affianced bride. I have no intentions of taking on both, and am on my way to terminate the matter with her family's repre-sentatives. Since I had to pass through Qaryma, I thought to pay my respects to the new ruler. And to bring you this.'

He handed Azhar a small package. 'You sent out word through your agents that you were looking to reclaim any property stolen from the Englishwoman. In particular jewellery, and a cus-tomised trunk? Our port sees a good deal of il-legal trade and contraband, unfortunately—or in this case, fortunately for you. This was con-fiscated from a known rogue trader. I cannot be sure it belongs to her, but it is certainly English.'

Azhar unwrapped the object and read the in-scription inside before setting it down on the table. For some reason, he was reluctant to touch it. 'Yes, there can be no doubt it is hers,' he said. 'It was very kind of you to take the trouble to bring it in person. Madam Trevelyan will be extremely grateful. She will wish to thank you herself.'

'For recovering her property, which a bunch of barbarous thieves who are my countrymen thought to profit from,' Kadar said grimly. 'That kind of trade, we can well do without.'

'Indeed. I have been putting considerable energy into tightening our own border controls,' Azhar said. 'That the theft took place within Qaryma still rankles with me.'

'Perhaps that is something upon which we can collaborate in the future. Please pass on my apologies to Madam Trevelyan. I am sorry not to be able to make her acquaintance. She must be a remarkable woman, to have captured your attention so.'

'What precisely have you heard?' Azhar asked sharply.

'An Englishwoman travelling alone through the desert gathering plants is fuel enough for idle gossip,' Kadar replied mildly. 'One with hair the colour of fire, who is the confidante to a future king—you must know perfectly well that will give rise to a great deal of speculation.'

'I had not thought of it,' Azhar said stiffly. 'Julia—Madam Trevelyan—has been—she is— there is nothing—her presence here relates to a matter of private business.'

His friend clapped his shoulder warmly. 'Unfortunately, you will learn soon enough for yourself that a ruler is afforded no privacy. I brought the matter to your attention only because I thought you should be aware of it. Another unfortunate fact—although our people love to gossip about us, they dare not gossip with us. Now I really must go. I hope that you will not permit another ten years to elapse before we meet again.'

The door closed behind him and Azhar sank on to the couch, picking up the pocket watch that Kadar had brought, opening the case to read the inscription once more. *To our beloved son Daniel Adam Edward Trevelyan on the occasion of his coming of age.* He set the time and wound the mechanism. The watch ticked as sedately and fastidiously as Azhar imagined its owner to have been.

He snapped the case shut and put it back on the table, eyeing it distastefully. He had not forgotten

that Julia was a widow, but he had somehow forgotten that she had once been a wife. The wife of
the man who had owned this watch. A man who
had singularly failed to appreciate her. Who had
thought of Julia, clever, witty, brave, determined
Julia, as a mere amanuensis. His dogsbody. His
chattel. A man who had denied her the right to
speak for herself, had imbued her with the belief that her thoughts were irrelevant, and to add
to those heinous crimes, who had denied her the
pleasures of the flesh.

Such flesh. Such pleasure. And not nearly
enough time to indulge in it. In the last five days,
between Azhar's commitments and her completing her cataloguing, they had scraped only a few
precious hours together. Azhar closed his eyes,
reliving last night. When they were together he
could lose himself in her delightful company,
forget the mountain of work he must get through
on Kamal's behalf before he left.

Though he had also come to enjoy discussing
that mountain of work with her. In fact it was becoming something of a habit. He had never discussed his business with anyone before. It was
not that he needed Julia's advice, nor even her
affirmation but—but it was simply that he en-

joyed her company. No, not only that. There had been several occasions when discussing a thorny matter with her had served to both clarify and resolve it, and a number of times her proposed solution was better than his. And the odd thing was, he didn't mind.

Azhar stared down at the watch. Its relentless ticking seemed to be mocking him, reminding him that his time with Julia was rapidly coming to a conclusion. *Tick-tock.* Less than two weeks left before she left for England. The day he had looked forward to for so long, when he would leave Qaryma for ever was also approaching at a frightening rate. *Tick-tock.* So little time to accomplish so much. Precious little to spend with Julia. It hadn't occurred to him until now that he would miss her, but he would. There was no other woman like her. Daniel Adam Edward Trevelyan had not appreciated Julia, but Azhar did.

Tick-tock. Azhar pushed the watch away from him with the tip of his index finger. In the days they had left together, he would do his best to demonstrate that to her.

It was late afternoon. Julia opened her notebook with some reluctance. Though cataloguing and cross-referencing was a crucial element of her botanical work, it was also the part she disliked the most. This was partly due to the fact that there was a tedious and repetitive element to it, but mostly, she realised with a flash of insight, because it had been a task which her husband had regularly delegated to her when he found something more interesting to occupy him.

'Your diligence is proof that you are a true woman of science,' he had once said to her. And on more than one occasion, when she had protested at his demand for her to make yet another fair copy of something, 'But your elegant feminine hand is much neater than my masculine scrawl.' Julia rolled her eyes. Daniel would have vehemently rejected any suggestion of condescension, but then he would have equally vehemently denied Julia's ability to execute any component of his research on her own initiative—even though that was exactly what he'd been forced to demand of her on his deathbed.

It was that, she thought broodingly, the assumption that she had no mind of her own, that she had resented more than anything. No, actually what she had resented was her own inability to tell him so. She would not be such a timid little mouse now.

She rearranged several specimens which she had laid out on the table. Was that true? In the five days since they had returned from the desert, there had been several occasions when she could have shared her concerns regarding Kamal with Azhar, yet she had deliberately refrained from doing so.

They had had so little time together. Like him, she had been very busy, documenting and painting and consulting with Johara, who had made two trips to the palace with her precious book. And Azhar—for a man set upon renouncing his kingdom, Azhar was putting a great deal of effort into setting it to rights. No one understood better than Julia his desire to be free, but while the duties she must discharge to gain that freedom were finite, Azhar's sense of duty to his kingdom seemed to her quite the opposite. With every passing day, he assumed more and more responsibilities under the guise of easing Kamal's path. As he increasingly embraced matters of state, and dug deeper into the issue of the diamond mines, she became more convinced that Azhar's fate was to rule Qaryma. If he could have refrained from pursuing the anomaly of the diamond yields, if he could delegate more tasks, if he could force Kamal to make some of the decisions he was taking upon himself, it might be different. But his conscience and his deep sense of honour made it impossible for him to do any of these things.

The personal consequences were potentially ruinous for him. No wonder Azhar did not want to face them. With a sickening jolt, Julia discovered that she was not particularly eager to think about them either. Despite her resolution not to wish for more time with him, she had been hoping there would be some times in the future that they might spend together. She had fantasised about trips she might make once she was free, when Azhar had resumed his old life, to visit him in his home in Naples perhaps, or even return to Damascus again. Her dreams were vague, she had no idea the form these visits might take, or whether Azhar would welcome them, but they existed none the less.

Julia swore under her breath. 'What the *devil* are you thinking?' she demanded of herself. 'That once you have finally freed yourself from Daniel, you will immediately set about attaching yourself to a man who has made it perfectly clear that he wants no attachments?'

But she wasn't contemplating any sort of formal arrangement. She did not want to marry any more than Azhar did. 'What, then?' she asked. 'You become his occasional mistress, spending nine months of the year pining for the three months or three weeks or whatever it is he allots to you? And you think a man as attractive as Azhar would take no other lovers? How would you feel about that?'

She did not want to think about that, and that fact should be caution enough for her. She cared. She was very, very close to caring too much. Azhar liked women, he'd told her so. Women. Plural, not singular. Stupid, foolish, *unrealistic* Julia to imagine that he would want only her when there was a world of women for him to choose from while she waited alone for a summons as if she was part of a harem. Where was the freedom in that?

The answer was starkly simple. There was none. It was folly, utter folly to allow herself to think that way—or even to dream. She had come to care for Azhar, there was no harm in admitting that, but to cherish any notion that this was anything other than a moment out of time was madness.

Outside, the sky was a strange shade of violet. Aisha, bringing her afternoon mint tea, closed the windows leading on to the terrace, indicating that there was a storm brewing. 'Prince Azhar had a visitor today,' she said, speaking in the mixture of English, Arabic and gestures in which she and Julia customarily communicated. 'The Prince of Murimon, an old friend. For ten years, since Prince Azhar left, he has not been here, but he is every bit as tall and handsome as I remember,' she added with a saucy smile. 'After our Prince, the second most handsome man in Arabia. Now they will be rulers together.'

After Aisha had gone, Julia sipped her mint tea pensively. Outside, the sky looked bruised, a mixture of violet and pink, the clouds an odd golden brown, leaden with dust. She felt tense and edgy, a little like the weather, as the sky grew more ominous. On impulse, she opened the long window and stepped out on to the terrace. The paving was gritty, covered with a thin film of sand. She sat down on the edge of the pool, dabbling her feet in the water. The surface of the water was gritty too.

Azhar had not mentioned any friends in their various conversations. Another bond he had cut from his life when he left Qaryma, determined to set himself free of his past. He had severed every single tie, and now he would have to sever them all afresh, if he were to leave again.

If?

She lay back on her hands and gazed up at the sky. A single large drop of rain fell on to the tiles. Above her, the clouds swirled. The surface of the pool rippled and the leaves of the lemon tree shivered as a breeze blew up. Another fat drop of rain fell, followed by a distant rumble of thunder, and then the skies opened.

It was warm, soft rain, not the cold, sharp rain of home. The thunder grew closer, more muffled than the sharp cracks of noise that used to split the sky above Marazion Bay, but she relished both all the same, leaning back on her hands, closing her eyes, letting the rain fall on her face, soak through her tunic, darken her hair and empty her mind.

Having received no answer to his knock on Julia's door, Azhar entered, calling her name. The window was open, the gauzy curtains flapping in the breeze. A rumble of thunder was followed almost immediately by a bolt of lightning that lit up the rain-drenched courtyard outside. And illuminated Julia, splayed like a fallen angel on the tiles beside the pool, her feet in the water, her hair streaming out behind her.

His heart in his mouth, Azhar dashed out into the storm, calling her name. So convinced was he that she had been hit by the lightning, when she sat up Azhar thought he was hallucinating.

'Julia?'

She smiled at him dreamily. 'Isn't it fantastic?'

'It's dangerous to be out here in a storm. Come in.'

Her clothes clung to her body. Her hair hung in long ropes down her back. Her feet were bare. 'I love it,' she said, making no move.

A clap of thunder sounded in the distance. The rain stopped with a suddenness that made the silence seem to ring. Above them, the clouds began to part, and the sun shone weakly through. Julia stared up at the sky looking acutely disappointed. 'It's finished.'

'When I saw you lying there on the ground, for a horrible moment I thought you were dead, struck by lightning.'

'I was imagining being on the beach at Marazion Bay.'

'Then you must have a very vivid imagination, because you look as if you *have* been swimming in the sea there. This bay, it is in Cornwall?'

'Marazion Bay. Near my father's home. I learned to swim in the surf there, and to sail.' Julia's eyes lit up. 'It is almost a perfect crescent of sand, set into the cliffs. The path down is almost as steep as a staircase. In the winter, the sea is treacherous, the waves can be thirty feet high. The noise they make as they crash on to the sand is like a lion's roar, and even when you're sitting high above the tide line, the spray can drench you.'

'You are drenched now. Come inside,' Azhar said, leading her back into the sitting room and closing the latch on the window.

'Aisha told me you had a visit from an old friend today,' Julia said a few moments later, having changed her tunic for a flowing robe of soft lemon muslin sprigged with pale blue flowers.

'Kadar. Prince Kadar of Murimon, as he is now. The kingdom of Murimon is on the coast, some distance from here.'

'Was he here on official state business? You must have been delighted to see him after all this time.'

'Kadar was merely passing through. Yes, it was good to see him. You also have good reason to be glad he came to Qaryma.'

'Whatever do you mean?'

'He brought you a present.' Azhar handed her a small package.

'A present? But I've never even met him.'

'Open it.'

Julia did as he bid her, staring incredulously at the timepiece. 'It is Daniel's watch. How on earth did your friend come by it?'

'It was recovered from rogue traders at the port in Murimon. He asked me to pass on his apologies, and his regrets that urgent business prevented him from making your acquaintance.'

'But how did he know it was mine, or that I was here?'

'When we first arrived at Qaryma I sent out word of the crime which had been committed against you. I know the markets, I know the places where such thieves operate, but I confess, I held out little hope of recovering any of your possessions. It is not your trunk containing your precious notebooks and sketches unfortunately, but I remember you said this watch held great sentimental value for you.'

'It does.' Julia pressed it open and read the inscription. 'It is so—symbolic of Daniel,' she said softly. 'Practical and reliable.' She blinked, for she was close to tears. 'I'm sorry, it is not like me to be at a loss for words. I hadn't realised how much I've missed it. Thank you, Azhar. What a considerate gesture.'

'It was nothing.'

'No,' she said fiercely, 'it is not nothing. It matters a great deal to me that you thought of this, of me, when you had so much else to deal with—I am—I don't know what to say.'

Azhar kissed her forehead. 'You have said enough. My reward is seeing your delight at being reunited with it.'

Julia sank on to the divan, flicking open the case once more and studying the fascia. The mechanism vibrated slightly in her hand. 'Daniel is buried in the family plot beside his father, but his mother is still alive. I wonder if I should return this to her when I am back in Cornwall.' She gazed, mesmerised by the second hand as it relentlessly counted down the time she had left

here in Qaryma, second by inexorable second.
She wished it would go slower. Absurd thought.
Snapping the case shut, she set it down on the
table beside her painting materials. 'Only one
more week after the end of this one, and I shall
be setting out on that journey,' she said.

She had meant it as a warning to herself. Her
voice wobbled. Azhar flinched. 'Your task will
definitely be completed by then?' he asked.

How she longed to lie. 'Yes,' Julia said. 'I will
even have time to do some paintings of the secret garden in the Fourth Court.'

'I wish...' Azhar picked up Daniel's watch and
opened it, staring at the second hand mesmerised,
just as she had done. Setting it down, he cleared
his throat. 'If you had time to spare, I would very
much like a painting of your bay in Cornwall. It
would be good to imagine you there. Looking at
it would make you seem not so far away, somehow. Does that make sense?'

'Perfect sense, I shall make time,' Julia whispered. Azhar took her hands between his, rested
his forehead against hers. A tear escaped from her
eye, trickling down her cheek, and was swiftly
followed by another, which splashed on to his
hands. 'I'm sorry,' she said.

'Don't be. Don't cry, Julia. Please don't cry.'

'I am not crying,' she said, but another tear fell, and then another. 'I'm sorry.'

'Julia.' He caught her in his arms, pressing her tight against his chest, stroking her hair. 'Julia, don't be sad.'

She hugged him tightly, breathing in the warm male scent of him, relishing the familiar hard strength of him. 'I'm going to miss you so much, Azhar.'

He did not reply, but her yearning was reflected in his eyes as he picked her up and carried her into her bedchamber. Their kisses was all-consuming, urgent, kisses fuelled by hunger, a primal craving to amass as many kisses as they could before the time arrived when there could be no more. They made love with the same passionate abandonment, pressing themselves together, clinging together, skin on skin, as if trying to meld themselves together, become one entity, crying out together, then lying together, sated, slick with sweat, their hearts hammering, mindless at last.

Azhar sat on the throne in the Audience Chamber of the Royal Kiosk awaiting the arrival of the

Chief Overseer of the diamond mines. He had made the decision to summon the man last night, after leaving Julia's chamber. The watch—that fateful watch—ticking away the hours and minutes relentlessly, had compelled him to take the action which he had known in his heart for some days was inevitable.

This summons would, he knew, set in motion an inexorable chain of events which would bind him to Qaryma for ever. He could not bear to think about it. If he thought about it he would hesitate, and he had hesitated too long already. Honour forced his hand. He would pay a heavy personal price for his sense of honour.

A sharp rap on the door of the kiosk heralded the beginnings of proceedings. It did not take long. In the face of the compelling evidence which Azhar cited, the Chief Overseer prostrated himself at his Prince's feet, sobbing and begging incoherently for mercy.

Azhar ordered the guard to take him to the Cage, noting with satisfaction the surprise on the guard's face and the horror on his prisoner's. The name, he well knew, conjured up dark dungeons, perhaps even a torture chamber. In fact, the Cage was a suite of disused rooms which had once, many, many years ago, housed the illegitimate progeny from the harem, in the days when it held more than one wife and many concubines. In recent times the Cage had served as the schoolroom for the King's legitimate sons, and was comfortably furnished. Azhar had chosen it merely as a secure place to hold the Chief Overseer until his fate was decided. He pitied the man, who was in one sense nothing more than a greedy puppet, but even a greedy puppet must be punished for the dishonour he had brought to the Council and to the kingdom he served.

The puppet master himself threw open the door of the kiosk a mere ten minutes later. Kamal flew into the chamber, his face red with rage. 'Why did you summon my Chief Overseer? What game are you playing?'

'Once again I must correct you, Brother. *My* Chief Overseer, and this is no game. I am the future King of Qaryma,' Azhar said, surveying his brother haughtily from the throne. 'Or had you forgotten? My actions are not to be questioned, even by you.'

Kamal made a show of dropping slowly to his

knees. 'I see you have overcome your dislike of standing on ceremony.'

'I have been forced to reassess my opinion on many matters since my arrival.'

'You have certainly made your opinion of my regency very clear,' Kama said, glaring at him defiantly. 'I doubt there is any aspect of my rule which has met with your approval.'

'It is not for want of trying, believe me, Brother.'

Kamal swore. 'Do not take me for a fool. Ever since you arrived here, you have been determined to undermine me, systematically removing my supporters from the Council, interfering in countless petty matters of state, questioning my Treasurer and examining my accounts. You travel to our villages with that English woman trailing behind you to whip up support—as if you needed to—and now I discover you have been interrogating a man who...'

'Has been helping you misappropriate my diamonds.' Azhar waited, but Kamal said nothing. 'I know all about the whole sordid scheme,' he said. 'Not only has the Chief Overseer confessed fully to his role—'

'But has implicated me in order to save his own skin,' Kamal interrupted with a sneer. 'By the heavens, Azhar, is it not obvious! If there has been any pilfering...'

'The scale of the theft goes far beyond pilfering.'

Kamal waved his hand impatiently. 'You cannot possibly think that I would be involved in this.'

'And you cannot possibly grasp how very much I have wanted to prove you innocent.'

Something in his voice put fear in Kamal's eyes. He scrambled to his feet. 'Brother...'

Azhar shook his arm free. 'I came here intending to abdicate,' he said. 'I came here with the sole purpose of handing Qaryma over to you. You think I cannot resist claiming the crown and power. How wrong you are, Kamal. How very, very wrong. I wanted you to have it because you deserved it more, wanted it more.'

'Then give it to me, I still want it. Free yourself from the burden, leave Qaryma in my hands.'

'No. You have forfeited any right to be trusted with the safekeeping of the kingdom.' With cold precision, Azhar ticked off the facts he had uncovered. Sick at heart, he watched as Kamal's bravado turned to blustering rage, removing any faint hope that he would do the honourable thing and confess his guilt.

'I hope you are not expecting me to apologise,' Kamal spat at the end of the damning summation. 'For ten years, I have remained here doing our father's bidding while you indulged your selfish desire to see the world, making your personal fortune, earning your pathetically important reputation. For ten years I have served our father, this kingdom and these people, and for what? A few diamonds are as nothing compared to what I am owed for my sacrifice.'

That the 'few diamonds' amounted to a significant part of Qaryma's wealth was beside the point. It had never, for Azhar, been the value of the stolen goods which mattered, but the greed and the lies which motivated the crime. 'You had ten years in which to prove yourself worthy,' he said. 'Ten years to prove to our father that you were fit to be his heir.'

'Do you think I did not try?' Kamal replied with a snarl. 'I reminded you when you returned that you were always his favourite. Do you think I said that to flatter you? Oh, yes, in the early days he was angry enough with you to turn to me, but he made it clear even then that I was second best.

He never trusted me. Always, he watched me and questioned me. Always, he made it clear that I was but a poor substitute. And later—' Kamal broke off abruptly.

'Later?' Azhar repeated. His brother shrugged. 'What happened later?' Azhar persisted.

Kamal snorted with derision. 'I thought you might have guessed, since you pride yourself on your astuteness. Didn't you ask yourself how we knew where to send that summons, Azhar? Didn't you ask yourself why, when he knew he was dying, our dear father did not summon his nominated heir earlier, why he settled for making me acting Regent instead?'

'I did ask,' Azhar said with a horrible sense of premonition. 'I remember very clearly that I asked you, Kamal, when I first arrived here in Qaryma, why our father insisted the summons was sent after his death.'

'And I told you that it was because he believed you wouldn't return while he was alive,' Kamal replied. 'Which was true enough, but far from the whole truth. Our dear father knew all about your houses in Europe and Damascus and Cairo. He was so secretly proud of you, his wealthy, successful trader son, he arranged to have bulletins on your progress sent every six months.'

Azhar felt faint. He sat down on the throne, gazing at his brother in disbelief.

Witnessing the effect of his words, Kamal continued with renewed malice. 'When he became ill he asked me to send for you. I told him that I had done so, and then I am afraid I informed him that your response had been singularly disappointing. You would not come to Qaryma, I told him. You made it clear that you never wanted to see Father again. He was most upset, as you can imagine. And bitterly disappointed.'

Azhar clenched his fists so tightly his nails dug into his palms, drawing blood. 'So you gave him no choice but to appoint you his Regent, which was your plan all along.'

'Not quite. My plan was to make him so angry he disowned you completely and named me his heir.'

'But he didn't.' Azhar got to his feet once more. 'I thought my father bequeathed me Qaryma to punish me for leaving. I see now that he did it to keep the kingdom safe from your treacherous clutches. He knew—or he must have strongly suspected—that you lied about the first summons, why else would he insist the second was made in the presence of Council?'

'The act of a dying autocrat, no more,' Kamal protested. 'He cannot possibly have guessed that I...'

'...deceived him. He must have,' Azhar interrupted, his mind racing. 'To swallow his pride, to be prepared to make the first move to heal the rift between us, my father must have feared greatly for Qaryma's future at your hands. It must have cost him dearly to be forced to appoint you Regent.'

'It was my right. It was my *right*.'

Kamal, fists clenched, expression sulky, took a hasty step forward. Azhar put a restraining hand on his brother's chest. 'Attempt to strike me,' he said with icy calmness, 'and we will be spared the need to secure the services of an executioner to despatch you for a treasonable act, for I will throttle you myself with my bare hands.'

He would never mete out such draconian punishment, but Kamal did not know that. The colour drained from his face, his knees gave way and he crumpled, prostrate on the tiled floor below the throne, sobbing and begging for mercy, just as the Chief Overseer had done an hour previously.

'Get up,' Azhar said, sickened.

'What will you do with me? I am your brother, your only brother of true royal blood, you cannot possibly mean to...'

But Azhar had had enough. 'You have brought nothing but shame and dishonour to our royal lineage,' he hissed, white with fury. 'I came here willing to overlook your weaknesses, to help you to become the King that Qaryma deserves, and you have done nothing but lie to me, cheat me, deceive me. I came here, Kamal, to give you what you wanted most because I thought you deserved it, and because it is the last thing that I wanted. You have not only done your best to ruin our kingdom, you have destroyed my life in the process. Get out! Get out and do not dare show your face to me again. I will decide your fate when I am ready.'

Kamal hesitated, but whatever he saw in Azhar's face persuaded him that further pleas for mercy would fall on stony ground. Deliberately refraining from bowing, he turned his back and left the kiosk, head defiantly high. Azhar watched him go, waiting for the door to close behind him, another moment for the garden door to close, and then he slumped down on the throne, dropping his head into his hands. Ten years ago, he had been on the other side of that door when it had slammed shut. Now, he was on the inside. Not just inside but locked inside. For ever.

Chapter Ten

Wearily rubbing her neck and rolling her shoulders, for she had been working since first light, Julia took a sliver of melon from her untouched luncheon tray. Outside, the sky was newly washed by yesterday's storm, a celestial blue with not a single cloud to mar it. Though she had any number of loose ends to tie up in order to complete Daniel's treatise, and despite Daniel's watch ticking away remorselessly, almost reproachfully, Julia decided that she was going to steal some of the remaining time for herself, and start work on capturing the hidden garden in the Fourth Court.

Half an hour later, bathed and changed into her favourite tunic of lemon muslin, pale-green trousers and matching slippers, Julia turned the key in the door which connected the two gardens. It was like stepping into a perfumed bath, scented by all the familiar flowers and herbs of home, mingling with the exotic, more heady scents of the desert. She closed her eyes, trying to fix every single element in her head in the elusive hope that one day she would be able to recapture it, perhaps even recreate it in a garden of her own. But for the moment she would try to preserve it in watercolours.

Azhar was sitting on a stone bench in the shade of an archway where roses grew in wild profusion. He was staring out over the parapet at the desert, lost in his own thoughts, and did not see her. He was dressed in white silk, his formal robes, though he had cast off his cloak and headdress. His hair, recently cropped, sat like a silk cap on his head, the ruthlessly short cut drawing attention to the sharp planes of his cheeks. The starkness of his beauty stole her breath away, but the bleakness of his expression twisted her heart. Setting her painting equipment on to the path, she stepped lightly forward, joining him on the bench.

'Julia.'

Azhar put his arm around her, tilting her head on to his shoulder, pulling her tight against him.

She could feel the rise and fall of his chest. The soap he used was scented with lemons. Through the silk of his tunic, his skin was warm. Their legs were touching, thigh to knee. She shifted her foot to rest her slipper against his boot, and he stirred, kissing the top of her head, releasing her but only to push back her headdress, to run his fingers through her hair, and then to kiss her slowly, lingeringly, with a hint of desperation, before releasing her a second time.

'Julia. How did you know I would be here?'

'I didn't. I came to paint.' She smoothed out the frown which furrowed his brow.

'The first time I showed you this garden—this secret garden—you said you thought it would give my father solace, a private place of refuge. I didn't understand you then, but I do now.'

'What has happened, Azhar?' she asked, already dreading the answer.

He shook his head, the sensuous curve of his mouth turned down in an expression of such pain that she almost couldn't bear to look at it. 'Kamal?' she whispered, taking his hand.

His fingers gripped hers painfully as he nodded. 'I realised last night that I could put it off no longer,' he said harshly. 'That cursed watch I brought you. So little time left to set matters to rights, I thought. And now…' His voice cracked. 'Now I have all the time in the world.'

'You have decided to stay?'

He swallowed hard. 'I have no choice.'

She listened as he recounted his interview with Kamal, biting back indignant exclamations, while a deep, burning anger at the weak, selfish, unworthy man who called himself Azhar's brother grew inexorably.

'He was completely unrepentant,' Azhar finished. 'He seemed to think that the diamonds were some sort of legitimate compensation for his regency.'

'How do you intend to deal with him?'

Azhar shook his head dejectedly. 'It will bring shame and dishonour to our royal name if I publicly accuse him, and shame and dishonour upon myself if I do not.'

'I don't know what to say. I can't even begin to imagine how you must feel.'

'You are the only person on this earth who can,' Azhar replied with a ghost of a smile. 'No one knows me as you do. You know what a poisoned chalice the crown of Qaryma will be to me. You, and only you, understand what it will cost me.'

'Oh, Azhar, I wish with all my heart that you did not have to do this. If there was any other way...' Julia stopped, her voice clogged with tears.

'Don't cry, I beg you. It had to be done and cannot be undone.'

'Then I shall not cry,' she said with a sniff and a faltering smile. 'To learn that your father actually kept track of your whereabouts—that he was proud of you—that at least, is one positive thing to emerge from this, is it not?'

'Another poisoned chalice. If I am completely honest, I am not at all sure that I would have responded to that first summons, had Kamal actually sent it,' Azhar said, looking troubled. 'It would have been my opportunity to make my peace with my father, but I fear I would have seen the price as too high to pay, Julia, suspecting that if I came back I would not be capable of leaving a second time. A suspicion that I have just now managed to prove was well founded. But I deeply regret that I did not make my peace with my father.'

'You cannot bear the sole burden of guilt,' Julia said decidedly. 'Your father waited nine years before extending the olive branch, and even then he did it only because he fell ill. Nine years which have served to make you the man you are, and that man will be a better ruler for the experience.'

'Thank you,' Azhar said, kissing her hand. 'I know you say these things only to ease my guilt, but I appreciate the sentiments.'

'I say these things because they are true. And the most important truth of all is that it is the— the essence of you, the man in here,' she said, laying her hand over his heart, 'the honourable man who can give nothing less than his all, whether it is to his business or his country, that's what makes you the best King Qaryma will ever have.'

'And now I have made you cry again.'

Julia shook her head. 'I'm not—it is not you. I wish—oh, Azhar, I wish there was something I could do to help you.'

He brushed a tear from her cheek with his thumb. His eyes were dark, still troubled. 'Do you mean that?'

The way he looked at her made icy fingers of fear clutch at her heart. 'What do you require of me?'

Azhar got to his feet, clasping his hands behind his back, looking out over the parapet at the desert. 'If I am to do this, if I am to wear the crown, then it is best that I do so as soon as possible. From now on, my time will not be my own—I cannot afford to be distracted, Julia.'

Her heart plummeted. 'I see,' she said, trying to keep the disappointment and sense of rejection from her voice. She knew she had no right to feel that way but there it was regardless.

'No, you don't.' Azhar caught her as she made to turn away from him. 'These last few weeks, the precious time we have spent together has been the only ray of sunshine in what has been a torrid experience. I have come to greatly value your judgement, to rely on being able to talk matters over with you, knowing that you will always be honest with me, no matter what the cost. A rarity for a man in my position, believe me, since no one dares challenge my judgement.'

'You will be Sheikh al-Farid, King Azhar of Qaryma,' Julia intoned, quoting the words he had once recited from the coronation. 'You will be the font of all wisdom, the provider of all happiness. The infallible one, whom none may question. Do I have that right?'

'Almost word perfect,' Azhar said. 'Unfortunately,' he added with a twisted smile. 'Which means that our spending time together must come to a halt. I must start as I mean to go on Julia—alone. My decisions must be my own, and my desire for you—you know how strongly I desire you—but it can have no place in my life now either. I must dedicate myself to my kingdom. When they place the crown on my head, I will belong to Qaryma. And I plan to be crowned as soon as it can be arranged.'

'Are you afraid that if you delay, you might not go through with it?'

He flinched, for her tone was sharp, but he met her gaze openly. 'Yes.'

The simple admission broke down all her defences. 'I'm sorry. I'm so sorry. I couldn't bear to make things more difficult for you. I will do whatever you ask.'

The relief which flooded his face was her reward. He pulled her into his arms, kissing her gently. 'I ask only that you understand.'

'I do.'

'Thank you.' He kissed her again. 'You will use the extra time usefully, I hope?'

'I—yes. Johara told me of an oasis where there is a unique kind of moss, I had hoped—but it is not necessary. I have more than enough to occupy my last—the time I have remaining here, thank you.' Was this the end? Was he expecting her to say goodbye? No, she could not believe it, there were arrangements to be made, a guide to hire—no, she would not allow herself to think that this was the last time she would see him. Utterly dejected, Julia cast around for her drawing equipment. 'I wanted to paint this secret garden, but if you are going to be in residence at the Royal Kiosk...'

'I will have someone inform you when the garden is unoccupied so you may work undisturbed.'

She could feel the tears welling. She *would not* allow them to fall. Muttering another thank you, Julia picked up her painting box and fled.

Julia set down her paintbrush and studied the two landscapes critically. In the three days since she had last seen Azhar, she had been working on them almost exclusively. The light was not yet perfectly captured in the seascape, but she was pleased with the mood.

Aisha, setting the dinner tray down on the table, studied the almost-finished works. 'These are beautiful. This is your home?' she asked. 'I have never seen the sea. It is vast and so beautiful.'

Julia nodded. 'Much as your desert is for me.' She had always considered Marazion Bay her home, though she had not lived there since she married Daniel. The house she had shared with her husband near Truro, leased from an acquaintance of her father's, would be occupied by someone else by now. After the funeral, Julia had boxed up their few possessions and had them placed in storage at her father's house. He had assumed that she would come to live with him when she returned from her supposed visit to the Highlands.

Julia had no idea what she was going to do with her freedom once she attained it. She had not thought beyond fulfilling her promises to Daniel, but those would take her perhaps three, at the most six months more to execute. Her work here in Arabia was already completed. Now that she had finished the landscapes for Azhar, she intended to spend what time remained painting the pictures which would become her own personal mementos of her momentous time here.

Aisha had finished setting out the dainty array of dishes on the table. 'Prince Azhar is very busy preparing for his coronation,' she said.

There was sympathy in her eyes. 'Yes, I know,'

Julia said. Now that it was almost over, she could not see the point in pretending that Aisha didn't know how often Azhar visited her here. Aisha had proven herself the soul of discretion and Julia was happy to have her company. 'He told me he would be unable to visit again.'

Aisha ushered her to the table. 'As it should be,' she said with a smile. 'Prince Azhar is an honourable man. It is known that he spends much time with you. You are a foreigner, you have no husband and you are so skinny,' she said with a small smile. 'People cannot understand why he does not take a more suitable mistress.'

Colour flooded Julia's cheeks. Living so isolated from the rest of the palace, it had been easy for her to pretend that the nature of her relationship with Azhar was privy to no one save Aisha. Knowing that she had been the subject of gossip, none of it flattering, was mortifying. 'I have caused a scandal,' she said, putting her hands to her flaming cheeks.

Aisha shook her head. 'No, people understand that Prince Azhar is a virile man with needs...' Her mime made it quite clear what she thought Azhar needed. 'It is shocking that you are a foreigner, but we are not shocked by his having a mistress.'

'But after his coronation?' Julia asked with a sinking feeling.

'After, it would be unthinkable,' Aisha said, shaking her head vehemently. 'A king must be above reproach. But I tell everyone that you are returning to England, and that when you are back there,' she concluded with a reassuring smile, pointing to Julia's painting, 'you will find a fine English husband. So when he has been crowned, King Azhar can find a fine Arabian princess. As it should be, yes? Both happy.'

Both happy. As the door closed behind Aisha, Julia pushed the plate of delicious food she had been served aside. Aisha had not meant to hurt her. She had only said what Azhar had told her more obliquely himself. He must be aware of the scandal she would cause if she remained here after he had been crowned, yet he had said nothing of the damage her simple presence would do to his reputation—though when she thought back to that conversation, she could see that he had implied it. If he had made the situation so starkly clear, she would have insisted on leaving as soon as possible, but even in extremis, when his world was crashing down around him, Azhar had been thoughtful enough to ensure she had enough time to finish that blasted book of Daniel's. While she had been selfishly focused only on being deprived of Azhar's company.

How long after he was crowned, would it be before he was expected to marry? For he would marry. Being Azhar, incapable of half-measures, he would do everything in his powers to be the best King possible. Which meant ensuring that there was a Crown Prince waiting to take his place when the time came. He'd told her that himself, in the Divan room—was it really less than two weeks ago?

Abandoning any notion of eating, Julia opened the window and stepped out into the cool evening air, making for her favourite spot under the lemon tree. Azhar would marry and produce an heir for the sake of his kingdom. She would never marry, for the sake of her hard-won freedom. That much had not changed, but something else had. And quite profoundly so. She leaned back against the bark of the tree, closing her eyes. She loved him. Dear heavens, how she loved him. A most fundamental shift, and a very, very unwise thing for her to have allowed to happen, for it changed nothing. None the less, she loved him.

The scent of the lemons reminded her of the soap Azhar used. Julia wrapped her arms around herself. When they lay on her divan in the aftermath of making love, his skin was salty, slick with sweat. He liked to pull her tight against him then, her bottom snuggled into his groin, one hand heavy on her waist, the other cupping her breast. When she touched him, when he was aroused and she stroked him slowly, her hand curled around his girth, tight and then looser, tight and then looser, his expression was almost one of pain. His fingers curled into the sheets in his efforts to control himself, but Julia had learned how to send him out of control. She knew how to touch the most sensitive spot to make him climax almost immediately. She had a similar spot and he knew exactly how to touch that too. She knew how to hold him tight inside her, to make him pulse, pulse, pulse, but to prevent his release. He could do things with his fingers and his mouth that kept her on the edge of her climax for what seemed like hours, and he could do other things that sustained her climax beyond what she thought possible. He had taught her to take delight in her body.

He was the perfect lover. If only she had been able to confine him to that role, but love was an insidious thing, like a desert flower lurking below the surface for years, waiting for the rains to give it life and make it bloom. How long had she been in love with Azhar without knowing it? She had known him less than a month. Was it possible to fall in love in such a short time? Apparently it was. She had known Daniel most of her life, her love for him had grown steadily and surely, but had she ever been passionately in love with him?

'No,' Julia said, 'definitely not. Nothing compares to this.'

And nothing could ever come of it. She knew that, as surely as she knew that she was in love with Azhar. Her freedom meant everything to her, and freedom most certainly did not encompass tying herself to a man again. She had no idea what she wanted to do with her life, but she wanted the freedom to decide for herself. To make and learn from her own mistakes as Azhar had done during the last ten years, and to celebrate her own successes as he had done. Perhaps she would travel. Perhaps she would find a way to earn her living with her landscapes. It didn't matter. What mattered was that she was free to choose, while Azhar...

Her heart contracted as it did every time she thought of his predicament. She longed to comfort him, but he had already locked her out of his life, already denied himself any solace. Daniel's first love was his book. Azhar had made it clear that his one and only love must be Qaryma. Not even his wife, when he took one, would take precedence over his kingdom. Even were Julia considered suitable to be the wife of a king—which she most clearly was not—she would never want such a role.

Not even if it meant being by Azhar's side?

'No,' she said aloud, this time even more firmly than the last, 'because I would not be by his side. Qaryma would be his, and I would be his, but neither Azhar nor Qaryma would ever be mine.'

But dear heavens, how she loved him.

Azhar listened with one ear as his Council debated the exact route of the coronation procession, his mind racing ahead to consider the other equally tedious details to be discussed at the meeting, none of which he gave a camel's hump about. He was resigned to going through the formality of a coronation, but the minutiae of the ceremony simply didn't interest him.

The two most pressing matters which did occupy his thoughts were for the moment in abeyance, awaiting the response of the two men concerned. He was a man of action, he'd told Julia once. Certainly, in the three days that had passed since he saw her he had made countless decisions, but he had also spent an inordinate amount of time trying *not* to act, not to do the one thing he wanted above all, which was to go to Julia and lose himself in her arms.

He missed her. It would be easier when she was no longer resident in the palace, easier still when she had crossed Qaryma's border *en route* to England, but for now, knowing that there were only a few walls separating them was making it ridiculously difficult to resist temptation.

He missed the sound of her laughter, and the tone of her voice. He missed the almost guilty expression she wore when she was about to tell him something she thought he didn't want to hear. He missed the frown of concentration that wrinkled her brow when she sketched and the way she pressed her lips together when she painted—to prevent herself nibbling on the end of her paint-brush, she had once confessed to him. He missed the silkiness of her hair strewn across his chest after lovemaking, and the way her mouth curved then too, into an unashamedly satisfied smile that made him unaccountably proud to have been the cause of it.

This morning she would most likely be in the Fourth Court painting what she called the secret garden, since he had sent word that he would not be there. He would like to see how her work was progressing. Would she give him one of the paintings if he asked? He'd like to have some-thing tangible to remember her by.

The Council had moved on to the menus for the various feasts, which they were debating with some gusto. The coronation was to take place in three days' time, almost four weeks exactly since he and Julia had made their agreement. The desire to see her was painful. He had known from the moment that he had decided to stay, how vital it was that Julia left, how deeply improper it would be for him to consort with her after his coronation.

But would it really be such a sin for him to see

her again before he was crowned? He had not informed her of the arrangements he was making on her behalf for her journey, and he ought to. In fact, his time would be far better spent doing that, than worrying about what people would eat on the day he handed his life over to his kingdom.

He was not fooling himself. Azhar sighed in irritation. He did not need an excuse to spend time with Julia. He had not handed his life over just yet. He had the right to claim one more day of freedom, and to spend it with the woman who was about to leave him for ever, to claim freedom for herself!

Azhar jumped to his feet, startling his Council into silence. 'I have decided to entrust the final details of the ceremony to you,' he said 'In three days' time I will dedicate my life to Qaryma. I require some time to prepare myself for this solemn undertaking, time to close the door on my old life, to ensure that when I begin this new life as your King, I come to you unburdened.'

This last remark drew some murmurs of approval and knowing looks that reminded Azhar of Kadar's warning. No one would dare question Julia's presence here, but everyone would be speculating. Until he was formally crowned,

Julia's position in Azhar's life was none of their business but after—surveying his Council, he could see the relief in some of the older faces.

They wanted their King unburdened of the Englishwoman. Despite the fact that it merely confirmed what he already knew, it sickened him to be faced with this evidence of the silent pressure, the unspoken rules and traditions he would be forced to conform to in the future. It also fixed his resolve and decided him to grasp not one but every day he had left. 'Until the eve of the coronation, my time will be exclusively my own. Any decisions to be made on anything other than the ceremony must be deferred.'

He waited, but not a single man seemed inclined to suggest the most logical alternative, which was to hand matters over to Kamal. None had questioned his brother's sudden absence from council meetings either, nor that of the Chief Overseer, though they must know that Kamal was under informal house arrest, that the Chief Overseer was confined to the Cage. They would no doubt speculate as to the reasons for this.

He sighed. For the time being it would have to remain just that, idle speculation, until he was in a position to implement his planned solution. But that, and everything else, would have to wait. In three days' time he would be King of Qaryma. Until then he would be simply Azhar.

It was dusk by the time they reached the oasis. 'It is known as Little Zazim, not because it is close to the Zazim Oasis, but because it is...'

'Almost a perfect replica, in miniature,' Julia exclaimed, surveying the spot from her vantage point on the seat of her camel.

The lagoon was small, elliptical in shape, the water had the same silver-green sheen she remembered from the oasis where they had first met. A belt of lush vegetation encircled the waters almost entirely, leaving only one end of the lagoon exposed where the soft desert sands met the waters in what looked like a small crescent-shaped bay. Julia stared around her in wonder. 'There is no one else here. Did you...?'

'I wanted to ensure our privacy. There are some advantages to being a member of the royal family,' Azhar said drily.

'But people will know that you are here with me. They will be talking, Azhar, and—and they will be wishing me gone. I had no idea until Aisha said...'

'I wish that Aisha had kept her mouth closed.' Azhar leaned across to press her hand. 'We discussed this before we left. I do not deny that your remaining here in Qaryma after the coronation would be unacceptable to my people, Julia, but I am not theirs to command just yet. I am sacrificing everything in three days' time, I will not sacrifice this final opportunity to spend time with you, unless you have changed your mind. Do I ask too much of you? Would it have been easier for you if I had done as I said I would, and left you alone?'

'No.' She clutched his hand tightly. 'If you can brazen out the scandal of my presence, then I can bear the shame of being the subject of palace gossip.'

'I will not have you bear any shame,' Azhar said fiercely.

Julia laughed. 'You are not my King, Azhar. My feelings are my own to command.'

He smiled, twining his fingers in hers. 'Your feelings and your life will be yours to command entirely very soon. You should be proud of yourself, Julia. I am proud of you.'

'Thank you.' The words were bittersweet, reminding her of all that she would be leaving behind, reminding her of all that Azhar would be giving up. She had wrestled with her conscience when he had come to her rooms this afternoon, having escaped his Council meeting, but her conscience had been no match for her heart. He did not love her, he would soon enough be duty-bound to love another woman, but for these next few precious days he would be hers alone.

Carefully holding on to the pommel, Julia leaned closer to Azhar and kissed him fully on the mouth. 'There,' she teased, 'that is to prove that you were wrong when you said it was not possible to make love on a camel.'

'I will accept that it is possible to *begin* to make love on a camel,' Azhar replied, 'but as to whether or not we can continue...' He moved so swiftly that he left her breathless, commanding both beasts to their knees before sweeping Julia from the saddle, holding her high against his chest. 'I prefer not to have to worry about controlling a camel, when I have sufficient to worry about, in controlling my appetite for you, Julia.'

She laced her arms around his neck. 'Are you hungry, Azhar?'

His smile made her blood fizz. 'Ravenous, Julia.'

'Then please, abandon any attempt at controlling your appetite for me,' she whispered into his ear, 'because I too am starving.'

Her words made his eyes darken. Grabbing a blanket, leaving the mules and camels which formed their little caravan still tethered together in the care of his Saluki hound and his hawk, Azhar carried her swiftly across the sand, to the point where the trees and shrubs screened them from the rippling sands of the desert. Lying down on the blanket beside her, he kissed her softly, but Julia desired kisses as fierce and as wild as her love. She rolled on top of him, trapping his body underneath hers, and claimed his mouth, kissing him urgently, until his mouth and his hands became urgent too, pulling her tightly against the pulsing length of his erection.

Julia moaned. She wriggled, struggling to free herself of her pantaloons and relishing the way the movement made Azhar shudder, made her shiver. She kicked herself free of the garment as Azhar tore himself free of his trousers. She was struggling to pull her tunic over her head when he pulled her back on top of him, fastening his mouth around one of her nipples, and she could feel her climax building, already peaking.

'Wait,' Azhar said, trying to claim her mouth again, but Julia couldn't wait. One more swift kiss, and then she slid him inside her, not slowly as she had done before, but urgently, drawing him in swiftly and deeply, making them both gasp with delight. The rhythm she set was fast, but he matched her, arching underneath her, pulling her tight against him with each thrust, with each thrust pushing hard, high, so that the illusion of control she harboured was quite lost as her climax ripped through her, and it was only his own last vestige of control that allowed him to lift her clear as he came too, crying out her name into the desert sky.

Their simple camp had none of the glamour of their previous trip to the desert, for they carried everything with them on the pack mules, but Julia knew that it would be this night she would remember most fondly. The Bedouin tent was Azhar's own, a simple wooden frame covered with animal skins. As he set it up, Julia laid the fire. Dinner consisted of hare and vegetable stew, the meat more succulent than that first one they had shared, and Julia had to admit, far tastier, thanks to the palace cook who had prepared it for them. Afterwards, they sat together by the dying embers of the fire, looking up at the stars, watching the moon's ghostly reflection dance on the gently rippling waters of the lagoon.

Julia was reluctant to disturb the perfect peace, but at the same time, she wanted to make the most of the opportunity to discover as much as possible about Azhar's future. She would never know it, but she would like to try to imagine it. 'Have you decided what to do with your brother?'

'I think I have come up with a fitting solution,' he said with a wry smile, 'that is if I can persuade my friend Kadar to co-operate.'

'The Prince who brought Daniel's watch? What has he to do with it? Are you going to send Kamal into exile in his kingdom—what was it called?'

'Murimon. No, I am not sending my brother into exile there, though he will certainly be spending some time in that kingdom—that is, as I said, if Kadar is agreeable.'

Julia must have looked as confused as she felt, for Azhar laughed. 'Border controls,' he said. 'You know from personal experience that the black-market trade unfortunately flourishes. It is a much bigger problem for Kadar, whose kingdom has a very large coastline. As a trader myself, I thought that I had a good understanding of the shadier side of the business, but when I questioned Kamal as to how he had disposed of the diamonds he stole, I was quite taken aback at the extent of his knowledge. It made me realise how vulnerable we are, and how much work has to be done to put an end to it.' Azhar grinned. 'It also made me realise that I had the ideal man for the job.'

Julia burst into astonished laughter. 'You plan to make your brother responsible for stamping out illegal trade?'

'Unfortunately, no one knows better where to root out that illegal trade than Kamal.'

'He surely won't agree?'

Azhar's expression hardened. 'Offered the choice of that position or permanent house arrest, he had little option.'

'You are right, it is a peculiarly apt solution, and one that avoids shaming your family name, as exile would. In England, we would say you had forced the poacher to become the gamekeeper. I think you have been very clever.'

'Thank you. I wish my little brother was more grateful, but I fear I have earned his eternal enmity.'

'Oh, I think you simply have to accept that you will endure Kamal's enmity no matter what you do. Even if you had abdicated in his favour, he would have found a way to blame you for the chaos his rule would most certainly have brought to Qaryma,' Julia said.

Azhar put his arm around her, pulling her head on to his shoulder. 'I wish I could disagree with you.'

'And what of his partner-in-crime, the Chief Overseer?'

'Once I had settled on Kamal's fate, I applied the same principle to his accomplice,' Azhar said. 'What you call poacher cum gamekeeper again. He has been stripped of his position on the Council, obviously, and has returned to the diamond mine in the rather less exalted position of guard, searching the miners at the end of every shift for any purloined gems.'

'You do not fear that he will reveal your brother's role in the crime?'

'I made it crystal clear that I would have no compunction in exiling him if I heard so much as a rumour to that effect. I think his silence is ensured.' Azhar sighed. 'I thought long and hard about whether I was treating Kamal more leniently because he was my brother, but I honestly believe that he will suffer far more from the loss of prestige and the loss of his luxurious lifestyle than the Chief Overseer.'

'I think you have been more than fair,' Julia said. 'I think you have been creatively just.'

She felt the rumble of his laughter against his cheek. 'Have I told you that you have a unique perspective on life?'

She sat up, pulling his face towards her. 'I like this perspective very much.'

Azhar ran his thumb along her lower lip. 'Truly,' he said, 'it is a view I don't think I could ever tire of either,' he said, and kissed her.

Chapter Eleven

'But this is the rare moss Johara told me about,' Julia exclaimed animatedly, 'I am sure of it, the one which she says has special healing qualities. How on earth did you know about it, far less where to find it?'

They had ridden out early from their encampment at the Little Zazim to this place which even Azhar had had some difficultly in locating. He smiled as Julia gazed at the thick reddish-brown slime which grew on the stones in the shallow pool with the delight that other women would reserve for jewellery. 'You seemed excited about it after your last conversation with Johara, so I dispatched someone to find out more from her.'

'I did not expect—you should not have gone to such trouble on my behalf, especially when you have so many more weighty matters to deal with.'

'Julia, everyone else causes me nothing but trouble, you are the one person in my life who gives me nothing but pleasure,' Azhar replied. 'When you said this rather revolting slime was unique, I knew that it must be very special, and I wanted you to be able to include it in your book.'

'Daniel's book.'

He considered this for a moment. There had been a time, not so very long ago, when he had resented Daniel Trevelyan's ghostly presence, when he could not have cared less about the content of the man's botanical treatise. Not now. 'For me, it will always be your book,' Azhar said, 'and as such, I want you to make it the best you can possibly make it.'

'I couldn't have finished it at all if I had not met you,' Julia said.

'Nonsense, you are the most determined woman I have ever met. You would have found a way. If I had not stumbled upon you that day, someone else would have come to your aid. The Zazim is a busy oasis.'

'I am very, very glad that it was you who stumbled upon me, Azhar. More glad than you will ever know.'

There was a catch in her voice. There was

something in her eyes that squeezed his heart. He knew she cared. He did not want to know how much. 'Will you be comfortable here on your own for today?' he asked.

He saw her expression reflect the slight brusqueness in his voice. He could see her pondering whether to accept the deliberate change of subject, or whether to pursue her train of thought. When she decided the former, he felt guilt as well as relief. 'Of course I will,' she said. 'You know that I can easily lose myself in my sketching, and drawing this moss will tax my ability to its limits. Have you business elsewhere?'

The notion had come to him in the night. He wasn't at all certain if it was a good idea, and until he knew that, he wasn't prepared to share it, not even with Julia. 'I will return in good time for us to ride back to Al-Qaryma before nightfall,' Azhar said briskly.

Julia didn't look intimidated, she looked hurt, but once again, unusually, she bit her tongue. He almost wished she would not. 'That gives me plenty of time to get to work,' she said brightly.

'Julia.'

'Yes?'

He paused. 'Let me get your drawing materials from the saddlebags.'

She was settled with her sketchbook and pencil by the side of the small pool when Azhar left, though he was fairly sure she was not as engrossed as she contrived to look, and even more certain he could feel her gaze burning into his back as he headed into the desert. He knew she had come to care for him, and not only as a lover. Her anguish at his plight was obvious, far beyond that of a mere friend. She meant it when she said she wanted to spare him pain. She meant it when she had said, before they set out yesterday, that she would rather sacrifice their last few days together if doing so was best for him and his blasted kingdom. Julia cared. He knew that, of course he knew that, but knowing was one thing, hearing how much she cared—was it cowardly of him to have cut her short?

What was he afraid of? The answer was obvious, but it was not fear which kept him silent, even to himself, on the subject of his own feelings. Duty again, cursed duty. He had no right to feelings. When he married, as he must, he would have to be able to try to love his chosen wife with a clean conscience. He could not care for Julia. He would not allow himself to care for Julia. And so he must not allow Julia to care for him.

So deep in his musings had Azhar been that he had not noticed how far he had travelled. No one knew when the first King had been buried in the Royal City of the Dead, for the epitaphs on the earliest tombs had been worn away by the desert winds. Unlike the mighty pyramids and the vast underground tombs filled with necessities for the afterlife now being excavated in Egypt, Qaryma's royal dead were buried in simple sarcophagi hewn from the indigenous red rock, one large monument at the centre for the King, his family ranged around him, their final resting places meriting only small markers.

Azhar was familiar with the site, for he had visited his mother's grave every year. The marker had sat in isolation on the outer edges of the sprawling city of tombs. Now, it was in the shadow of the newest, largest sarcophagus. In death as in life, he thought wryly. Faced with this incontrovertible evidence of his father's death, sorrow took a wrenching hold of him, squeezing the breath from him. Dropping to his knees and bowing his head, Azhar tried to fight the tears. Kings did not cry.

He read the simple inscription. Kings did not cry, but he was not yet a king. Leaning his head against the warm red rock of his father's tomb, Azhar wept.

His tears did not persist for long but they cleansed him, and they brought his father closer to him here, in the City of the Dead, than he had ever been in life. 'I wish that we could have made our peace while you still breathed, but I hope you are listening now,' Azhar said in a low voice, still husky from emotion, his head bowed as he stood by the tomb. 'I am sorry for the long silence that existed between us, but it would be to fly in the face of nature to expect anything else from either of us. You called my bluff. I called yours. In that way I am made in your image, Father, but in so many others, I have made myself. I will not be the man you were. I will be a better king. I will try to be a loving husband and father. I will grant my son the freedom you did not grant me. I will allow my son the true freedom to choose.'

The words were a vow. His own solemn oath, to which he would be true even before the oaths he would take at his coronation. Azhar touched the sarcophagus in farewell. He knelt before his mother's marker and promised once more to make a better husband than his father had. And then he turned away, out of the Royal City of the Dead, to ride his camel back to Julia, knowing now that he would tell her where he had been and why, knowing now that it had been absolutely the right thing to do.

They returned to the palace in the late afternoon, to be met in the First Court by the Head of the Royal Guards.

'I am informed that an Englishman crossed the border without official papers,' Azhar told Julia. 'The border guards intercepted him and brought him here. I can only assume that the British Consul in Damascus has become concerned by your lengthy absence and has despatched an official to search for you. Does the name Christopher Fordyce mean anything to you?'

'I've never heard of him,' Julia replied.

'He is currently being detained in the Second Court, in the waiting room of the Divan, will you accompany me while I interview him?'

'Of course. I cannot imagine that he can have any connection with me,' Julia said, following him through the gate to the Second Court. 'Though I admit it does seem an odd coincidence that Qaryma should have two English visitors in such a short space of time.'

'We do not have that honour,' Azhar said with a smile. 'One of you is Cornish, remember.'

However, Christopher Fordyce appeared more Arabian than English or even Cornish. He looked to be in his late twenties, and was dressed for the desert in a simple cotton tunic and trousers which were either very dirty or had been dyed the colour of sand. Slung around his hips was a plain brown belt holding a sheathed scimitar and a long, thin dagger, also sheathed. His head-dress was also pale cotton of some indeterminate colour tied with a plain brown scarf. Beneath it, his skin was tanned almost mahogany, his fair brows bleached by the sun.

The first impression Julia had of Christopher Fordyce however, was by no means either brown or nondescript. Like Azhar, this tall, lithe figure had a presence, an indefinable air of command. Like Azhar, his features were almost perfect, and like Azhar he had a patrician air about him. Even more like Azhar, it was his eyes which drew her attention, though the Englishman's were a deep and brilliant blue, almost exactly the colour of cornflowers. She would never have forgotten this man if she had met him before. Whatever his business here in Qaryma, it was nothing to do with her. He looked nothing like any servant of the British crown she had ever encountered on her travels.

'Mr Fordyce,' Azhar said, holding out his hand in the English manner. 'How do you do. Allow me to present Madam Julia Trevelyan, an eminent English botanist, who has been studying our native flora.'

'How do you do, madam?' Christopher Fordyce made his bow to her curtsy. 'How very extraordinary, to meet an Englishwoman so far east in the desert.'

The emotion he expressed was not reflected in either his expression or his tone. Mr Fordyce wasn't in the least bit surprised nor very interested to find one of his countrywomen here, dressed as he was, in native clothing. Which made Julia extremely curious indeed.

Turning towards Azhar, she saw her feelings reflected in his eyes, if not his face. 'I am told you have been trespassing on my lands,' he said.

'Yes.'

Azhar's brows quirked. 'May I enquire why?'

'I am embarked on what one might call a personal quest.'

Azhar sighed. 'Is it incumbent on everyone in England to have a quest? A royal decree perhaps?'

Julia stifled a giggle, though Mr Fordyce looked puzzled. 'My quest has nothing to do with the British crown. As I said, it is of a personal nature.'

'So personal that it precludes you obtaining the appropriate permissions to travel within our borders.'

'Frankly, I find it the most effective method of obtaining an audience with someone in authority,' the English man replied. 'Much quicker than going through the palaver of getting official papers and jumping through any number of diplomatic hoops to get to the man at the top.'

'A very risky strategy, if I may venture an opinion,' Azhar said.

Mr Fordyce smiled disarmingly. 'But successful, on most occasions. Such as today. Shall we get down to business?'

'Do we have business to—er—get down to?'

'Indeed.' Like a conjurer producing a rabbit

from a hat, Christopher Fordyce produced a bracelet. 'I don't suppose you've ever seen this, or anything like it?'

It was not a bracelet but an amulet, intricately worked and set with diamonds and enamel. 'It looks very old,' Julia ventured.

'It is. Thousands of years old. And very valuable too. In fact it's priceless.'

'There is some damage. It looks as if a stone has been lost or removed.'

'You are very observant, madam. I'm not sure what it is that is missing, but I am sure that whoever the true owner is will provide me with the answer.'

'True owner?' Azhar frowned, turning the delicate item over in his hands. 'May I ask how you came by this, sir?'

'Oh, quite legitimately, I assure you. It was left to me by my mother. As to how she came by it,' Christopher Fordyce said, his expression darkening, 'that is another matter entirely. I presume it is not part of Qaryma's crown jewels, Prince Azhar?'

'No, it is not.'

'You are sure?'

'Certain. We produce our own diamonds here

in Qaryma. They have a very distinctive colour and clarity. The stones in this bracelet are quite different. Of magnificent quality but definitely not from here. This bracelet is certainly Arabian but I'm afraid your search for the rightful owner must continue.'

'Then I will thank you for your time, assuming I'm no longer under arrest.' Mr Fordyce hid the amulet in the folds of his tunic, turning to go with an insouciance that Julia couldn't help but admire.

Azhar, however, was less sanguine. 'Wait! Where are you going now? You surely do not plan to wander Arabia, casually dropping in on each kingdom and asking if they happen to have lost any of the family jewels.'

'More or less, though I have it narrowed its place of origin down to six likely candidates, and you're now the third I've eliminated. The quality of the gold and the gems, together with the distinctive style of the enamelling act as a sort of signature. It's astonishing that such exquisite workmanship was possible more than two millennia ago.' Mr Fordyce smiled ruefully. 'You must forgive my over-enthusiasm. 'I'm a bit of an amateur archaeologist.'

'I suspect you are more expert than you modestly claim, Mr Fordyce. And please do not apologise for your overenthusiasm. It seems to be another English trait. Only this morning I witnessed Madam Trevelyan here become excited by a patch of green slime. Where do you intend to go next? Perhaps I can help you with permissions?'

'A kind offer but there is no need. I shall stick to my tried-and-tested method.'

Azhar laughed and held out his hand. 'Then I will wish you good luck.'

'I don't need luck. It is a mere process of elimination, but thank you. Good day, sir...madam.'

'What an extraordinary man,' Julia said, as the door closed behind the Englishman and the guard.

'With extraordinarily bad timing,' Azhar said. 'I have plans for tonight.'

'To be fair to him, he hardly overstayed his welcome. What plans?'

Smiling, Azhar held out his hand. 'Come with me, and I'll reveal all.'

'What is this place? Where are you taking me?' Julia clung to the rope which served as a banister on the spiral stair of the turret. She had lost count of the number of steps they had climbed at somewhere around eighty-something. In front of her, Azhar held the lantern high, but she still had to take great care not to miss her footing.

'Only ten more steps,' Azhar said. 'There are one hundred and fifteen in total,' he added, pre-empting her question.

The door was curved to fit snugly into the turret wall. With some relief, Julia stepped through it, and found herself on the roof of the palace. 'Azhar!'

'What do you think?'

She gazed around her in wonder. The roof was huge, almost like an outdoor room with a knee-high parapet for walls and the star-filled night sky above forming a celestial ceiling more beautiful than the most ornately decorated ceiling in the most opulent of rooms. A tent had been set up in the middle, but it was not at all a practical tent. It was the kind of tent a child would dream up, made of scarlet silk, decorated with gold tassels. Open on one side to face out to the desert, the interior was a decadent haven of silk and velvet, luxurious rugs, huge cushions and one even larger divan. A crystal chandelier hung from the centre, the candles casting flickering shadows. Flowers floated in huge glass bowls, throwing their exotic scent out into the night.

And what a night. Leaning precariously out over the parapet, Julia saw the desert, soft undulating sands, peaked dunes, the distant high mountains. And above, casting the chandelier into shadow, the waxing buttery moon, the huge slivery discs of the stars. 'Azhar,' Julia said, 'it is breathtakingly beautiful. But how on earth did you manage to get all of this up those narrow stairs?'

He laughed. 'There is another, much easier way to access this roof. Do you really wish me to spoil the effect with practicalities?'

She gazed up at him, quite entranced. 'No.'

'This will be our last night together. Tomorrow, on the eve of the coronation, there are many rituals I must endure, and after that...'

'I will watch the ceremony and then I will leave with my escort,' Julia said. 'The arrangements you have made are faultless, but if you don't mind, I'd rather not talk them over again. As you say, this will be our last night...'

Her throat clogged with tears. She stared out over the desert defying them to fall. She would

not cry. She had promised herself she would not
cry. She did not want to mar the perfection of
this last night.

'Julia, have I upset you? Is it too much?'

'No,' she said, 'on the contrary, it is not enough,
but it is all we will ever have.'

Azhar flinched at the raw emotion in her voice.
He had deduced that she cared too much, and
was reluctant to acknowledge it, she knew that.
This morning she had allowed him to prevent
her speaking out, but she had been wrong to do
so. So close to the beginning of her new life, she
would not allow Azhar to smother her feelings.

She smiled up at him. She fluttered her fingers
over his hair, his cheek, let her hand rest on his
shoulder. She had thought it would take courage,
but it was actually straightforward. 'I love you,'
Julia said. 'I love you with all my heart.'

He did not flinch this time, he froze.

'I know you can't love me or won't love me or
don't love me, but I love you. I love you, Azhar,
and if I allowed you to prevent me telling you
that, I would have left Qaryma feeling I had been
untrue to myself.'

'Julia.'

He tried to pull her into his arms, but she resisted. 'I know it doesn't change a thing,' she said gently. 'Even if you did love me, I know that it would be impossible for us to make a life together. Your duty is to Qaryma. Your kingdom requires all of you. Aside from the fact that I would never be considered an acceptable wife, I don't want to be a wife who will be second best. I don't know what my life will be but it is mine, Azhar, as you said last night. I am not offering you my heart, but I want you to know that I carry you in it, and always will. So you see,' she whispered, brushing his lips with hers, 'you have nothing to fear from my love, and nothing to feel guilty about.'

He was silent for a long moment, staring out at the desert, the pulse beating in his throat the only indication of the strength of whatever emotion held him in its grip. 'You are right,' he said finally, slowly. 'I cannot love you, Julia, I have not that right, but nor do I have the right to deny you your feelings. I am…' He stopped to clear his throat, his hands clenching and unclenching. 'I was about to say that I am honoured, but in fact I am humbled by your courage and your honesty. I can say without any doubt at all that I will never meet another woman like you.'

His crooked smile, his trembling voice, melted her heart. 'And I can say without any doubt at all that I will never meet another man like you,' Julia said. 'I know you can't love me, but you can make love to me, one last time.'

This time when he swept her into his arms she did not resist. 'And that I will do, my brave desert rose,' Azhar said, kissing her fervently.

Julia loved him. Julia, brave Julia, had told him that she loved him because she wanted him to know, and for no other reason. She loved him, and she was right, it changed nothing, though what she said could feel momentous if he allowed it to. His feelings for her ran far, far deeper than they should. He could not articulate them, but he could show her. He could do as she asked, and make love to her. He could be hers tonight, for all of tonight, and in the morning—he would deal with that when the sun rose.

'Julia,' he said, simply for the pleasure of saying her name. 'Julia.' She tasted so sweet, he could never tire of kissing her. Their mouths were formed perfectly for each other. The soft little sigh she made when he stroked the curve of her breast through her tunic stirred his blood.

The marble rooftop bath, no longer in regular use, had once been part of the *hamam* bath complex below. Julia's face lit up with surprised pleasure when he led her round the side of the tent to show her it. He undressed her slowly, covering every new inch of skin with kisses as it was revealed. The hollow of her shoulder fascinated him. The valley between her breasts. The curve of her spine. The soft flesh of her belly and her thighs. In the moonlight, her skin gleamed like porcelain. Her eyes gleamed with desire for him. Though she waited, taking her cue from him tonight, he knew there would be a moment when her passion would be unleashed, and that moment would be his undoing.

Azhar quickly stripped himself of his clothes. She watched him, supremely confident now in her own nakedness, her eyes devouring him unashamedly. She fluttered her fingers over his skin, shoulder, chest, flank, before languidly stroking his manhood, making him shudder involuntarily. She smiled that slow, sensuous smile that never failed to make his pulse quicken.

He led her down the shallow steps which led into the huge bath. The water was warm, the bath deep enough for it to lap just above his knees.

She twined her arms around him, pressing her breasts against his chest, and kissed him deeply. His erection pressed insistently between her legs.

He angled her against the side of the bath and dropped to his knees before her, easing her legs apart. The scent of her arousal made his senses spin. He tilted her towards him, his hands on her bottom, his favourite of her curves, and kissed her between the thighs. So wet and so sweet she tasted. Her hands clutched at his shoulders. Her breathing quickened, making her belly contract. He licked his way over her, around her, into her, relishing the way each touch of his tongue made her tighter, wetter, made him harder. He knew her intimately now, knew how to take her to the brink and keep her there, before sending her over the edge at a moment of his choosing. That moment had arrived.

She came fiercely. He pulled her into his arms, wrapping her legs around his waist. Then Julia kissed him. Holding him tight inside her, Julia whispered in his ear, a guttural command that should have shocked him to the core, but instead elicited a much more primal reaction.

He set her down on the shallow steps and thrust deeply into her, just as she had demanded. She cried out and arched up against him, taking him higher. He thrust again, harder. She wrapped her legs around his waist. The steps were slippery. Her hair was trailing in the water, her breasts thrust upwards by her arched back. He had never seen such an arousing image. He thrust again. Julia moaned and tightened around him. 'Harder,' she urged, but by then Azhar needed no urging, losing himself inside her, feasting his eyes on her, the combination of heat and wet skin and lapping water and the scent of her, and that cry she gave as she came again, tightening around him, sending him over the edge so quickly that he barely had time to pull himself from her, could do nothing but cling to her helplessly as he came, feeling as if he was being torn asunder.

Afterwards, they sat on cushions in the doorway of the tent watching the stars, a blanket draped loosely over them. There was food, but neither of them had eaten much. Nor did they have much to say, speaking with their eyes and their hands. The desert stretched out below them, darker and more mysterious now that night had fully descended, the moon partially obscured by a cloud. The air had that distinctive salty taste to it that on some days cast a dew, prompting the most rare of desert flowers to push their petals through the sands' surface and bask in the sun for a few precious hours.

As she and Azhar had done, basking in the sun for an all-too-fleeting period. 'Salt and sand,' Julia mused. 'In Cornwall, the sand is every bit as golden as it is here, and the air is every bit as salty, and yet the effect is quite different.'

'You prefer the Cornish version, naturally,' Azhar teased. 'Cornwall is the most beautiful county in England, after all.'

'Did I say that? It's true enough, but Qaryma is the most beautiful kingdom in Arabia.'

'You have not seen them all.'

'I don't need to,' Julia replied. 'This is the most beautiful kingdom, and you are the most beautiful man.'

'You cannot call a man beautiful.'

'I am an artist, you told me so yourself, which means I have an eye for beauty, and I have always thought you beautiful Azhar, from the very first moment I saw you. Of course, I also thought you arrogant and selfish and just a little bit intimidating...'

Azhar laughed. 'I have never once managed to intimidate you.'

'Not for the lack of trying, on occasion.'

'I should have known better.'

'You do now,' Julia said. She was suddenly close to tears. She would miss this closeness they shared more than anything. Determined not to spoil things, knowing that any further declarations of love would sound horribly needy, she decided instead to show him. Pushing back the blanket, she kissed him, easing him on to his back. Her lips clung to his, silently telling him over and over how much she loved him, how very much she loved him. She kissed his mouth and his eyes and his cheeks and his throat. She kissed his chest, sucking gently on his nipples. She kissed around the curve of his ribs, and she kissed the dip in his belly.

Her kisses had made him hard again. She touched the silken skin of his erection, circling her thumb over the tip. Azhar exhaled sharply. She put her lips where her thumb had been and kissed him. He let out a groan.

She did it again, and was rewarded with another groan. Dare she? It was one of the most delightful things he did to her. Would he feel the same? She wrapped her hand around him. One slow stroke, and then a kiss. He throbbed in her hand. She did that again. No doubting that he liked it. And so did she. She wanted to do this, she wanted to give him what he had given her, and her desire emboldened her.

'For you, Azhar,' she said, positioning herself between his legs.

'Julia, you do not have to…'

'But I want to,' she said, bending her head and taking him into her mouth.

They did not sleep. They sat entwined in the tent watching dawn break with its usual spectacle. The stars faded, the night sky lightened to soft grey, and the sun appeared, rising swiftly on the horizon, streaking the sky with orange and pink, before it settled, a pale yellow glow in a pale blue sky, and it was over.

And so too was their desert idyll.

'I have to go,' Azhar said.

'Yes.' She had not permitted herself to imagine this moment, and now it had arrived.

'Aisha has the details of your travel arrangements.'

'Yes.'

'Would it be easier for you to leave before the coronation?'

'No, I want to be there.' To witness him bind himself to his kingdom. To ensure that she could never, at any point in the future, fool herself into thinking that there could be a future for them.

She knew that a clean break would be best, but Julia could not resist throwing herself into his arms one last time and clinging to him, though she did manage to resist the urge to beg him to stay. Later, she would be grateful for this small mercy. 'Kiss me,' she said.

He did, but carefully, as if he was afraid he would break her. Little did he know her heart was already broken. 'I love you,' Julia said, 'and I will never forget you.'

'Julia...'

His voice cracked. She had barely any control left over hers, but she managed a smile. 'Goodbye, Azhar.'

He hesitated. Stepped towards her. Changed his mind. 'Goodbye, Julia,' he said. And then he left her, taking the exit that led down to the *hamam* baths.

Julia stood frozen to the spot in her rumpled clothes staring out over the desert. It was over.

Tomorrow, Azhar would wed his kingdom and she would set out for home.

No, it was not over, she told herself sternly, for her life was just beginning. Even if it felt quite the opposite.

Azhar stood on the dais which had been set up in the middle of the Divan. Heavily veiled, Julia watched from a position in a far corner where her presence would not cause offence. His tunic was made of simple white silk, but his cloak and headdress were cloth of gold. Diamonds weighted the cloak down. Diamonds glittered in the band which held his headdress in place, and there were diamonds and pearls in the slippers he wore too. He had always carried an air of authority, no matter what he wore, but today, Azhar was without doubt a king.

'By anointing thy hands with this sacred oil, we give to thee, our King, the strength and the power to rule your kingdom, to wage just wars, and to defend our people from the unjust.'

Julia, reading from the translation which Azhar had thoughtfully sent to her, watched as he held out his hands to the Chief Celebrant. Beside her, Aisha craned forward excitedly. The maidservant had explained every step of the ceremony yesterday as she helped her to pack up her things. Julia knew that the oil was made of frankincense, the resin taken from the trees which grew in the far south of Arabia, many thousands of miles from Qaryma. The distinctive scent mingled with the heady perfume of the rose petals strewn at Azhar's feet.

Like every other subject in the kingdom—with the notable exception, presumably, of Kamal—Aisha saw this day as a cause for jubilation. What Azhar thought, Julia was finding it difficult to discern. She knew he would embrace his role as King, she knew he would give everything of himself, but what did he feel? What was he feeling right now? Where had his resentment gone, and his anger at being forced into this role he so desperately didn't want? What had he done with his pride in his own trading business, and his love of travel? Was it possible to bottle all of that up and throw it away?

'By anointing thy head,' the Chief Celebrant intoned, 'we give to thee, our King, the wisdom to govern justly, to rule absolutely and infallibly.'

As Azhar bent his head obediently, Julia had the horrible sensation that the words of the cer-

emony to mark the beginning of his reign also
served to mark the end of something precious.
The oil dribbling from the ornately chased, heavily jewelled spoon would be viscous on his skin.
Was he aware of her presence in this crowded
room? Was he thinking of her? Had he slept since
he left her on the rooftop yesterday morning?

She had not. He did not look as if he had. The
glow of their lovemaking had been replaced by
a sallow tinge to his skin, dark shadows under
his eyes. She wanted to go to him, to take him
in her arms, to soothe away his cares. It was an
agony to be able to do none of these preposterous things, and the very fact that she was thinking them made enduring this occasion to the very
end a very necessary agony. Common sense and
logic were weak defences against irrational love,
Julia was discovering

'By anointing thy heart, we give to thee, our
King, the enduring and unquestioning love of our
people. In the name of your revered father, King
Farid, so suddenly stolen from his magnificent
life, we do name you, Sheikh al-Farid, his most
revered and most high successor, King Azhar of
Qaryma.'

King Azhar of Qaryma. He would never be her

Azhar. He had never been her Azhar, Julia reminded herself sternly. But she wished he could have been. Stupid, stupid Julia, but still she wished he could have been.

The Chief Celebrant handed Azhar the glittering ceremonial sword of Qaryma clad in its diamond-encrusted sheath. The huge emerald glittering in the hilt was reputed to have been discovered in a tomb thousands of years old, Aisha had told her. The first row of men in the audience, the most powerful in this kingdom and the members of Azhar's Council, stood to play their allotted roles in the ceremony. Kamal, Julia noted, looked sullen and sulky, but nevertheless played his part dutifully. 'Receive this kingly sword, our King, from our unworthy hands, and with this sword do justice, stamp out iniquity, and protect and defend your people.'

The final words were spoken by all, echoing around the high walls of the throne room. 'With this sword, our King, we most humbly beg that you restore the things that are gone to decay, punish and reform what is amiss, and confirm what is in good order.'

The heavy ring of office was placed before Azhar on a velvet cushion as the sun crossed the dome above the throne. Golden rays bounced onto the crescent suspended over Azhar's head, and onto the walls and pillars of the Divan. Azhar was enveloped in a golden glow, the sunlight setting his cloak ablaze, making him look like a golden deity.

He pulled the sword from its sheath and raised it above his head. 'I am Azhar, King of Qaryma,' he declared. 'I am the source of all power, all wisdom, all happiness. I am the infallible one. I make the laws and I enact the laws. None can question me. None can harm me. I am Azhar, King of Qaryma. Beloved and revered.'

The familiar words brought a lump to Julia's throat. She had no option but to accept that it truly was over. He was Azhar, King of Qaryma, and she was Julia Trevelyan, botanist cum artist from Cornwall with some outstanding deathbed promises to fulfil. Soon they would be separated by thousands of miles. The distance made no difference. The vows Azhar made had already torn them asunder. Azhar, King of Qaryma, stood alone at the pinnacle of power, quite out of her reach.

For ever.

* * *

Julia said no farewells. Her journey from the palace through the deserted streets of Al-Qaryma was very different from the one she had made just a few weeks before. The streets were carpeted with the rose petals which had been thrown at the feet of the new King's cavalcade as he paraded through the city, while she made her final preparations to leave. It looked as if everyone in Al-Qaryma was at the palace joining in the celebrations. All was silent apart from the jangle of the bells on the reins of her own much more modest cavalcade.

She was escorted by a guard to her first overnight stop, the name of the oasis unfamiliar to her. There, she would meet her new dragoman and the men who would escort her all the way to Cairo. Azhar had obtained all the relevant papers for her. He had arranged for the caravan of camels and mules, a fresh supply of gold, and he had armed her guard. He had refused to accept her bank notes, asking instead that she carry his letters to his agent in Cairo. The letters would put an end to his trading business. Ten years of work, ten years of Azhar's determination and dedication, of his ambition and his flair, to be ended by a packet of letters. Julia patted the package, tied in a leather purse around her waist, along with Daniel's watch. Now that it was no longer ticking away her time in Qaryma, she found the watch reassuring. It reminded her of Daniel, but it also reminded her of Azhar, who had gone to such trouble to get it back for her.

The two landscapes she had painted of Cornwall, she had left for Azhar in her rooms, along with one of the paintings she had made of the secret garden in the Fourth Court. She hoped he would not find them a painful reminder. She hoped he would look at them and think of her. She hoped, she was ashamed to admit, that he would miss her.

The camels left the city streets and turned towards the desert. Tonight she would sleep under the stars once more. She would take solace in their beauty. She would not look back in sorrow to the desert Prince she had left behind, she would look forward in anticipation to the life she would make for herself. She would not regret her time here in Qaryma because she was done with looking back. There could have been no more perfect idyll.

But it was over. She allowed herself one final

glance over her shoulder. The heat haze made the city shimmer like a mirage. And like all mirages, it was not real. It really was over.

Chapter Twelve

Qaryma—two months later

'And so, as I've just explained, this is where the source of the problem is located,' Kamal said, pointing at a map of the entire region. 'The centre of the illegal trade network lies here.' He circled an area of the map with his finger. 'I have come up with several strategies for dismantling this web of corruption.'

Azhar listened with half an ear as his brother began to expound each of his proposals in detail. After a most reluctant beginning, Kamal was thriving in his new role with all the zeal of a convert. The qualities which had made him an accomplished thief served to make him an equally accomplished thief-hunter. His devious mind was proving the scourge of the vagabonds he had once consorted with.

As a result, their relationship was on a slightly better footing. They would never be close, that was impossible after all he had done. Kamal's ambition and sense of entitlement would always leave him vulnerable to corruption, his weak character would always cloud his judgement. Azhar was not fooled into thinking his brother was either reformed or redeemed. He would never trust him, but he could respect the work he was doing and the difference he was making.

And he did envy his brother's new zest for life, his sense of purpose. For Kamal—at the moment at least—every day brought a new challenge to be embraced. Azhar's life did not lack challenges, but Julia seemed to have taken his sense of purpose with her. As time passed, the pain of her leaving did not lessen. On the contrary, he missed her more now than yesterday, and more yesterday than…

'What do you think? My own view is that we should go with the first option.'

Azhar stared at Kamal blankly. Another thing that was happening more and more recently. Julia had always helped him see more clearly, helped focus his mind. But Julia was not here. 'The first option,' he hazarded. 'Remind me again of the advantages.'

Kamal rolled his eyes, but obliged. This time Azhar managed to keep his mind on the matter, and to agree with his brother's proposal. 'Thank you. Does this mean you will be leaving us again soon?'

Kamal nodded. 'I set off tomorrow. I must confess, I am very much enjoying the freedom this role gives me to see the world outside Qaryma. I can understand a little of your wanderlust, Brother. You must miss it.'

The barb was deliberate and it was well aimed, but Azhar was accustomed to such sallies. 'I have more than enough to occupy me within our own borders, thank you very much.'

'Indeed, I hear that the Council has a proposal for you that will occupy you a great deal more,' Kamal said. 'Is it premature of me to offer my felicitations?'

'Extremely,' Azhar said. 'I have no intentions of taking a wife yet.'

'And to the best of my knowledge, you have taken no mistress either. Two months of celibacy is not healthy for any red-blooded man, Azhar.' Kamal's voice hardened. 'And two months of pining for an English widow is not good for Qaryma.'

'What do you mean by that?'

Kamal flinched at Azhar's tone, but he stood his ground. 'We were all relieved when you did the right thing and sent that woman packing after your coronation. Her presence here was most improper.'

'You dare to take the moral high ground with me?'

Kamal had the grace to look shame-faced. 'I am, I hope, a reformed man,' he said. 'But you—Azhar, you must realise that until you take a bride—or at the very least a new mistress—our people will live in fear of that woman returning.'

If only! If only Julia was here. If only she had not gone away. If only there had been some way to legitimately keep her here. The longing for her hit Azhar with some force. The desire for her simple presence, for her smile, for the sound of her voice, was actually painful enough to make him wince. If only she could return. 'Would it be so very terrible if she did come back?' he asked.

'You cannot be serious!'

He had not been, because he had not permitted himself to consider it, but now he did, his yearning for Julia washed over him like one of the waves in the Cornish bay she had painted for him. Two months here without her had seemed like an eternity. He *missed* her, and every day he missed her more, and he didn't want to spend the rest of his life missing her.

Could he be serious? His heart beat faster at the idea. The sluggishness left his body, leaving him tingling with energy. Could he be serious? Yes, he could. Could he do anything about it? That was another question entirely, and one he needed to address in peace.

Kamal was still staring at him in horror. 'Was there anything further you wished to discuss with me?' Azhar asked haughtily.

His brother took the hint, rolling up his maps and picking up his papers. 'The people worship you, you know. They always did, and now you are back—you have made all their dreams come true by delivering them from me. You have it all, Brother, but you act as if you have nothing. It is not good for a man to live without a woman. It is not good for a kingdom to be without an heir. Take my advice, forget that English woman and accept the wife the Council is proposing for you. You will be much happier sleeping in a warm bed.'

* * *

The door of the Audience Chamber closed softly, and Azhar headed towards the rear of the Royal Kiosk and the sanctuary of his private rooms. The paintings had been hung on the wall of his bedchamber. He wondered, as he did every time he looked at them, where Julia was, what she was doing. Had she published her book? Had she managed to persuade the prestigious Royal Society to grant her husband posthumous membership? Was she still living in the little fishing village depicted on the canvas? The sun shone brightly in the painting, where the white cottages tumbled down towards the harbour, though it was subtly different from the bright desert light. He had tried several times to work out how Julia had conveyed a colder sun, but had concluded it didn't matter. What mattered was that he knew it was colder, that he knew if he stepped into that vivid sea with its silver-crested waves, they would wash over him like a bucket of iced water.

He turned to the seascape. Marazion Bay, where Julia had learned to swim. 'Salt and sand,' he remembered her saying that last night they had spent together. 'In Cornwall, the sand is every bit as golden as it is here, and the air is every bit as salty, and yet the effect is quite different.'

Azhar traced the arc of the beach with his finger. Did she play their conversations over in her head as he did? Did she lie awake at night torturing herself with memories of their lovemaking as he did? Did her body ache for him as his did for hers? Did she still love him as he loved her?

He loved her?

He loved her.

Of course he loved her. He had known he loved her that last night they spent together on the roof, when she had told him that she loved him. He had known then, though he had not allowed himself to admit it because he had also known the limits of his own resolution. If he'd let his feelings loose, he'd never have been able to let her go, and he'd had to let her go for the sake of Qaryma. He had known he loved her when they had put the crown on his head, because he'd needed her to witness that too. To show her that it was final, to prove to himself that it was over. He'd tried to use the power of majesty to extinguish his love.

But it hadn't worked.

You cannot be serious! One short sentence that his brother would never have uttered had he known the consequences, and all of Azhar's defences crumbled. He could be serious. He *was* serious, because he loved her.

He stared at the paintings. He imagined Julia hunched over the paper, paintbrush in hand, lips pursed to prevent her chewing the tip of it. He remembered the night of the storm, the way his heart had turned over when he had thought her lying dead on the terrace, struck by lightning. He remembered the way she relished the wildness of the elements that night. It was June now, wasn't that summer in Cornwall?

He loved her.

He loved her, but what did it change, after all? What did his admitting it do, save make life without her more intolerable? Azhar groaned, running his fingers through his hair. Julia had said she loved him, but it changed nothing even if he did return her love. Which he did, though he had not recognised it. Or would not admit to it. It didn't matter which. What mattered was that he loved her.

And where did that leave him? His duty was to Qaryma. Ruling his kingdom had been all-consuming, just as Julia had said it would be, just as Azhar had promised it would be. He had sacri-

ficed everything for Qaryma, including his love
for Julia. The one sacrifice it was now abundantly
clear that he could not live with.

Qaryma or Julia. Must he really choose? Qaryma or Julia. His heart knew the answer, even if
his head did not. But even if he let his heart rule
his head it wasn't that simple, it was not his decision alone. Julia had made it crystal clear she
would not sacrifice her freedom, even for love.

But he loved her. And she loved him—or she
had, two months ago. Would she love him still?
What if she had put him, like her past, behind
her, relegated him to a pleasant memory? What if
she had found someone else? It was possible. She
was confident of her allure now, and she had set
her passionate nature free. She had left Qaryma
certain that they had no future together, but that
was no reason for Julia to face her future alone.
By the heavens, it was very possible that she had
found someone else…that he had thrown away
the chance to love and be loved for the sake of
a crown.

He couldn't think that way. He had to believe
there was a chance, because already, he was too
far down the path of walking away from this life
as it was. If she loved him as he loved her, then

there had to be a way for them to be together. If he could not cut Julia from his life, then something else had to go. He needed to think.

Outside, the secret garden was in full bloom. Like his father before him, Azhar took solace in this faux-wilderness. There had been many days when ten minutes' contemplation here had cleared his mind, readied him for the next meeting and the next. He could not abandon Qaryma. To break the vows he had made at his coronation and before that, at his father's grave, would be to tear out an integral part of himself. For better or worse, he was King of Qaryma until he died. Which meant he would have to find a way of ruling which did not devour his entire life.

Could he turn the impossible into the possible? Instead of thinking of what he could not have, could he turn his mind to working out what he could do to change things?

Space. That was a start. He had to make space. It went against the grain with him, but there were ways he could delegate, weren't there? He could grant more powers to his Council. This compulsion he had to make every decision himself, how much of it was really necessary? How much of it was driven by his need to fill his days in order to prevent himself from missing Julia? Was it possible for him to mould his kingdom to his needs rather than to mould himself to the insatiable needs of his kingdom?

Possible. It must be possible if he wanted it enough. And he did. Which left him with the other side of the problem. He would be a far better king with Julia by his side, but how to persuade Julia to be by his side? What could he possibly offer her to compensate for the sacrifice of her freedom?

Love? Julia said it changed nothing, but Julia was wrong. It changed everything—or it would do, if they made it so. He was a king. He had the power to move mountains. Azhar jumped to his feet, filled with excitement and hope. There was no perfect solution. There would have to be compromise and there would be sacrifice and it would therefore be painful, but he was determined upon one thing. He was going to do everything in his considerable powers to persuade Julia to give their love a chance to flourish. He owed that to them both, even if he failed.

But he did not intend to fail.

Cornwall, six weeks later

The folio edition was bound, as Daniel had requested, in fine Morocco leather, tooled with gold leaf. It was a very handsome book indeed, but it had proved extraordinarily expensive to have printed. Julia had been able to afford only five copies, with another twenty in quarto. All of them bore the dedication to Mr Joseph Banks which Daniel had requested, and to which Mr Banks had graciously acceded. Julia felt that Azhar deserved the dedication more, but that would mean breaking her solemn promise to Daniel. Besides, Mr Banks's dedication played its intended part in Daniel's successful nomination for posthumous membership of the Royal Society. Membership of the London Horticultural Society quickly followed, again thanks to Mr Banks's influence. All the quarto editions had been sent out to the designated recipients. The entire process had made a pauper of her, forcing her to move back into her childhood home and to strenuously resist all her father's attempts to embroil her in his work.

Julia leafed idly through the pages of the edition destined for her father. There was no doubting that her Qaryma illustrations were the very best. Without exception, it had been the desert succulents which had elicited admiring comments from Mr Banks and his fellow experts. What would Daniel think of that? No question, he would have preferred his collection of South American species to underpin his fame, but she had long ago concluded that it was the fame he coveted. She was glad to have achieved it for him.

Those drawings were painful to view, but she could not stop looking at them. They spoke of the unique scent of the desert and the heat. And Azhar.

It was almost four months since she had left him on the day of his coronation. Since she had landed back on Cornish soil, she had worked like a fiend, driven by the need to use action to avoid thinking about what she had lost. Now her quest was complete. Her promises to Daniel had been fulfilled. And instead of feeling liberated, Julia was acutely conscious of the huge gap in her life which she longed for Azhar to fill.

She missed him. She ached for him. Barely a day went by when she did not wonder what he was doing, whether he still thought of her, whether he had taken a wife yet. Most likely he would be married. Marriage was part of his commitment to Qaryma, and Azhar was completely committed to Qaryma.

She really, really missed him. She loved him so much. The freedom which she had so longed for now stretched painfully in front of her like a void. She had been so certain that her love for Azhar changed nothing. Now she wasn't at all sure that her hard-won freedom would change much either. She was free, but she was not happy. In all honesty, she had never been as happy as when she was with Azhar. She wanted that wild exhilaration that only his company provided. She wanted that heady combination of being able to say anything she chose, knowing that she would be understood. She had confused independence with freedom. Love changed nothing, she had said. She wondered, she was sick of wondering, if she had been wrong.

The schooner lay at anchor in the bay. She was three-masted. The sleek lines of the hull, so clearly built for speed, were painted glossy black trimmed with gold. Further along the coast at the tin-mining ports, she would still have been an extraordinary sight. Here at Marazion Bay, where the biggest ship afloat was the excise man's small sloop, almost every person in the village was gathered at the end of the quay to take a look at her.

'Can't even read her name,' a fisherman's wife told Julia. 'Odd sort of writing, looks like something my four-year-old would do. Can't imagine what she's doing here. Perhaps she's strayed off course.'

Julia squinted at the ship, which rocked contentedly on the gentle swell. 'How long has she been here?'

'Only just dropped anchor. Do you think the King is mad enough now to come to Cornwall?'

'Maybe it is Napoleon, escaped again,' one of the other locals ventured.

'Or Wellington,' someone else suggested. 'I hope he's not intending to put up yet another bloody statue of himself here.'

'Well it certainly ain't Prinny. Not even a schooner that size could keep him afloat.'

'Whoever it is, he's coming ashore.'

A rowing boat was being lowered over the side. There were four oarsmen, and one other man sitting in the prow. He was dressed in white. White tunic. White cloak. White headdress.

'He's wearing some sort of bedsheet.'

'Hush. Look at him, he's—he's a *foreigner.*'

'Anyone not from Cornwall is a foreigner in my book.'

'Well foreigner or no, I'm happy to welcome him,' another fishwife said. 'Did you ever see a finer-looking man?'

'Hush now, Peggy, you're spoken for. What would your Tom make of such talk?'

'We'd have to drag him kicking and screaming out of the tavern to find out!'

The crowd continued to laugh and to speculate, pushing and jostling on the jetty for a better view. Julia stood stock still. It could not possibly be him. She must be hallucinating. She could hear the splash of the oars now. The rowing boat, at least, was real. She couldn't see through the crowd. It simply couldn't be him. Her heart could stop thumping because it definitely wasn't him. No cause for her palms to sweat, or for her face to flush, because without question of a doubt it could not be...

The crowd fell back. Some of the women dropped into curtsies. Most of the men simply stared. Azhar stood on the end of the jetty. The breeze whipped at his thin clothes, outlining the lines of his body, as sleek and as exotic as the lines of the schooner from which he had just emerged. Julia's mouth went dry. Her knees threatened to buckle.

He had not seen her.

He was speaking to one of the fishermen.

Who was pointing over at her father's house until someone grabbed his arm and pointed straight at Julia.

Their eyes met. She saw it there on his face, exactly what must be written on her face, for he strode towards her and she fell towards him and there was nothing else, no one else, save the two of them, as their lips met, and his arms went around her, holding her in an embrace that stole away what very little breath she had left.

'You're here.' Azhar stared down at her in wonder. 'I had no idea if you would still be in Cornwall, and yet here you are, waiting on the jetty for me. I can't believe you are here.'

Julia seemed as dazed as he. 'I wasn't waiting. I was admiring your ship.'

'She's not mine. I borrowed her from my friend Kadar.'

'Was your magic carpet out of commission?'

'I would have flown here if I could. Kadar's

ship is the fastest on the Red Sea, but no ship on earth could be fast enough for my purposes.'

Julia's expression became serious. 'Azhar, why are you here?'

He had had several weeks at sea to prepare a speech. Several weeks to rehearse every possible argument, to perfect the words with which to persuade her that she could still love him. He had swung from certainty to doubt, from determination to despair. Looking into her eyes, holding her close, he spoke the most important words of all, which came unbidden. 'I love you,' he said simply.

Julia paled. Azhar's stomach plummeted. 'I love you, Julia,' he said more urgently. Forgetting all his carefully planned stratagems, carefully weighted arguments, he simply spoke from the heart. 'I came here because—because—do you remember? Do you remember that you told me on that last night that you were not offering me your heart? Well I came here to offer you mine instead, Julia. I came because you were wrong when you said love didn't change everything. I came knowing that there was a possibility we may still not be able to find a way to share our love, knowing that our lives may yet be destined to be lived apart, but wanting and hoping that we could find a way, because my love for you is the one thing I cannot compromise. That is why I came.'

Tears were streaming down her face.

'I love you,' Azhar said tenderly. 'I love you so much. All I ask is that you listen. If you do love me. Or if you think you could love me again. Please, Julia...'

'I love you.' She threw her arms around his neck. 'I love you so much, but I don't know what to do about it. If there is any way, *any* way, then, yes. Please. Let us find it.'

Julia barely remembered the short trip out to the schooner. She sat in the rowing boat in a complete daze clutching Azhar's hand, clinging to him as if he were a mirage that might disappear at any moment. On board the ship, she followed him down past the wheelhouse below decks. It was surprisingly spacious down there. They passed through the galley. Along a narrow passageway where doors were fitted on either side, towards the prow. A bigger door opened on to a luxurious sitting room which took up the width of the ship. Through a curtain, she glimpsed a smaller room, equally luxuriously kitted out as a bedchamber.

Azhar closed the door behind them, and hesitated. 'We have much to discuss,' he said.

'Yes,' Julia agreed.

She held out her arms. He stepped into them. 'It won't be easy, Julia.'

'No.'

He kissed her deeply. She pressed herself urgently against him.

'There are things—many things, that we need to resolve.'

'Yes.'

This time their kiss was starving. Mouths and lips and tongues and hands, clinging and urgent.

'But perhaps not yet.'

'No.'

More kisses as they dropped on to the cushions. More as they tore at each other's clothes, removing only the essentials, kissing frantically, passionately, stopping only for breath before they kissed again. They made love swiftly and without any finesse, caring only to have skin on skin, flesh on flesh, and to show their love for each other in the most primal way.

* * *

'I intended a rational discussion, not a ravishment,' Azhar said afterwards, holding her tightly against him, unable to stop his hands from roaming over her body, checking that she really was here in his arms.

Julia chuckled. 'I am not sure that the ravishing was entirely one-sided.'

'I have missed you.'

She rolled around to face him. 'And I have missed you dreadfully. But what are we to do?'

His expression became serious. He sat up, pulling her with him. 'I don't know, exactly,' he said. 'I must rule Qaryma, but I must find a way to do that which allows me to put you before all else. Most of the time at least, for there will be times when I cannot. I have already put a number of measures into place.'

He told her of his plans for delegating more power to the Council, and of his many other ideas, some already set in motion, some requiring a good deal of further thought. She listened intently, but she made no comment. 'You are worried that you will be living in my shadow,' Azhar said.

'It is a very much bigger shadow than Daniel's.'

'I wish I could disagree.'

'It's not only that,' Julia said, worrying at a button on her blouse. 'You will be expected to marry someone your people think fitting, and that is never by any stretch of the imagination going to be an English widow.'

'I convinced myself I could marry for the sake of my kingdom, but I know now that I never could. My people will have no choice but to accept you, but I hope in time that they will do so from love and respect rather than duty. There will be many who resent you at first, I will not pretend otherwise, but when they see how much I love you, and when they get to know you, I believe their feelings will change. I love you, Julia, and only you. I will not marry a woman I cannot love, which means I can only marry you.'

'You told me once that you never wanted to marry.'

'That was true until I met you.'

'Would you have wanted to marry me if you were not King of Qaryma?'

Azhar considered this carefully. 'King or trader, it matters naught. Either way I would have realised eventually that I need you to complete me.'

'Oh.' Julia blinked furiously. 'You have such perfect answers.'

'Honest answers. I am not the only one who said they would never marry, Julia.'

She nodded, biting her lip. 'I thought freedom was the same thing as independence. I thought I had to be alone to be free. But I am only ever truly myself when I am with you, Azhar. I know, that is such an—an extravagant thing to say, but it is true. I have come to realise that freedom means having the ability to choose. To choose to share your life, to choose to love unconditionally. The two are inseparable. There is no freedom without love and there is no love without freedom. Or am I just twisting my own logic to fit what I want?'

'Your logic, like you, is beautiful and flawless.'

'Oh, Azhar, now you've made me cry again.'

'Tell me I've said enough for you to consider being my wife.'

'You haven't asked me.'

Azhar's heart skipped a beat. 'Does that mean you will?'

'It won't be easy, will it?'

'No. It will be at times very difficult.'

'I won't be locked away in a harem.'

'I would not dare! You will be as free as I will be. Which at times, will not be very free at all, but I have been thinking—if we cannot leave Qaryma to see the world, then why not find a way to bring the world to Qaryma? Trade is one obvious way, I don't know why I didn't think of that before—but the other is you, Julia. You told me once that people travelled from all over England to see your father's gardens. Do you not think that they would travel much further to see our magnificent gardens? How would you like to establish a botanical garden that would put the recently established one in Cairo to shame? And perhaps to document it, to write your own treatise, publish your own botanical textbook?'

'Azhar!'

He laughed. 'I'll take that as a yes.'

'Yes.' She kissed him softly. 'It won't be plain sailing, but we will be together. That is what matters more than anything isn't it?'

'Yes, it is. More important than anything else. I love you, Julia. Say you will be my wife. Let us choose to share our lives and our love.'

She hesitated. He saw her considering every angle, watched her give a little nod as she ticked each point from her internal list. Then she gave a final decisive nod and smiled at him. 'Yes,' she said simply.

He kissed her, secure in the knowledge that he would want to kiss her every single day, and, for the first time in his life, with the absolute certainty that he would do exactly that.

* * * * *

If you enjoyed this story, make sure you don't miss the second book in Marguerite Kaye's HOT ARABIAN NIGHTS *miniseries* SHEIKH'S MAIL-ORDER BRIDE

And watch out for two more books in this sizzling series, coming soon!

Historical Note

As usual, when researching this book I've unearthed a great deal more historical facts than I've actually included in the story. Which is as it should be, since romance is the true core of the book, not history. Having said that, I can't resist sharing some of my period research with you. I hope it enhances your reading experience.

A fascination with what we now call 'natural science' expanded rapidly in the late eighteenth and early nineteenth century. Richard Holmes's excellent book, *The Age of Wonder*, is a great introduction to scientific thinking of the time, including the field of botany and the key figures who promulgated it. Joseph Banks was a prime architect in the establishment of the royal collection at Kew Gardens, bringing back a number of exotic specimens from his famous voyage around the world with Captain Cook—and his infamous stay on Tahiti. Before he set out on this voyage Banks was informally betrothed to Harriet Blosset, ward of the famous botanist James Lee and a botanist in her own right. In a very minor way, this pair served as my models for Julia and her father.

Banks, by then the hugely influential President of the Royal Society, was one of the founder members of the Horticultural Society of London. Established in 1804, and now known as the Royal Horticultural Society, it is membership of this exclusive group to which Daniel aspired. I'll be honest: I have no idea whether a volume which included succulents and desert plants actually existed in Daniel's time, but I am pretty certain that no Western woman had travelled so deeply into the desert as I imagine the Kingdom of Qaryma to be in order to discover such exotic specimens.

For my descriptions of the gardens in the royal palace, and the various imagined environs of Qaryma, I owe much to N. M. Penzer's somewhat dated but brilliantly detailed book *The Harem*. It was left behind by the previous occupants of my parents' house, and I first read it as a teenager, when I devoured every book I could find. My fascination with the harem stems from that first reading, though more recent readings have enhanced this: Lady Mary Wortley-Montagu's letters; the travels of Lady Hester Stanhope and Lady Jane Digby; and the excellent anthology *The Illustrated Virago Book of Women Travellers*, which I must thank Alison L. for most kindly sending to me.

Consul General Henry Salt, at the time this book is set, was taking up his post in Cairo. And although he gets a fleeting mention in this story, he deserves credit as the inspiration for a certain Egyptologist who has a walk-on part in this book. His second name is Fordyce, but he's actually related to the five Armstrong sisters whose stories I've already told in the series of that name, but although he has a small part in each of the next two books I'm afraid you'll have to wait until the fourth story for him to play a starring role.

The spelling and naming of 'period' Arabian clothes is a tricky call. I've gone mostly with Lady Jane Digby's usage—and, since she was married to a sheikh, she should know.

I'm sure there's more I should be sharing with you, but I've got the luxury of three more historical notes to write for the remaining books, so I'll keep my powder dry, as they say. I do hope you've enjoyed Azhar and Julia's story. In fact, I hope you loved it so much that you'll be looking forward to the next in my Hot Desert Nights series. A shipwrecked heroine, a dark and broody hero, of course… And now you know as much as I do at this moment in time!

MILLS & BOON®

Why shop at millsandboon.co.uk?

Each year, thousands of romance readers find their perfect read at millsandboon.co.uk. That's because we're passionate about bringing you the very best romantic fiction. Here are some of the advantages of shopping at www.millsandboon.co.uk:

* **Get new books first**—you'll be able to buy your favourite books one month before they hit the shops

* **Get exclusive discounts**—you'll also be able to buy our specially created monthly collections, with up to 50% off the RRP

* **Find your favourite authors**—latest news, interviews and new releases for all your favourite authors and series on our website, plus ideas for what to try next

* **Join in**—once you've bought your favourite books, don't forget to register with us to rate, review and join in the discussions

Visit **www.millsandboon.co.uk**
for all this and more today!